Riggs Crossing

Michelle Heeter has written short fiction for Australian magazines That's Life and Family Circle under the pen name Renee Dunn. Her work has also appeared in the American titles True Story and True Confessions. Michelle has been a full-time technical writer for the past several years, and enjoys working with software developers.

Michelle grew up in the American Midwest. After earning a master's degree from Michigan State University, Michelle left America for good. She moved to Japan, where she was a lecturer in English for six years. Michelle was living in Kobe when the 1995 earthquake struck. Five weeks later, she moved to Australia.

Michelle loves cats and dogs, swims, practises yoga, wishes she could go horseback riding more often, and commutes to work by bicycle. She lives a short walk from the Sydney Harbour Bridge.

This book is dedicated to my high school English teacher, Mr. William Murphy. I owe special thanks to Dyan Blacklock and Meredith Costain, along with all the readers and editors who helped make *Riggs Crossing* a better book.

RIGGS CROSSING

Michelle Heeter

FORD ST

First published by Ford Street Publishing, an imprint of
Hybrid Publishers, PO Box 52, Ormond VIC 3204

Melbourne Victoria Australia

© Michelle Heeter 2012

2 4 6 8 10 9 7 5 3 1

This publication is copyright. Apart from any use as permitted under the Copyright Act 1968, no part may be reproduced by any process without prior written permission from the publisher. Requests and inquiries concerning reproduction should be addressed to Ford Street Publishing Pty Ltd, 2 Ford Street, Clifton Hill VIC 3068.

www.fordstreetpublishing.com

First published 2012

Dewey Number: A823.4

National Library of Australia Cataloguing-in-Publication data:

Heeter, Michelle, 1964–

Riggs crossing / Michelle Heeter

ISBN: 9781921665707 (pbk.)

For young adults.

Accident victims – Fiction.

Cover design: Gittus Graphics ©

Printing and quality control in China by Tingleman Pty Ltd

PROLOGUE

Case Summary

Samantha Rose Patterson [aka Len Russell]
Adolescent female, age approximately fourteen, found alone and suffering serious injuries in the wreckage of a car near Wollomombi. Police contend Samantha's father, suspected commercial marijuana grower Michael Patterson, was murdered by rival drug traffickers, although the body has not been found and no charges have yet been laid. Spent bullet casings, bloody clothing, and other signs of a violent altercation were found near the scene of the accident.

No identification was found in Samantha's possession. Her birth seems never to have been registered, her name does not appear on Medicare records, and she is not enrolled at any school in New South Wales. Hospital staff called her 'Len Russell', a nickname that seems to suit her androgynous appearance and manner and with which she seems comfortable.

Samantha was positively identified after a police investigation led officers to the isolated logging town of Riggs Crossing, where a handful of local residents admitted knowing Samantha after being shown photos of her taken during her hospital recovery. The information gained from the people of Riggs Crossing about Samantha was sparse and grudgingly provided, fuelling the suspicion held by police that Samantha's father was involved in criminal activities that led him to his violent death.

Samantha reacted badly when two social workers attempted to explain what police had learned about her identity and past, verbally abusing the caseworkers and exhibiting compulsive hand-washing behaviour over the next several days. As a result, it was decided to continue addressing Samantha as 'Len Russell' and allow her to recover her memories in her own time.

Samantha appears well-nourished and is recovering quickly from the injuries sustained in the auto accident. Nevertheless, she exhibits a confusing, even contradictory, range of physical and psychological symptoms with no clear etiology. Samantha claims not to remember anything prior to waking up in hospital. However, CAT and MRI scans show no evidence of concussion or brain damage sufficient to cause cognitive impairment or memory loss. The examining neurologist and psychiatrist agree that Samantha is either (1) suffering from hysterical amnesia following the emotional shock of her father's violent death, or (2) refusing to discuss her past due to fears of reprisals from her father's killers, or out of distrust of law enforcement and other authority figures.

Two months after the accident, Samantha underwent a range of psychometric tests. Samantha's verbal ability, spatial visualisation, and mathematical reasoning skills were measured by a team consisting of a cognitive psychologist and a representative from the Department of Education. Samantha cooperated fully and seemed to enjoy the testing process. Results indicate that Samantha's intelligence is in the top ten per cent of the population.

Samantha's emotional health is less easy to determine. She presents as a well-spoken but reserved teenager who appears most comfortable dealing with adults in structured, formal situations. Samantha, during her stay in hospital, was observed avoiding interactions with patients her own age. When such encounters were unavoidable, Samantha behaved in a surly and abrasive manner, perhaps in an unconscious attempt to mask her own social anxieties and poor interpersonal skills.

Elements of Samantha's behaviour observed by hospital staff indicate at least some degree of Obsessive-Compulsive Disorder. Samantha maintains an elaborate personal hygiene routine and registers disgust at others' actual or perceived lack of cleanliness. One nursing sister observed that while Samantha never asked personal questions or engaged in small talk, she expressed interest in the disposal of contaminated waste, asked how hospital equipment was sterilised, and paid close attention as her room was cleaned and disinfected each day. Samantha has maintained a rigorous attention to personal hygiene since her discharge from hospital. Resident caseworkers at the Inner West Youth Refuge report that Samantha takes at least one shower a day, keeps her room meticulously ordered, and exhibits moderate anxiety at the less stringent personal habits of other children at the Refuge.

Anita Gibson, Samantha's mother and the former de facto partner of Michael Patterson, went missing in 1998. Anita Gibson was a known hitchhiker and was last seen near Bellingen. Anita Gibson's remains, identified through dental records, were found in New England National Park, where the notorious backpacker killer murdered at least four of his victims.

Police investigations revealed that

Samantha Patterson's nearest known relation is her maternal grandmother, Mrs Rose Gibson. Mrs Gibson, who has suffered from a psychiatric disorder since learning of her daughter Anita's death, lives in a Housing Commission flat in Campbelltown. Mrs Gibson has unresolved anger toward Anita for abandoning the family and is ambivalent about meeting Samantha. Anita's three surviving siblings all wish to establish a relationship with Samantha but are fearful of the effect this would have on Mrs Gibson.

It was arranged for Samantha to be placed at the Inner West Youth Refuge. IWYR is a youth care facility of an experimental and sometimes controversial nature. IWYR receives funding from government and private sources. IWYR's non-intrusive philosophy and high carer/child ratio was judged best suited to an adolescent who is recovering from physical injuries, suffering from psychological trauma, and resistant to psychotherapy.

It is normal practice for children and adolescents to be reunited with their families or moved into foster homes as soon as possible. However, in view of the sensitive nature of Samantha's case, it has been agreed that Samantha will remain at IWYR indefinitely.

Chapter 1

I wake up with the sun shining through the cracks in the dusty, crooked blinds. Down the hall, other girls are using the showers and toilets. I need to go, but I close my eyes and hold it in. I usually wait until everyone's been gone a while before I go to the bathroom, because fat Karen always leaves the place smelling like a sewerage treatment plant. Considering how much she eats, she probably drops a huge elephant turd every morning. Wouldn't that be the definition of a home, a place where you don't mind the smell of the other people who've gone to the toilet before you? Where there are proper curtains on the windows, not dingy blinds? No matter how homely they try to make this place, it looks, smells and feels like what it is: an institution.

I hear Bindi and Cinnamon laughing about something as they head off to the kitchen. A minute later, I hear Karen slam the toilet door behind her, then go clomping down the hallway on her camel feet, each huge paddle sending reverberations through the whole house. *Stomp clomp stomp clomp stomp clomp.* Fat moron.

I look at the clock radio. Eight-twenty. I roll over onto my side and draw one knee up toward my chest, which for some reason makes my full bladder less uncomfortable. I close my eyes and try to remember what the bathroom was like where I lived before the accident, but end up falling back to sleep.

It's just after sunrise on a winter morning and I don't want to get out of bed, but I'm busting for a wee. I put on my shoes and coat and walk through the cold house. When I open the door to the lounge room, a blast of warmth hits me in the face. Someone left the kerosene heater on. I tiptoe through the lounge room, past a woman sleeping on the couch under a leather jacket. The ashtray on the coffee table is full of cigarette butts and there's a plastic juice bottle with a piece of garden hose coming out the side and dirty water in the bottom. A man with a beard is snoring in an armchair. I step on a beer can and it makes a crunching sound. The woman shifts and pulls the jacket over her head, the man mumbles something in his sleep. I cross the room, walk through the kitchen, and go out the back. Twenty paces through long grass and I'm there. The smell is bad. I leave the door open even though my teeth are chattering, partly to let in some air and partly because I'm afraid of spiders. No one can see me – the dunny faces away from the house. In front of me, across the canyon, is endless forest and sky and mist. We are on the edge of the escarpment that drops to the river below. The Nymboida River.

'Len? Are you awake?'

Nymboida. Escarpment.

The vision fades and the words fly away as Lyyssa, the Resident Counsellor, pounds on my door and I remember how badly I have to go to the toilet.

Chapter 2

I'm at the Inner West Youth Refuge. They brought me here after the accident. Not right after the accident – I spent a month in hospital, floating in a painkiller haze while surgeons put me back together again – but when the doctors said I was 'well' enough to go home.

I don't know where my home is, if I even have one. That's why they sent me here.

At least I know my name, my nickname, anyway. When they found me, I was wearing a jumper with 'Len' stitched over the heart. Would that mean my proper Christian name is Leni? Helen? Elaine? And my surname is anybody's guess. They put it down as 'Russell' on my papers, because I was wearing a Russell Athletics T-shirt. Pretty stupid, if you ask me. What if I'd been wearing Tommy Hilfiger?

On my first night here, Karen asked me why I couldn't remember anything. I told her I'd taken a bump on the head in a car wreck, because Karen didn't look smart enough to understand the truth.

There's no such thing as 'bump on the head' amnesia – that's something that only happens on TV. Dr Mengers explained it to me when I was still in hospital. If I'd taken a knock on the head severe enough to cause memory loss, there would be evident brain damage. I don't have any brain damage, and the test results prove it. They've taken squillions of CATs and MRIs and other assorted tests with fancy names. Sometimes I had my head hooked up to electrodes, sometimes I had to drink a whole glass of chalky-tasting glop, sometimes I had to lie still for an hour inside some scanner that reminded me of a tube-shaped coffin. All of those tests said the same thing: my brain survived the accident unharmed.

It's my soul that got knocked around.

Hysterical amnesia was the official diagnosis. That's why Dr Mengers referred me to Lyyssa. I have an appointment with Lyyssa in a few minutes, and I'm looking forward to it like I'd look forward to having a tooth pulled or getting a tetanus injection.

Lyyssa is a psychologist and a social worker. She lives at the Youth Refuge with us, and I'm supposed to see her privately for an hour once a week. I know Lyyssa means well, but our sessions seem kind of pointless. Dr Mengers is good at taking complicated ideas, like 'synaptic transmissions' and 'declarative memory' and 'consolidation in cortical networks' and explaining them in simple terms. Lyyssa is just the opposite. She takes simple ideas, and explains them in the most complicated words possible. Instead of 'acting out', Lyyssa talks about 'maladaptive coping responses'. Instead of 'praise', Lyyssa talks about 'positive reinforcement'. I bet Lyyssa wishes she was a neurologist, so she could have an excuse for using multi-syllable words all day.

I leave my room, walk down the hall and pass through the common area where Karen is sitting in front of the TV like an obese toad, staring at the screen with her mouth slightly open. Karen is about ten years old with frizzy red hair sprouting from a huge, pumpkin-shaped head that's attached directly to her neckless blob of a body.

'An insect's exoskeleton serves as a protective covering,' someone on the TV is saying. 'The exoskeleton also functions as a surface for muscle attachment, and as a sensory interface with the insect's environment.'

What the person on the TV means is that the exoskeleton is for the bug what a normal skeleton is for us, and that the bug can feel things through its exoskeleton, like we feel and see and hear. But Karen doesn't understand any of this. That person talking on TV could be saying that a bug's exoskeleton is made of the same stuff as the chocolate coating on a Magnum ice-cream, and Karen wouldn't know any different. She's just watching the TV for something to watch. She might as well be watching a goldfish swimming around in its bowl.

Ignoring Karen, I go down another hall, past the so-called library with its dog-eared books and broken computers. Next is the supplies room where Sky Morningstar, a Non-Resident Counsellor, is showing Jo, a new Non-Resident Counsellor, where to find stuff. Lyyssa's office is the room on the end. I hesitate a moment, then knock.

'Hello, Len.' Lyyssa opens the door to her office. 'Come in and have a seat. I'll be with you in a moment.' Today, Lyyssa's wearing jeans and a Big Day Out T-shirt. I can't believe that Lyyssa really went to Big Day Out. Dressing like a kid just out of high school is one of her transparent techniques to make her more 'accessible', and so all the better to 'relate to' juvenile clients like me.

With Dr Mengers, I feel like a patient. With Lyyssa, I feel like a laboratory experiment.

I sit down at the table and study the only poster on Lyyssa's wall that interests me: the illegal drug chart. Most of Lyyssa's posters are illustrated with cute animals, hot air balloons, or rainbows, and feature vaguely inspirational quotations. But the drug poster just lays things out and lets you decide what to think. *Drug: cannabis, also known as marijuana, mull, pot, grass, weed. Usually smoked in a hand-rolled cigarette (joint, reefer) or a water pipe (bong). Active ingredient: THC. Effects: relaxation, euphoria, increased appetite, reduced inhibitions. Causes paranoia in some individuals. Long-term side-effects: decreased fertility in males after prolonged heavy usage.* To the right of the chart is a picture of a cannabis leaf, some dried marijuana, and a fat joint.

'So,' Lyyssa says, taking the seat opposite me, 'why don't we start with you telling me about your week.'

I can't see the point of this, as Lyyssa knows everything I've done this week, but I tell her anyway. 'Um, on Monday I went with you to a school and I took some tests.'

Lyyssa nods encouragingly. 'And what else?'

'Well, on Sunday you drove us to the Westgardens Metro.' Every other week, Lyyssa drives us to a shopping centre so we can spend our pocket money.

'Did you have a good time?' Lyyssa asks.

That's difficult to answer. I was having a good time, in spite of Bindi and Cinnamon sticking together and making rude comments about everyone, but then Karen pissed her pants and we had to cut short our trip. Karen has some weird form of diabetes that makes her wee every five minutes if she forgets to take her medicine. It wasn't much fun riding home in the van sitting next to Karen, who smelled like a dirty nappy.

'Yeah, it was all right.'

'And what else happened to you this week?' Lyyssa prods.

I got up. I went to bed. In between, I ate and watched television. I worried that they'll make me go to the same school as Bindi and Cinnamon. Yesterday, I walked around the neighbourhood and looked at all the old houses. This morning, Bindi told me not to touch her skateboard or she'd kill me, even though I was only looking at it.

'Nothing, really,' I say to Lyyssa.

A few more minutes of this and I'm allowed to leave. As I close the door to Lyyssa's office behind me, I see Sky Morningstar and Jo leave the storeroom. I hang back until they disappear around the corner of the hallway, chatting about paperwork and house rules. I'm not sure what Sky Morningstar or Jo do, exactly. They help Lyyssa somehow. They're both vegetarians. Sky Morningstar is small and pretty, with curly brown hair and brown eyes. She wears skinny jeans and black Converse All-Stars. She's here four days a week. Jo is taking over from somebody who recently left. Jo will be here one day during the week and on the weekends. She is tall and pale, and wears long plain dresses that come to her ankles, long strings of wooden beads, and thick sandals. She brings her laptop with her to the Refuge and works on it in the dining room.

I wonder what to do with myself for the rest of the day. This morning, I got some paper towels and spray cleaner and cleaned the grime off the blinds in my room, then I got a knife and scraped off all the stupid Lila-Rose & LeeLee stickers that the previous occupant of my room had pasted all over the desk. Lila-Rose & LeeLee Nelson, the tanned, blonde, skinny Malibu Twins. They have their own

TV show, their own line of clothing, and starred in four straight-to-video movies. LeeLee went solo for a while and recorded her own CD before she went into treatment for anorexia. Then Lila-Rose went into rehab for alcohol and drug dependence. Tweens all over the world have girl-crushes on both of them. How vomitous.

Karen told me that a girl named Kim used to have this room, but Karen didn't know what happened to her. Probably, Kim got sent to the Planet for Dorks Who Like Lila-Rose & LeeLee.

In the Refuge, there are safe and unsafe places, safe and unsafe times. I feel safe in my own room with the door shut. When Bindi is gone, I feel safe.

Bindi has hated me since the moment I got here. I don't know why. Bindi is about fifteen. She's not what I'd call pretty, but she's dark and thin and striking, like one of those models in fashion magazines who's made up to look sick and heroin-addicted. Bindi has papered her walls with pictures of those blank-eyed models that she's torn from magazines. Whoever decides what goes in those stupid magazines needs to have a look at the methadone clinic a few blocks up the street from here. Then they'd get a clue as to what heroin-addicted really looks like. Real junkies don't wear ropes of gold necklaces or shoes that cost five hundred dollars.

Bindi has decided that she's bound for better things than this boring Refuge, like being a dickhead fashion model or a 'high-class hooker' (that's another look that the fashion mags love), so she's trying to be as troublesome as she can so they'll let her go. She breaks the house rules, is rude to Lyyssa, bullies Karen, and is working out what she can do to intimidate me. She hasn't really done anything to me yet except stare at me in a mean way and make a few threats, like the one about her skateboard. I keep quiet when she's around and pretend I'm not afraid of her. If I don't show her anything, if she doesn't know what I want or what I care about or what I'm afraid of, she won't know how to get at me.

Cinnamon is Bindi's little hanger-on. Cinnamon is more conventionally pretty than Bindi, with thick brown hair that falls to her waist, a straight nose, and a bee-stung mouth. She's a bit heavy, but I've seen guys turn and stare at her boobs and butt. It's her eyes that ruin her looks. They're big, brown, and empty. In one of the old magazines in the library, there's an interview with a dog breeder who talks about Irish setters, which have been bred for their looks for so many generations that they no longer have any brain to speak of. 'Those dogs are so dumb, they get lost on the end of their leads,' the breeder said. That dog breeder could have been talking about Cinnamon.

Cinnamon's lack of intelligence is probably why she follows Bindi around. I don't have to worry about Cinnamon unless Bindi is here.

Anyway, both of them will be at school until around four. I decide to have another look in the library, even though my first look in there didn't exactly thrill me. I open the door and look at the books, some of them lined up neatly, some just piled on top of each other. There are all the standard-issue kids' books, from *Winnie the Pooh* to *Little House on the Prairie*. Nothing new there for me. I move on to the next shelf. *Sweet Valley High*, *The Baby-sitters Club*, *The Saddle Club*, and, wouldn't you know it, *A Twinning Team*, by druggy Lila-Rose and skinny LeeLee. Modern trash for tweens.

Tweens. Nobody who is a tween would want to be called a tween. Anyway, I'm older than a tween.

I move on to the next shelf. Issues of Christian magazines probably sent to us by the Foundation, the group of church people who started the Refuge and who are still partly in charge of it. A stupid-looking kids' book called *Bessie Bunton Joins the Circus*, with a picture of a fat girl in a tutu on the cover. A dozen or so yellowed and dusty volumes of Reader's Digest Condensed Books. God knows where those came from. And why would anybody want a *condensed* book? Then there are the brightly coloured paperbacks, obviously bought by Lyyssa, stuff about self-esteem and life choices and mapping your own destiny. These are all in mint condition.

There are a few Mills & Boon novels and a few

historical romances. When I came in here the other day, I opened one written by a lady named Serena Delacroix because it had a picture on the cover of a dark-haired man pashing a girl who looked like Cinnamon, but it was so embarrassing I had to stop reading. The story was about Riana, a young English noblewoman who's kidnapped by a pirate named Cade. The beginning was kind of boring, so I skipped some pages and ended up reading the part where Cade forcibly takes Riana to his bed. She sobs and says she hates him, but secretly realises that she loves him and desperately hopes that she has conceived his son. I closed the book feeling embarrassed to be female. Before I put the book back on the shelf, I wiped the cover with my shirt so that no one can ever find my fingerprints on it and prove that I touched such a stupid book. I have to wonder, who owned that book to begin with, and why the hell did they give it to us?

There are rows of old school textbooks: algebra and trigonometry and history and grammar. A few books seem utterly pointless: *Advanced Machine Quilting*, *Colour Schemes for Australian Homes*, and *Birthday Cakes for Children*.

As I come to the end of the third bookshelf, I see three huge boxes of books stacked on top of one another in the corner. Probably, no one has got around to sorting them yet. The boxes are too heavy for me to lift, so I open the flaps of the top box, pull the books out a few at a time, and set them on the table.

I have hit the jackpot.

I tiptoe to the door and close it very carefully, so that the latch doesn't even click. Then, working as quietly as possible, I sort the books into three piles.

OKAY

These are the ones I'm too old for, or too young for, or that just don't interest me. I also put schoolbooks and cookbooks into this pile.

CRAP

All the Mills & Boon-type books go into this pile, along with condensed books, religious stuff, and stupid girl books. Just when I think I've got the CRAP sorted, I find *So Rich, So Famous* by June Collins and two *Star Trek* books. Three more for the CRAP pile.

MINE

These are the good ones. Or at least they look good. They say you can't judge a book by its cover, but what choice do you have? There's a book on Chinese astrology and a smaller paperback on regular astrology. The dust jacket of the Chinese astrology book is blood red, with black lettering and a gold stencilled picture of a dragon. There are a couple of biographies that look interesting. The biography of Georges Sand is perfectly new – I can tell by the stiffness of the pages that no one has ever opened it.

I'm going to take these books up to my room now

and hide them. After all, I'm the one who went to the trouble of sorting them.

A few of the books are just so weird as to defy classification. There's a very old blue paperback called *Memoirs of a Midget* by Walter de la Mare. There's an even older blue hardback called *The Story of a Piece of Coal: What it is, Whence it Comes, Whither it Goes*. I open it – the paper lining the front cover has a pretty floral pattern. It was published in London in 1896, written by Edward A Martin, FGS. I wonder what FGS means. It doesn't seem very interesting, but there are some nice illustrations of the prehistoric plants that became coal, and of the machines that cleaned and refined the coal.

Before I can stop myself, I've constructed one of those impossible dilemmas that I hate but can't stop making up. What if I'd read every single book in the library and had nothing left except *Memoirs of a Midget*, *The Story of a Piece of Coal*, or *So Rich, So Famous*? And I wasn't allowed to have any new books until I'd read at least one of them? Which one would I read?

Before I've solved that dilemma, I remember the time and glance at my watch. A quarter to four. I'd better get the books up to my room in a hurry. Only one problem: there are too many to carry in one trip. I put the OKAY and CRAP ones back into the boxes, hide half of the MINE pile behind the shelves, and sprint out of the library and up the stairs with the others, which I hide under my bed. I can get the rest of them tomorrow.

I make it to my room just in time. Five minutes later, Bindi and Cinnamon come back from school, slamming the front door behind them. At six we have dinner. Lyyssa or Sky cooks for us four nights a week; on the other three days it's our own responsibility to look after our meals.

Lyyssa is a good cook, which is surprising, considering how bad she is at everything else. Tonight, she's cooked a lamb roast so tender it falls off the bone, with mashed potatoes, roast vegetables and gravy. Despite the food always being nice, I don't enjoy mealtimes. Lyyssa sits at the head of the table, trying to start a conversation that includes everyone. Cinnamon and Bindi ignore everyone else, talking to each other about how much they hate all the teachers at school. Karen pours tomato sauce on everything on her plate, takes huge mouthfuls, and makes disgusting smacking noises as she chews.

I sit at the table eating quietly, trying to tune out Karen's chewing and Bindi and Cinnamon's bitchy chattering. I wonder which of the books I'll start to read first. Maybe I'll start with one of the astrology books, then . . .

'You haven't said much this evening, Len,' Lyyssa says, breaking my concentration.

I think for a moment. 'The roast was really nice. You did a really good job cooking.'

Lyyssa beams. 'Thank you, Len.'

When we're finished eating, we carry our dishes to the kitchen. Bindi comes up behind me. 'Suck-arse,' she hisses into my ear.

Chapter 3

Today, a lady from the Salvation Army, Major Heath, took me to Kmart and let me pick out some underwear and stuff. Ten pairs of socks. Ten pairs of knickers. A couple of bras. And two sets of pyjamas: one pair in plain blue cotton flannelette, and the other with a flower design all over them.

It was kind of fun going to Kmart and having things bought for me, even if it was a little embarrassing. Everybody noticed Major Heath's Salvation Army uniform and paid more attention to us than normal.

We didn't go to the Kmart in Westgardens Metro – we went to the one in the city. Since I came to the Refuge, I've only been out a few times. I like taking short walks around the neighbourhood, and once I walked as far as University Road. I've also been to the Westgardens Metro with Lyyssa and everybody else.

On the way, we passed a million shops and restaurants and saw all sorts of people with weird hair and wearing weird clothes. The University.

The University Regiment. And just before we got there, on the left, a big park with a swimming pool shimmering in the afternoon sun.

Before bed, I order all my clothes in the bureau. My underwear drawer is my favourite, because all my underwear is brand new. My other clothes are second-hand, mostly jeans and jumpers. Oh, my shoes and watch are new – the nursing staff bought me a pair of trainers and a digital Casio as a goodbye present when I left the hospital.

I feel bad that the people at the hospital seemed to have got more attached to me than I was to them. A few of the nurses even cried when I left. It bothers me that I didn't feel like crying. It wasn't that I didn't feel grateful that they'd taken care of me, or that I didn't appreciate being given a pair of shoes and a watch. But I couldn't feel sad about leaving.

I knew there was something else that I should feel even sadder about. But I didn't know what.

Chapter 4

Just when I'm really getting fed up with being the new kid in this crappy place, someone else shows up to distract everyone's attention from me, which suits me just fine.

They bring him here one evening when we're all in the TV room. Bindi and Cinnamon are on the couch, Karen is sprawled in an armchair, and I'm lying on the floor, propped up on one elbow. Lyyssa answers the door and speaks for a few minutes to someone with the front door wide open. A blast of winter air blows into the lounge room.

'Close the effin' door,' Bindi says loudly, and Cinnamon giggles.

The front door shuts and Lyyssa, pretending she didn't hear Bindi, brings a kid into the lounge room. 'Everyone, we have a new member of our household. This is Shane.' We look at Shane. He drops his eyes to the floor as Lyyssa introduces each one of us.

Shane is about eight, blond, and scared-looking. He's wearing a ski cap, and he's rugged up with so many jumpers that his ski jacket won't close in the front.

'Shane, would you like to take off your jacket?' Lyyssa asks him. He doesn't really want to, but he thinks that this is what Lyyssa wants him to do, so he takes off his jacket and holds it tightly to his chest.

'Maybe you'd like to watch some TV with the rest of the house,' Lyyssa suggests. 'I'll take your bag up to your room. You can get settled later.' Lyyssa picks up Shane's duffle bag and trudges up the stairs, not noticing that there isn't any place for Shane to sit. Shane stands there frozen, paralysed.

'Geez, if they're gonna send a guy to the house, couldn't they have sent one ten years older?' Bindi says. Once again, Cinnamon giggles at Bindi's stupid remark.

'You can sit over here, Shane,' I say, as much to piss off Bindi as for any other reason. Shane slowly walks over, puts his jacket on the floor next to me, and sits cross-legged on top of it.

In two minutes, I'm silently cursing Shane and bitterly regretting my attempt to be nice. Shane *smells*. As if Karen wasn't bad enough, they've sent us another stink bomb. Shane smells like stale farts and sweat and socks that have been worn for weeks. Where the hell did he come from, anyway?

I've been breathing through my mouth for five minutes when Lyyssa reappears. I raise my hand. 'Is it okay if I go to bed now, Lyyssa?' I think my brain is deprived of oxygen, having to breathe Shane's miasma. At the Refuge you don't have to ask for permission to go to bed, nor do you raise your hand before you speak.

'Sure, Len,' Lyyssa says. I get up and run out of the room, not caring that Bindi and Cinnamon are sniggering at me. I dash up the stairs and into my bedroom, closing the door behind me and taking gasps of fresh air. When my head clears, I take a towel and my robe and go down to the girls' showers and soap myself until every centimetre of my body that was contaminated by Shane is cleansed.

Purified, I return to my room and lie on my bed. I hear Lyyssa coming up the stairs with Shane, chattering to him about house rules, fumbling with the keys to the boys' toilet and the boys' showers, which have been locked because there haven't been any boys at the Refuge for a while. Then Lyyssa unlocks the door to Shane's room and they go inside. For a few minutes, I can hear them talking, but I can't hear what they're saying. Then Lyyssa's voice rises. 'Shane, you need to have a shower. Or at least a quick wash.'

'NO!' Shane yells.

'Shane, this is not negotiable,' Lyyssa says firmly. 'You don't have to spend an hour in the bathtub, but you must at least make an effort to be clean.' Shane makes protesting, whimpering noises; probably Lyyssa has taken him by the arm and is trying to pull him toward the shower.

Then Shane lets out a scream that makes me hold my ears. It's not the volume of the scream that makes me shudder; it's the history behind that scream. You don't even have to think very much about what it means. Why was Shane removed from whatever home he came from? Because he was abused. Sexually abused. Where was he abused? In the shower. Which is why he now wears three jumpers and a ski jacket like a protective exoskeleton and is terrified of taking his clothes off or going anywhere near a shower. Why doesn't Lyyssa know this? Hasn't she read Shane's file yet?

Lyyssa must have let go of Shane, because he's run back inside his room and slammed the door behind him.

'Shane?' Lyyssa says, her voice trembling. 'Shane, I didn't mean to scare you. If you want to lock your door, you can turn the lever right above the doorknob.'

A couple of seconds pass, then I hear the sound of Shane turning the deadbolt on his door. Of course, Lyyssa has a master key in case we try to commit suicide in our room and she has to get in, but Shane doesn't know this. Lyyssa slowly walks back along the hall and down the stairs.

Chapter 5

I was wrong to say the Refuge is crappy. It's a big old house with mouldings on the ceiling and marble counters and fireplaces that don't get used anymore. Some rich widow left it to charity, along with some money, with the instruction that they be used to help needy children. For a while, there were more kids than rooms, so they built an ugly modern wing that doesn't match the rest of the house. Now, only Lyyssa's office and bedroom, the guest rooms, library and storage rooms are in that wing. There's some fighting going on between the people from the Foundation and some people in the government over who's in charge of the Refuge. I don't really care about who's in charge, but it makes me nervous. If someone decides to shut this place down, then where will I go? The next place wouldn't be any better, and might be a lot worse.

Anyway, it really isn't crappy. It's just annoying sometimes. Like when Shane won't shower and stinks up the place.

The lady from the Salvation Army who took me shopping, Major Heath, ends up coming to the shelter to make sure Shane has a bath at least twice a week. Major Heath is plump and has white hair, like a TV grandmother. Lyyssa thanks her effusively each time she shows up. They're in the entryway, talking.

'It's my pleasure, Lyyssa. I seem to have a talent with children this age.'

'We've got to get this hygiene issue addressed,' Lyyssa says despairingly. 'Otherwise he'll have no chance of being placed with a family.'

I'm sitting at the kitchen table, having a glass of Milo. I'm pretending to read *Your Star Signs*, so Lyyssa and Major Heath assume I'm not listening.

A shadow falls over Major Heath's normally cheerful features. 'I don't think we can pin our hopes on that,' she says quietly. 'That young boy's faith in the family has been pretty thoroughly destroyed. Perhaps the best we can do is simply protect him from further harm.'

Major Heath sure isn't wrong about Shane being completely mental. It's not just showers he has a problem with. You should see him at the dinner table. I've never seen anyone so paranoid about the way he eats. Shane cuts his food into tiny pieces, makes absolutely no noise when he chews, takes a drink from his glass of milk after every fifth bite, then *very carefully* sets the glass back down on the table. Once, he knocked over his glass by accident and he sat there frozen in terror, like he thought someone was going to hit him. Lyyssa told him it was okay and cleaned up the mess, but she still couldn't convince him to finish the rest of his meal.

Lyyssa mumbles something and follows Major Heath upstairs. 'Where's my handsome young friend?' Major Heath calls out, and Shane comes out of his room to meet her. So as not to embarrass Shane when he takes his clothes off, Major Heath lets Shane go into the shower and throw his clothes out. She calls to him which body part to wash. 'And have you taken Little Shane out and washed him, too?' she says, without a trace of embarrassment, referring to Shane's dick and foreskin. Shane mustn't be circumcised. Shane even giggles when Major Heath says this.

This is the sort of thing that you would expect Bindi and Cinnamon to mercilessly make fun of, but they don't. At worst, they just roll their eyes, as if to say, 'What a big baby'.

Bindi is actually polite to Major Heath. She doesn't overdo it, being a goody-two-shoes, but all her normal attitude is gone. It isn't just that Major Heath is nice. Lyyssa is nice too, but she's annoying and Bindi is as rude to her as she can get away with. It's that there is never any hidden agenda with Major Heath. She accepts you as you are, and isn't always trying to 'improve' you in sneaky little ways.

Of course, Major Heath wanted Shane to shower,

in fact, she insisted that he shower. But Shane knew that Major Heath's goodwill toward him wouldn't change whether he stank or smelled like a daisy, so he figured why not make the lady happy and shower.

Shane has been packed off to bed, so Lyyssa and Major Heath come down the stairs. 'Hello, Len,' Major Heath says to me, pausing by the kitchen door.

I put my book down. 'Hello, Major Heath.'

Major Heath takes a few steps into the kitchen. '*Your Star Signs*,' she says, reading the cover of my book. 'That's pretty advanced for someone your age.'

'I'm good at reading,' I reply.

'Will you be starting school soon?'

Lyyssa takes a step into the room. 'Len's meeting with an education officer next week. She'll need to take a few more tests, and we'll go from there.'

Major Heath pats me on the shoulder. 'I'll be visiting twice a week for the time being. Let me know if there are any books you'd like.'

I thank her and watch as Lyyssa escorts her out the door to her car. *School.* That's something I hadn't put much thought into.

Have I ever been to school? That night, I try to remember as I drift off to sleep.

I'm playing with Kevvie. Daddy went into town and left me at Kevvie's place for a few hours. Kevvie is my school friend. We go to kindergarten together. We're playing in front of the house. Kevvie has pulled up some grass and leaves.

'This is mull,' Kevvie says. 'We've got to dry it and take out the kif.'

'That's Silly Stuff,' I tell him. 'We have Silly Stuff at home sometimes. My dad's a farmer.'

Kevvie laughs. 'It's mull,' he says. 'Your dad's a cropper, like my dad.'

Daddy doesn't say anything when I tell him what Kevvie said about mull and croppers. But I don't go to school anymore. Daddy sells our property, buys one further up the mountain, and starts teaching me at home.

I wake up feeling like the darkness is suffocating me. My chest hurts. I turn on the light and pick up *Your Star Signs*. I'm halfway through and I haven't really found a sign that sounds like me yet. I don't know when my birthday is, but if I can find the astrological sign that matches my personality, then I would at least know the month when I was born.

The Cancer chapter was pretty boring. I'm not placid, maternal, and home-loving, like Cancerians are supposed to be.

I turn the page to the next section. Leo.

Leos are expressive, spontaneous, and powerful. Leos are straightforward and uncomplicated people who know what they want and pursue it with determination and a creative spirit. Cities: Los Angeles, Chicago, Rome. Herbs: Saffron, Rosemary, Peppermint. Colours: Gold and Orange. Birthstone: Peridot.

There's a picture of a peridot – it's a pretty pale

green stone. Leos possess a positive nature and don't let any adverse circumstances get them down. Leos adore luxury and like to live on a grand scale. When it comes to travel, first class is the only way to go and only five-star will do.

This is me.

I'm going to decorate my room in orange and gold. Or at least get a peppermint-scented candle.

I shut the book, turn off the light, and fall asleep straight away.

Chapter 6

Mr Brentnall sits across from me. He's about forty, tall and lanky, with a pleasant, thoughtful-looking face. He's wearing black jeans, Blundstone steelcaps, and a neatly ironed long-sleeved white shirt. I can't work out whether he's a teacher or a social worker. It's his job to figure out which school I should go to and what year I should be in.

'I'm not sure what to make of your test results, Len,' he says, not as if this is a problem. His lack of curiosity is a relief. Most people get annoyed when they don't know what to make of me. 'Your mathematics scores are excellent. You didn't miss a single question in the weights and measures section.' Mr Brentnall looks up from the folder. 'Did you do all the problems in your head?'

I nod.

'I thought so. You didn't make any notes in the margins or on the scrap paper we gave you. Your reading comprehension and writing skills are similarly impressive. As for history and science . . .' Mr Brentnall frowns slightly and shakes his head.

'I bet you were home-schooled,' he says, more to himself than to me. 'These results don't make sense otherwise.' He closes the folder. 'Anyway, you've got some catching up to do in some areas. But that shouldn't be too hard.'

I tell Mr Brentnall that I don't want to go to Ramsay Training Institute if it's full of people like Bindi and Cinnamon.

Mr Brentnall looks surprised. 'Why, Len, have you been worried that we were going to send you to Ramsay?'

I nod again.

Mr Brentnall shakes his head and laughs a little. 'Ramsay Training Institute is a school for kids who've been in trouble with the law or who have serious behavioural problems. We'd never send someone like you to Ramsay.'

I look down. 'It's not just that I don't want to go to Ramsay. I really don't want to go to school anywhere.'

To my surprise, Mr Brentnall doesn't argue.

We agree that I'll study with a private tutor three days a week. If my progress is satisfactory, then I'll begin year nine at a normal school at the start of the next school year. If I do well enough on my exams, I might have a shot at going to a selective school, where there's guaranteed to be nobody like Bindi or Cinnamon.

'We can discuss other options further down the line, when you're settled in a foster home,' Mr

Brentnall says, putting my test results back into the manila folder. 'There's even some scholarship money available, if you're interested in going to a private college, like International Academy.'

I leave Mr Brentnall's office feeling relieved that I don't have to go to school right away. I push the part about the foster home to the back of my mind.

Chapter 7

It's a couple of weeks before anything actually happens. I fill my time reading the books I nicked from the library and taking walks through the neighbourhood. I overhear Lyyssa having arguments on the phone. I think she's arguing with Mr Brentnall, and I think they're arguing about me. Lyyssa's voice gets all shrill and she keeps saying things like 'importance of balanced and structured education' and 'healthy interaction with her peers'. I'm dead certain that whatever plans Lyyssa has for me would be a total disaster. Does she want me to go to Ramsay, where most of the kids are even worse than Bindi and Cinnamon? Does she want me to go to that snotty girls' school up the road, where the mothers drive up in Land Rovers and Mercedes to pick them up when school lets out?

Fortunately, Lyyssa loses. I can tell she didn't get her way by the tightness around her mouth when she calls me into her office, forces a smile and tells me that 'an arrangement has been agreed upon' where I'll be tutored privately, and intermittently tested by the

Department of Education to monitor my progress.

The arrangement goes like this. Three days a week I see Renate Dunn. She's Mr Brentnall's partner, which is how he got the idea for her to teach me. Miss Dunn is a professor of educational psychology at the University, where her office is. Miss Dunn is tall, maybe about thirty-five years old. She usually wears a black calf-length skirt with Doc Martens, a black jumper and a heavy silver necklace. I can't decide whether she's pretty or not. She has a straight nose, a firm jaw line, clear skin, and dark blue eyes, but she never wears any makeup. If she did wear makeup, get contacts instead of those glasses, and lost a bit of weight, she could look like one of those old-time actresses who made movies when they were black and white.

Miss Dunn's office is lined with bookshelves, and she has posters on her wall, but that's where the similarity with Lyyssa's office ends. Lyyssa's bookshelf is a brand-new metal one from OfficeWorks; Miss Dunn's is a huge old wooden thing that takes up a whole wall. Lyyssa's office is painted pale yellow; the walls of Miss Dunn's office are a nondescript off-white. Everything on Lyyssa's walls is meant to be instructive or inspiring; the stuff on Miss Dunn's walls is there because it's interesting or beautiful. The meaning of every single framed poster on Lyyssa's walls is always summed up in a cheesy slogan. *'Pot hurts'*. *'If you don't know where you're going, you'll probably end up somewhere . . . else'. 'One Day at a Time'. 'God grant me the strength to change the things I can, the serenity to accept the things I cannot change, and the wisdom to know the difference'.*

There are no slogans on Miss Dunn's pictures, and the point of the pictures isn't always obvious. There's a Japanese kimono on a hanger suspended from the ceiling behind Miss Dunn's desk, filling the space between the two windows. On the wall opposite the bookshelf, there's a framed Chinese character. I have no idea what it means, and there's no slogan or caption to explain it. There's also a pencil sketch of a building that looks like a church, and a photo of a sign taken in some tropical foreign country. The sign says 'Commit no Nuisance' in English, but above the English is writing in another language that has totally different letters. I bet it's something funny, but you'd have to understand what the foreign writing says before you'd get the joke.

Lyyssa wouldn't know any language except English. Miss Dunn would.

I take the bus by myself now, but first Lyyssa had to bring me here and introduce me to Miss Dunn. It was pretty embarrassing, bumbling into the parking lot in a van with 'Inner West Youth Refuge' written on the side. Then we had to walk across campus with everyone looking at me like, what's a kid doing here? Naturally, Lyyssa took us to the wrong building and we had to ask directions from a mean-looking secretary who didn't like being interrupted while she was photocopying.

Finally, we made it to Miss Dunn's office, ten minutes late. I remember Lyyssa breathlessly gabbling an apology to Miss Dunn, and Miss Dunn sizing up Lyyssa in one shrewd, penetrating glance. Miss Dunn handed Lyyssa a list of the books I needed, then gave me a page explaining what she wanted me to read before our first lesson. Lyyssa and Miss Dunn talked about lesson plans and such, but I didn't listen too closely to what they said. What they said to each other with their eyes and body language was more interesting. Lyyssa, with her stiff back and her fake smile, was saying, *You think you're better than me because you teach at university, but you'd better remember that I'm officially in charge of Len*. And Miss Dunn, with her cool blue gaze taking in Lyyssa's twee plaid tunic, was saying, *You're just a dumb social worker. All you do is put your nose in other people's business*.

We had to rush to the bookshop before it closed, then hurry back to the van so we could be back home before Bindi and Cinnamon. After we left, Lyyssa turned to me and asked brightly, 'So, Len, what do you think of Miss Dunn?'

What's the point of a question like that?

'She seems really smart,' I replied. 'I'm glad she's going to be my teacher.'

Lyyssa kept quiet for the rest of the short drive back to the shelter.

Chapter 8

My lessons are on Monday, Wednesday and Friday, for an hour or two at a time, depending on Miss Dunn's schedule. If there's no one else in the lounge room in the evening and I've finished all my homework, I sometimes watch TV.

I don't watch much TV, but there is one show that I like. It's called *Clarissa Hobbs, Attorney at Law*, and it's about a woman lawyer. Fortunately, nothing that anyone else wants to watch is on at the same time. Bindi and Cinnamon always watch stupid stuff like *Shop with LeeLee*, the reality TV show where LeeLee Nelson goes shopping with the people who are her friends this week.

Clarissa Hobbs is a divorced mature-age lady, and has grandkids because she married so young, but she doesn't look like a granny. Clarissa's hair is ash-blonde, not grey, and her face has character lines rather than wrinkles. She dresses in simple, elegant suits and keeps fit by playing racquetball at the local gym, which is where she met her boyfriend, a handsome silver-haired lawyer.

Clarissa is from the South in America, but now she lives in Los Angeles. She comes from a rich family, although her family lost their money when she was about my age.

Tonight, Clarissa is doing one of her pro bono cases, which means that she's helping a poor person by handling their case for free. In this case, Clarissa is defending a young black man named Trell. He's a gang member, and Clarissa knows he's no angel. She's helping him for two reasons. Number one, she thinks he's innocent. Number two, Trell's father has been on Death Row since he was a baby, so he's had a rough start in life.

Trell has been accused of arson and murder. A fire broke out in a local convenience store, killing the owner who lived upstairs. The prosecution says that Trell set the fire as revenge because the owner accused him of shoplifting. The prosecution doesn't have any physical evidence, but they do have an eyewitness. The eyewitness is Mrs Crabtree, an old lady who lives across the street from the shop. Mrs Crabtree was sleeping, and says she was woken up by the noise from the fire and saw Trell running away from the building.

Clarissa works out a strategy to attack the credibility of Mrs Crabtree, who is white. Clarissa, when she cross-examines Mrs Crabtree, casts doubt that Mrs Crabtree can tell one black man from another by asking Mrs Crabtree to describe Trell's features.

'Well, he's black,' Mrs Crabtree says.

'And how would you describe the features of that gentleman over there,' Clarissa asks, pointing to a black court officer.

'Well . . . he's . . . black,' Mrs Crabtree says, squinting and looking flustered. You can hear a few people in the courtroom laughing quietly.

'Can you be more specific, Mrs Crabtree?' Clarissa says, with exaggerated patience.

Mrs Crabtree splutters and stammers.

'Mrs Crabtree, are you *sure* it was Trell Anderson you saw running from that burning building?'

Mrs Crabtree turns red. 'Are you calling me a liar?' she squeals indignantly. 'Are you casting aspersions on my character?'

'No, Mrs Crabtree,' Clarissa replies acidly. 'I'm not casting aspersions of any sort. I am questioning your attitudes toward African-Americans, the reliability of your memory, and the accuracy of your eyesight.' Clarissa turns to the judge. 'No further questions, Your Honour,' she says.

Of course, Clarissa wins the case. She always does.

Even so, Clarissa isn't overjoyed. 'I have a feeling I'm going to be representing Trell again someday,' Clarissa says grimly, as she snaps her briefcase shut.

After the episode ends, there's the usual five minutes of ads. A model strides down a dark alley and knocks on a door. When the door opens, she pulls off her dress so she's wearing nothing but lacy red and black underthings. 'Ripper,' a voice whispers, as she steps into the darkened house. Then the screen goes black and *Ripper Intimates* is displayed in red type.

I switch off the TV when a McCain's frozen food commercial comes on. I hate that part at the end where they say, 'Ah, McCain's, you've done it a-GAIN'. One night, that commercial was the last thing I saw before I went to bed, and I heard it rolling through my brain about a hundred times before I could get to sleep.

I climb the stairs, put on my pyjamas, and climb into bed.

Ripperrr, the TV voice purrs.

'*Ripper!*' Daddy used to say, if something really pleased him. '*Ripper got me best patch*,' says Ernie.

I jerk awake, run to the light switch and turn on the light. It takes me a few minutes to calm down. I pull out a book out from under my bed. *Georges Sand: A Woman's Life Writ Large*. It's too advanced for me to understand. Or maybe it's just boring. That's the best kind of book to read if you're trying to go to sleep. I still haven't figured out why a woman is named Georges, or why George has an 's' on the end, or why it's 'writ' instead of 'written'. I put the book away, turn off the light, close my eyes, and think *sand, sand, sand, sand, sand, sand,* until I fall asleep.

Chapter 9

Today, instead of asking me lots of questions, Lyyssa has given me a notebook. 'You might want to use it to write down your feelings. You know, like a journal or diary.'

'Thanks,' I say, taking the notebook. It's spiral-bound with two hundred pages. I like it, even though I know it's another one of Lyyssa's techniques to get me to tell her things. I'm glad she gave me a regular notebook, instead of some twee little pink book with 'My Secret Diary' written on the front in fancy letters, and held shut by some tiny metal lock that anyone could break. Karen was looking at one like that at the two-dollar shop in Westgardens Metro like she wanted to buy it, but Bindi and Cinnamon made fun of her so she put it back. For once, I had to agree with Bindi and Cinnamon. I hate cutesy, phony things like that. They're embarrassing.

'You'll need a pen, too,' Lyyssa says, opening the supply cupboard and giving me a choice of four new pens. There's a black fine point, a black roller ball, a blue ballpoint stick pen, and a blue gel ink pen with a rubber grip. I pick the one with the rubber grip.

Lyyssa says I can stay and talk if I like, or we can skip today's session if I prefer.

'I don't really have anything to talk about. Is it okay if we skip the session?'

Lyyssa seems a little disappointed, but she says that's fine and lets me go. I take the notebook back to my room and sit on my bed for a few minutes, admiring the crisp, unspoiled white pages. I know I don't have to worry about hiding it. Lyyssa may be a stickybeak, but she's also a fanatic about 'respecting boundaries'. Just the same, I decide I'll keep it underneath my mattress.

There's a space on the front of the notebook to write your name. But since Len Russell isn't my real name, I don't bother.

I think about what I want to write in the notebook. Something has been floating in the back of my mind all day, bothering me, distracting me. I try to put my finger on what it is. I sit quietly for a few minutes, and then I remember. It was something I was thinking about last night before I fell asleep. I pick up my pen and start writing.

It's Saturday. A girlfriend of Daddy's is here, not one I've seen before. Now that she's curled her hair and put on all her makeup she doesn't have anything to do, so she's sitting in a lounge chair looking bored. I'm playing Milk Jug with our dog Reggie. Milk Jug is his favourite game. You take an empty plastic milk jug by the handle and Reggie jumps up and sinks his teeth into it. Then you play tug-o-war, trying to pull the jug toward you as Reggie pretend-growls and pulls in the opposite direction. Reggie could pull you off your feet if he really wanted to, but he's smart enough to know that doing that would ruin the game.

'Aren't you afraid to let her play with a pit bull?'

I don't know why she's so concerned about me playing with the dog. She didn't care when I burned my hand on the kettle earlier.

'Reggie's a staffie cross, not a pit bull.' Daddy's watching the cricket on TV and doesn't bother looking at the lady when he talks to her. He talks to the lady like he talks to all of them, like she's kind of stupid and not really worth talking to.

'Aren't you afraid he'll bite her?'

'He's a sook,' Daddy says, and turns up the sound.

'Don't you think you should get him de-sexed?' The lady raises her voice to be heard over the TV.

Daddy hits the mute button, sets his feet on the floor and looks directly at the lady. If she doesn't shut up after Daddy does this, then she really is stupid. 'A dog like that has two purposes in life: to fight, and to root. You take both those things away, he'll go crazy.'

Then Daddy turns the sound back on and puts his feet back up on the coffee table.

Once I've finished writing, I read what I've written. Then I close the notebook and put it under my mattress.

Chapter 10

Today is my last regular visit with Scott, the physiotherapist. We've been doing exercises to help me extend my range of movement. After being inactive those weeks in hospital, I was pretty stiff and inflexible. Since I'm working with a tutor rather than going to school, we have to decide on a type of exercise for me since I won't be doing sport as a class.

Scott is soft-spoken and gentle, not really the kind of person you'd think of as the 'sporty' type. He's broad-shouldered and tall. You wouldn't immediately guess how strong he is. I could feel the strength in his hands when he was working on my shoulders and lower back.

'Can I take up racquetball?' Clarissa Hobbs does racquetball.

'Racquetball?' Scott looks at me through his rimless glasses and blinks. 'Well, I don't see why not, but racquetball's not that popular. It might be difficult for you to find a place to take lessons. Why don't you try tennis?'

I figure tennis will do.

'And can I start lifting weights?'

Scott frowns slightly. 'You can do *light* weight training,' he says. 'Just dumbbells – no barbells and definitely no weight machines. Your bones and muscles are still developing – I don't want you pumping iron and risking injury. And don't even *think* of dieting,' Scott cautions me further. 'You're a mesomorph – stocky and muscular. There's no sense in starving yourself to make yourself look like Lila-Rose and LeeLee. You're not built that way.'

I'd rather be dead than look plastic and phony like Lila-Rose and LeeLee, who probably started wearing thick makeup at age three, but I take his point. Scott says he'll ask Lyyssa to order a tennis outfit for me, and arrange lessons at a gym twice a week.

'Can you swim?'

Can I swim? I think about this. When I scan my brain for swimming, I come up blank, just like when I try to remember anything about my mother.

'No.'

'Everyone should learn how to swim,' Scott says firmly. 'We'll sign you up for swimming lessons once a week.' He makes a note for Lyyssa to get me a swimsuit as well. 'That should be enough for the time being. If you decide you want to spend more time at the gym, speak to me or Lyyssa. We can look at getting you a pass so you can go as often as you like.'

Scott gives me some pamphlets about healthy eating and exercise, and tells me to call him if I have any problems.

It's a short walk from the physio's office to the Refuge. When I get back, I go into the kitchen and pour myself a glass of milk and spoon in some Milo. I'm planning on having a nice afternoon snack by myself, so naturally Bindi and Cinnamon have to ruin it by barging in.

'Better not drink too much Milo, Len,' Bindi snipes. 'You'll put on weight.' Bindi is an ectomorph, tall and angular, with razor-sharp cheekbones. Her hair is naturally curly, but she irons it straight every morning and pulls it back into a skin-tight ballerina's bun.

'Yeah, you'll get even fatter, as fat as Karen,' stupid Cinnamon chimes in. Cinnamon shouldn't talk – she's a pear-shaped endomorph. But she probably thinks her big boobs make it okay to have a big arse.

'I'm not *fat*,' I say. 'I'm a *mesomorph*.' I say the word slowly and carefully, so they'll understand. Bindi and Cinnamon have a vocabulary of about a hundred words between them, not counting the four-letter ones.

'A MESOMORPH!' Bindi screeches. She and Cinnamon start screaming with laughter. 'Come on, Cin, let's get some food and leave the *mesomorph* to pig out on her Milo.' Bindi grabs a bag of Doritos from the cupboard and Cinnamon gets two Cokes from the fridge and they clatter out of the kitchen, hooting and saying 'mesomorph' over and over. They've left their school books from Ramsay on the kitchen table. Remedial English. Mathematics for Morons. History for Retards. Design for Delinquents.

I stare at my glass of Milo. I spoon out the chocolatey grains floating on the top and flick them into the garbage. Then I make myself drink the rest of it, even though I feel like dumping the whole glass down the sink.

Chapter 11

I've been here for a couple of months now. My life has settled into a routine. I have lessons with Miss Dunn. No matter what they tell me, I'm afraid they're going to send me to Ramsay if I don't learn enough, so I always do my homework. I read books from the library. I go to tennis lessons and swimming lessons. I avoid Bindi and Cinnamon, without making it obvious that I'm walking around them. You can't let someone know you're afraid of them.

One night I don't have anything better to do, so I look into the lounge room where Bindi and Cinnamon are sprawled on the lounge and Karen is in the brown chair. I survey the room before going in, working out that I can sit on the red two-seater couch, across the room from Bindi and Cinnamon. Karen doesn't take her eyes from the TV. Even though there's only some noisy fast-food commercial playing, you'd think it was the most fascinating thing she'd ever seen. Cinnamon gives me a quick glance of mild dislike, and Bindi stares at me for a moment with her eyes narrowed. They don't try to keep me from coming in, though. The lounge room is common property and they know it.

I settle myself into the sagging, musty-smelling red couch. The couch got here just a few days after I did. Some man showed up at the door and made a big deal about having a 'donation' for us, when all he really had was an old piece of furniture that he couldn't sell at his garage sale and couldn't be bothered taking to the tip. Lyyssa helped him unload it from his lime-green ute and carry it inside. He never took off his sunglasses the whole time.

For some reason, I decided the couch was female and gave her a name. I called her Clementine. I didn't tell anyone this, of course, I just named the couch inside my own head.

Clementine the couch is *red*. Not burgundy, or maroon, but bright, screaming scarlet. And the fabric isn't just plain velvet, it's crushed velvet. New, Clementine probably looked fashionably outlandish, like something an artist would have in the house. Twenty or thirty years old, she just looks run-down and sad. But the lights in the lounge room are always turned down low, so Clementine's shabbiness isn't so obvious.

The noisy commercial ends and a Channel Eight News Bulletin with Dan Martin and Susan Simons comes on. After Dan Martin reads the national news, mostly boring stuff about the session of Parliament in Canberra, Susan starts on the world news. All female newsreaders are pretty, and Susan Simons is prettier than most. But she has a hard, determined edge that sets her apart. It makes you pay attention to what she says.

'In New York, a well-known publicist has been arrested for allegedly driving her four-wheel drive vehicle into a crowd outside a nightclub,' Susan says, looking straight into the camera. 'Witnesses say that Lucy Grubb, publicist for several prominent actors and the daughter of an influential New York attorney, was angry at being told to move her car because it was blocking a fire hydrant.'

They cut to some news footage. 'She just went postal!' some guy in a polo shirt says in an American accent. 'She yelled, "– you, white trash!" and just ploughed right into a whole crowd of people!'

They've bleeped out the dirty word, but you can tell it was 'screw'.

'Local authorities say that nine people were taken to hospital for injuries ranging from severe abrasions to a crushed pelvis,' Susan continues. 'Police have not yet disclosed whether Miss Grubb remains in custody, or whether bail has been set.'

Bindi and Cinnamon explode into a fit of laughter. They think the whole thing is hilarious. 'Screw you, white trash!' Bindi screams at Cinnamon.

'No, screw *you*, white trash!' Cinnamon screams back.

I just know they're going to go around saying 'Screw you, white trash' for the rest of the week. They're too stupid to realise that they really are white trash. They're slutty and common. Bindi brags about her boyfriend who's a dealer, and Cinnamon's always going on about how much money she made as a stripper in Kings Cross.

They're the sort of girls that toffs can get away with crushing under the tyres of their expensive cars. But if Bindi or Cinnamon got behind the wheel drunk or stoned and mowed someone down, they'd be sent straight to jail.

I burrow down further into Clementine and hope they shut up before the nine o'clock movie comes on.

'What's going on?' Lyyssa is standing in the doorway. She must have heard Bindi and Cinnamon screaming 'screw you' at each other.

'Nothing,' Bindi says sullenly.

'Bindi, I thought we had an agreement. We agreed that you wouldn't watch TV after nine o'clock until you –' Lyyssa catches herself in time, ever mindful of 'breaking confidentiality' or 'betraying trust'. Lyyssa bites her lip. 'You remember our agreement, don't you?'

Bindi's not exactly stupid, but she has trouble in school. Probably, Lyyssa wants her to stop watching so much TV until her marks improve.

'Yeah, right.' Bindi sighs and gets up from the couch, pushing past Lyyssa and stomping down the hall to her bedroom. Cinnamon follows her. 'Screw you, white trash!' 'No, screw *you*, white trash!' I hear them saying to each other, before going into their rooms.

Lyyssa looks confused. 'What was that all about?' she asks.

I tell Lyyssa I don't know. Karen turns her eyes back to the TV.

Chapter 12

To get to my tutoring sessions with Miss Dunn, I walk to the main road and catch a bus.

If you're over twelve at the Refuge, you get a MyMulti1 train, bus and ferry pass along with your pocket money. It's cool that you can go pretty much any place in Sydney, but the rule is that you're not supposed to go to a certain list of off-limits places, like Kings Cross and Redfern.

There are a couple of people I keep seeing on the bus. One is a dwarf man with dyed purple hair who always has headphones on. Another is an European-looking lady who always carries lots of shopping bags. Today, they're both on the bus. It's going to be the same bus ride as always, or so I think, until the woman sitting behind me starts talking.

'I am not a loose woman!' she says loudly.

I turn around in my seat and glance at her. She's older, wearing a daggy sweater, with short hair and a face set in a permanent frown. Her eyes have that million-miles-away look. *Not the full quid*, Daddy would have said.

'I said, I am *not a loose woman*!' she says, even louder. She's not talking to anyone on the bus; she's talking to someone who's not there. Even so, everybody on the bus, except the dwarf who's nodding to the music on his headphones, starts finding something else to do. The European lady pulls a letter from her purse and pretends to read it. A uni student pulls a textbook out of his backpack and opens it. Another student turns his head to the window.

'Please stop casting as-per-sions upon my character!' the woman says firmly. She has trouble pronouncing 'aspersions'. Why bother using words you can't pronounce?

The bus fills up gradually. A noisy group of teenage boys gets on, and their loud talk drowns out the woman who's not the full quid. They're also drowning out the dwarf's music – I see him purse his mouth, look annoyed, and turn up the volume.

'I do not sleep around,' I hear the woman mumble, as I pile out of the bus with all the people getting off at the University bus stop.

Miss Dunn has me wait in her office while she takes care of some business upstairs. While I'm waiting, I look up 'aspersion' in the dictionary that I find on one of the bookshelves. *Slander, calumnious report or remark.* In other words, telling lies about someone. I kind of figured that was what it meant.

'Sorry to keep you, Len,' Miss Dunn says, coming back into the office. She notices me putting the dictionary back on the shelf. 'Did you want to borrow one of my books?'

'I was just looking up a word,' I explain.

'Yeah?' Miss Dunn says. Today she looks tired, with dark circles under her eyes. 'What word, if you don't mind my asking?'

'Aspersions. As in "casting aspersions upon my character".'

Miss Dunn laughs a little. '*Casting aspersions upon my character*. How appropriate. There's certainly plenty of that in the academic world.' I get the feeling that the meeting that she just had upstairs didn't go very well. 'Anyway, let's get to work.'

After we've finished, Miss Dunn apologises for not offering me tea, explaining that she has to finish an article she's supposed to write. I'm disappointed, but not offended. I'm glad Miss Dunn thinks I'm mature enough that she can speak to me honestly.

Not staying for tea and a chat with Miss Dunn leaves a hole in my afternoon. I decide to walk back to the shelter instead of taking the bus.

Casting aspersions upon my character. The phrase keeps twisting itself around in my mind, annoying me like the whine of a mozzie right next to my ear. Everyone else on the bus has probably forgotten about the woman who was talking to herself. So why do I keep thinking about that peculiar thing she said?

I'm at the top of University Road when it hits me. *Casting aspersions upon my character* was a line in that

Clarissa Hobbs, Attorney at Law episode that aired a few weeks ago.

I've just about replayed the whole episode in my head by the time I make it back to the shelter. It pisses me off that the nutcase woman who says embarrassing things out loud on city buses is a *Clarissa Hobbs* fan, just like me. One of the things I've always liked about *Clarissa Hobbs* is that no one else at the Refuge watches it.

It takes me a whole week to stop being annoyed about that. Fortunately, I never see the woman on the bus again.

Chapter 13

It's a *Clarissa Hobbs*: *Attorney at Law* night, so I'm lying on Clementine in the lounge room. Shane is already in bed. Bindi has been sent to her room for the evening because she called Karen a fat little pig at the dinner table and made her cry.

'Yeah, like I really care about being sent to my room,' Bindi sneered. 'Youse all suck, anyway.'

She scraped back her chair, practically threw it against the table, and stomped out of the dining room without taking her plate to the kitchen. As soon as the dishes were washed, Cinnamon went to Bindi's room. The two of them are up there listening to music and laughing loudly. Lyyssa is in her office typing. Karen is sitting in her favourite armchair. I don't really like to be in the same room as Karen, but at least she's keeping quiet, apart from the occasional snuffle.

You know what's really stupid? Karen's crying because Bindi called her a fat little pig for taking all the mashed potatoes from the bowl before it had been around the table. If you're going to get upset if people call you a fat pig, the sensible thing to do would be, maybe, go on a diet? Or at least not get any fatter. So what does Karen do? After she's already eaten a huge dinner, she gets a bag of miniature candy bars from her room and starts eating them in front of the TV. I bet you she finishes the whole bag before the show is over.

After some stupid ad for a discount bedding warehouse, the opening sequence comes on, with Clarissa driving her BMW through sunny LA, Clarissa addressing a jury, Clarissa playing racquetball, Clarissa passionately kissing a handsome, grey-haired man. I block Karen out of my mind and concentrate on the story.

Sure enough, Clarissa Hobbs is defending Trell again, just like she said she would.

Last time, Clarissa got Trell acquitted when he was wrongfully accused of arson and manslaughter. This time, Trell has been accused of shooting dead a rival gang member outside a Burger King restaurant, and Clarissa knows that he's guilty.

Even so, Trell won't admit his guilt to Clarissa. He keeps crapping on about how he was with his girlfriend that night, but Clarissa isn't fooled. When Clarissa threatens not to represent him, Trell finally comes clean.

'So I did it. So what?' Trell looks sullen and angry.

'*So what*?!' Clarissa shouts. 'So you're going to be on Death Row right next to your old man if you don't take this seriously!'

Trell starts to look afraid. 'You the best lawyer in LA,' he whispers. 'You gotta get me off.'

'I can't do that without your help,' Clarissa says, her voice calmer.

They work out a strategy. Trell is going to admit to the shooting, but will plead self-defence. She'll also try to stack the jury with people likely to be sympathetic to someone like Trell. 'And we've got to get you a suit,' she concludes.

'I got one at home,' Trell says in a low voice. 'My mama can bring it.'

'By the way, Trell,' Clarissa adds, 'you said I was the best lawyer in LA. Actually, I'm the best lawyer in the state of California.'

Trell manages a wry smile as he is led away, cuffed and shackled.

As the closing credits roll, it's late at night and Clarissa is back at her office working on Trell's case with a bunch of junior lawyers. They're sitting around a huge table reading thick law books and eating takeaway food from Burger King.

Are there Burger King restaurants in Australia? If there are, they're probably about the same as McDonald's.

'Is there a Burger King any place around here?' I ask Lyyssa during our weekly counselling session.

Lyyssa is both thrilled that I've said something and flustered about what to say.

'Burger King? Well! Um . . . let's see. Burger King is an American fast-food chain, but we have a restaurant called Hungry Jack's that's the same thing. Why? Do you want to go there?'

So that's how the whole damn Refuge got to go to Hungry Jack's for dinner. Well, everyone except Jo and Sky Morningstar, who are boycotting Hungry Jack's because breeding cattle to make hamburgers causes soil erosion and greenhouse gases. Honestly, I don't know which is more embarrassing – being seen with the other Refuge kids at the Westgardens Metro, or being seen with them at Hungry Jack's. Karen, instead of whizzing her pants, spills her thick shake down her front. Bindi, instead of being mean to Karen about whizzing her pants, is mean to Karen about spilling her thick shake. Cinnamon, instead of flirting with some store clerk, starts making eyes at some teenage ethnic guys at the next table who are all wearing Lonsdale tracksuits and baseball caps on backwards. They're good-looking, but I wouldn't trust them for a minute. They're grinning at Cinnamon and saying stuff to each other in Arabic. Probably they're saying, 'Look at that slut's boobs'.

Cinnamon's so damn stupid. It's boys like them who got arrested some years back because they pack-raped some girl and hosed her down afterward. They think every girl who doesn't wear a headscarf is a moll.

I'm still safe from things like that. The guys don't

even notice me, because I'm still a girl, not even close to being a woman.

As if things weren't bad enough, now that stupid LeeLee Nelson song, 'I'm Still a Girl, Not Yet a Woman' is running through my head. How do you get rid of a song going through your head?

'Karen, stop crying, it's okay, I'll get you another thick shake,' Lyyssa is saying, on their way back from the ladies' room, where they've been cleaning up Karen's shirt as best they can. There's still a big wet spot and the trace of a chocolate stain across Karen's chest. Her face is as red as her hair and her eyes are nearly swollen shut from crying. As soon as she sits down, she starts chowing on the super-size fries that she left, even though they must be cold by now.

Lyyssa goes to the counter to get another thick shake for Karen and chocolate sundaes for Shane and me. I'm still drinking my Coke, watching Cinnamon flirting with the boys.

Bindi is staring at me. Why is she staring at me when she's got Karen to make fun of? I realise, with a flush of shame rising to my cheeks, that I've been humming 'I'm Still a Girl, Not Yet a Woman'.

'Hey, look!' Bindi screams, grabbing Cinnamon's arm. 'Len thinks she's LeeLee Nelson!' They start shrieking, and then do a piss-take of 'I'm Still a Girl, Not Yet a Woman' for the boys, who whistle and cheer.

I'm so humiliated I can barely eat my ice-cream

when Lyyssa brings it back. All the way home, Bindi, who's sitting behind me in the van, hums that stupid song in my ear.

I go straight to my room when we get back to the Refuge. I don't even care what Lyyssa and the rest of these morons are up to.

The best way to calm down and forget about something unpleasant is to read a book you don't care anything about. You don't even have to read the book; just skimming your eyes over the text and looking at the pictures is enough. There's a book called *Japanese Prints* that's really good for that. It was in another box that came from the Salvation Army. The book is only a little one, only ten centimetres square. I snapped it up because it had a picture of a huge wave on the front, but the pictures inside aren't as good. They're drawings of old-fashioned Japanese ladies with small, squinty eyes who carry parasols and wear chopsticks in their hair, and Japanese men with really weird haircuts. When I'm in a certain mood, I like to flick through the pictures until I feel nice and bored and ready to sleep.

A Woman Strolling. Woman Holding a Comb. Surimono: Stretching Cloth. Young Woman with a Caged Monkey.

That one makes me look more closely. Animals in cages make me sad, even though the monkey is in a wooden cage, not a cruel metal cage. He's reached out with one arm and grabbed the edge of the lady's kimono, and she's looking down at him. You can't tell from her expression whether she thinks the monkey is being cute, or whether she's annoyed that he's got hold of her dress. I wonder if it's her pet monkey, and whether she takes him out of his cage and plays with him when she's not so dressed up.

This book isn't working anymore. I'm getting interested in the pictures.

I turn off the light and try to sleep, even though Bindi and Cinnamon are still making noise in their rooms. I can't stop thinking about those ethnic boys we saw at Hungry Jack's. It's because they make me think of something else, something I don't want to think about.

I push it back for a while, trying to hear what Bindi and Cinnamon are up to, trying to think about the Japanese pictures. I finally give up, and the memory rises to the surface.

'Can't stand dealing with foreigners,' says Ernie. I'm lying on the floor. I was colouring in my new colouring books, but now I'm just lying on my stomach, half-asleep. Reggie is asleep in front of the fire, as close as he can get without being burned. Daddy keeps having to pull him back so he doesn't catch on fire, but Reggie's fur is so hot to the touch that Daddy has to put on gloves each time he does it. Then Ernie laughs at Daddy. Then Daddy says 'STAY!' to Reggie. Then Reggie inches back toward the fire a little bit at a time when Daddy isn't looking, then Daddy has to put his gloves on and do the

whole thing over, and Ernie laughs at Daddy again.

Ernie spits into the fire and there's a hiss. 'Send 'em all back where they come from, as far as I'm concerned.'

Reggie creeps a couple of inches toward the fire. 'Reggie!' Daddy says sharply. Reggie pretends not to hear, settles his head on his front paws, and closes his eyes.

'That is one spoiled dog,' says Ernie. 'One boot up the arse would teach him to do as he's told.'

'He's not a working dog, he's a pet,' says Daddy. 'It doesn't hurt to spoil a pet.' Daddy picks me up and sits me on his lap. I'm tired so I rest my head on his chest. He's wearing a flannie. There's something in the pocket that presses against my cheek.

Daddy ruffles my hair. 'Two things it doesn't hurt to spoil: your pet dog, and your daughter. With a son, you've got to make him into a man. But a daughter, you can spoil her and there's no harm done.'

I'm tired because we just got back from Coffs. Daddy bought me two My Little Ponys, one pink and one purple.

Chapter 14

Karen is up early the next morning, probably for a doctor's appointment. I hear her whining when Lyyssa wakes her, then I hear her clomping to the bathroom, then I hear the front door bang shut and a car drive off. I don't know where she's going or care whether she comes back.

I didn't sleep well last night. I dreamt of monkeys in cages, of me standing on a table at Hungry Jack's singing while Cinnamon and Bindi jeered and ethnic boys yelled *Hose her down, hose her down*.

My eyelids feel gummy. I don't want to get up. I try to go back to sleep, but I just lie awake, miserable, and remember something else I don't want to know.

The man in the flannelette shirt is cutting something into pieces on the kitchen table, which is why I can't sit there to colour in my colouring books. There's another man watching, and two yellow-haired women talking to each other and not paying any attention. I'm in the lounge room sitting on the couch being quiet. The man in the flannelette shirt puts the pieces onto a shiny scale the colour of pirate coins. That side falls down to the table. He puts a little brass thing onto the other side. Then that side falls down. He adds a smaller brass thing, and then takes the bigger one away. The two sides of the scale seesaw, then balance.

'Never seen a scale like that before,' says the man watching.

'Belonged to my granddad,' Daddy says. 'He owned a corner store in Bankstown before the foreigners took over.'

The light in the kitchen makes the scale and the pieces of brass sparkle like the doubloons in the book about pirates, or the gold in the pot at the end of the rainbow.

'Buried treasure!' I yell, pointing to the scales with my Texta.

Everyone laughs, but Daddy folds his arms across his chest and says, 'Possum, go outside and play.'

I throw the doona off, grab my notebook, and write down what I remembered about Daddy and the scales.

The shower's free, so I take my toiletries and bathrobe. Music is blasting from Bindi's room down the hall. It's Saturday, so Lyyssa's rule about no loud music on weekdays doesn't apply.

Bindi and Cinnamon must have heard me going into the showers; one of them screams a couple of bars from, 'I'm Still a Girl, Not Yet a Woman' over the music, then they both laugh. They'll probably rag me about that song for a week or two before they get tired of it.

When I come out of the shower, they've put on

some gangsta rap. They yell along with whoever's singing about bitches and ho's.

Lyyssa will probably tell them to turn it down when she gets back, but I don't think I can stand it that long. I've got to get out of the house. I cram a book, my bathing suit, towel and all the rest of my swimming stuff into my backpack. It's warm enough to swim and read in the park afterwards.

I grab a couple of muesli bars from the kitchen and write, 'Gone to the pool – back before curfew. Len' on the whiteboard.

The only stroke I like is freestyle. My swim teacher made me learn backstroke and breast stroke to get my certificate of completion, but I never do them on my own.

Lyyssa asked me once how many laps I do. For once, it was a question of hers that I didn't mind, but I couldn't answer because I don't know. I don't see the point in counting. Scott, the physio, tried to get me to start counting my laps and work up gradually, or at least time myself so that I don't strain anything. But I don't. I just swim until I get tired.

Stroke, two, three, breathe. Stroke, two, three, breathe. Don't lift your head out of the water and gasp for air. Turn your head to the side, let the water cushion your head like a pillow, inhale. Look straight at the bottom of the pool. Stroke, two, three, breathe.

If you're lucky, there aren't any screaming kids

splashing around or grannies puttering along at a snail's pace with their kickboards, afraid of getting their hair wet.

Once I'm warmed up, stroke-two-three-breathe becomes pull-pull-pull-breathe. I forget about everything except the blue of the water and the taste of chlorine. When my left shoulder starts to ache and my elbows feel funny and cold, I ease off, then pull myself out of the pool and run to the showers, where there are signs warning that inappropriate behaviour will not be tolerated.

I think I know why they'd put a sign like that in the men's showers. But why in the ladies?

At three o'clock I'm in the park with my swimsuit and towel spread across the grass to dry, when a shadow falls across my book.

The sun has dropped behind a tree. I could just move, but I'm getting hungry and I've already eaten the two muesli bars I brought. Where could I get something to eat?

I walk to Town Hall Station and fifteen minutes later, I'm riding up a long escalator. I go across a concourse with a newsagent and shoe-repair shop, then up another escalator. On street level to the left of the escalator, there's a shop selling all kinds of kinky shoes and boots.

Kings Cross. I'm not supposed to be here. I'll just get something to eat, then leave.

I come off the escalator right into the middle of a

fight between an Aboriginal girl and her boyfriend; she's yelling at him about how he never does this and he never does that. I dodge them and come to the footpath in front of the station.

There's an ambulance, and a small crowd. Everybody's looking at a guy lying on the ground with his head in a pile of his own puke. He's a young guy, wearing jeans and a plaid shirt. His skin is pale and he's out cold, but I guess he'll live. The ambos don't look too concerned as they lift him up and strap him to a gurney.

Nobody in the crowd looks too concerned, either. One blondish pimply flabby guy in a blue shirt is standing there eating KFC nuggets. A couple of tourists wearing sandals and bum bags are holding their cameras like they're trying to decide whether to take a picture or not.

'Hey, it's something to watch,' a dark-haired guy in an expensive-looking shirt says, with a shrug. The pretty, mini-skirted girl hanging onto his arm looks up at him and giggles. No matter what that guy said, she'd agree with it. Two Asian girls are speaking in Chinese or Korean or whatever, not taking any notice of the guy on the ground. Then the Aboriginal girl and her boyfriend come over, carrying on the same argument.

'Yeah, yeah,' the boyfriend says, annoyed. The girl only stops ragging on him when she hears the two Asian girls talking. She stares at them for a minute.

'Foreigners,' she mutters. 'They come to my country, they can speak my language.' Then she remembers that she's mad at her boyfriend and starts in on him again about that thing he didn't do, and they head off.

That Aboriginal girl was speaking English. Shouldn't she be mad at the Asians for not speaking Aboriginal? Can *she* speak Aboriginal?

I'm getting confused about this when a guy who's been hovering at the other side of the ambulance buzzes past me, circling the crowd. He's old, maybe fifty, and is wearing an army helmet. He's not normal. His clothes are dirty and his face, what you can see of it around his sunglasses, has that hard, crazy look. He's carrying three library books in one hand and a tambourine in the other. He starts skipping, shaking his tambourine, doing some jerky little dance as the ambos load the sick boy into the ambulance. When they slam the door shut, the weird guy gives his tambourine a long shake, then an abrupt smack – rrrrp, BANG! As if to say, 'That's all, folks!'

The ambulance drives off and everyone in the crowd stands there a few seconds just blinking and looking stupid, trying to remember what they were doing before the guy OD'd and the ambulance came. The guy in the expensive shirt reaches for his ringing mobile and flips it open. 'Hello? Yeah, we're on our way, be there in five.' His girlfriend squeezes his arm again, and they cross the street. A man outside a strip club says something to them, and the girlfriend squeals and does the arm-grab thing to Expensive Shirt. Does that girl ever talk? Does her arm work if it isn't hooked to some guy's arm?

The Asian girls move onto the footpath. The tourists amble off like a couple of confused cows. The flabby guy stuffs the rest of his chicken nuggets into his mouth and looks around for a rubbish container for the paper bag. I remember that I'm hungry.

I don't really like the look of most places I see. There's a KFC and a Hungry Jack's. KFC? No thank you, not after seeing some fat guy eating KFC while he's looking at some other guy lying in his own vomit. And I'll probably never go to Hungry Jack's again, after being embarrassed to death when Lyyssa took us there. There's a Copenhagen Ice-cream and an Asian place with fish in the windows. I walk as far as Potts Point, where there are nice restaurants with outside tables, but I don't want to blow all my pocket money on one meal. Anyway, they'd probably think I was weird if I walked in all by myself.

I walk back toward the station, passing a tattoo parlour with bikies hanging around outside. I don't look at them. They might be harmless, but you never know. I don't look too closely at the strip clubs, either. Normally, the men standing outside try to invite people inside, but when I walk past, they either pretend not to see me or else look a bit concerned.

'You all right, there, miss?' a big Samoan guy asks

me quietly. Usually, when someone says that in an area like this, what they really mean is, I've got drugs to sell, if you want to buy any. But this guy really does seem to care if I'm all right. He probably thinks I'm a runaway or a street kid.

There are men who would pay to have sex with someone as young as me, or who'd force themselves on someone as young as me, even though I'm nothing special to look at. Half a block back, some skinny moll in a tube top, tight shorts, and thigh-high boots gave me the evil eye like I was a competitor. Yeah, right. I'm wearing no makeup, my hair smells like chlorine, and I'm carrying a backpack. Who'd think I was on the game?

I ignored the moll, but I smile at the Samoan. 'I'm just getting some takeaway,' I tell him. The Samoan guy seems nice; I wouldn't mind talking to him some more. But I keep walking.

I'm almost back to the station and still haven't found any place I want to eat. I end up standing in front of a pizza place I passed by earlier. I look at the pizzas in the glass case. They have sausage, peperoni, Hawaiian, and vegetarian. The vegetarian pizza is still round and perfect; nobody has taken a slice yet. Three-fifty a slice, the sign says. I pull a five-dollar note from my back pocket and look for a shop assistant. There are two young Asian girls and one young Asian guy behind the counter, but no one makes a move to ask what I want.

'Excuse me,' I say. A girl standing next to the cash register looks at me and blinks. The other girl walks into the back room, then walks back out again. The boy is sitting at the table doing nothing. All of them have a kind of glazed look in their eyes.

'Ex-*cuse* me,' I say a little louder. 'Could I get a slice of vegetarian, please?'

The girl who came out of the back room says something to the boy in Vietnamese or whatever, and he says something back. She says something to the girl standing next to the cash register, who looks over her shoulder, then slowly turns her head back to me and tries to get her eyes to focus.

I put the five-dollar note on the counter. 'Veg-e-tar-i-an,' I say, loudly. '*One* slice.'

The girl has no idea what I want. She makes a squeaking noise that means, 'What?'

I point at the pizza and make a 'one' sign with my index finger.

The girl finally gets it and picks up a pair of tongs. She grabs a piece of pizza, drops it on the floor, and shrieks. The boy at the table gabbles at her in Vietnamese, then gabbles something at the girl who keeps going in and out of the back room. She grabs the tongs and puts another slice of pizza in a paper bag for me. The first girl just stands there looking at the floor where she dropped the first piece. I'm annoyed that the slice I got was the second slice from the pizza, not the first slice. I push the five dollar note to the second girl, who has to think a minute before she can work out how much change to give me. I pull some serviettes from a dispenser and leave in disgust.

Chapter 15

I get back to the Refuge just five minutes before eight. Lyyssa is in the kitchen with Cinnamon, drying the dishes from dinner. 'Just in time, Len,' she says to me, looking at the clock.

'I'm never late, am I?' I say.

'No, you're not,' Lyyssa says. 'But we missed you at dinner.' Cinnamon gives me a nasty look meaning *she* didn't miss me, and neither did Bindi. Bindi is up in her room. Lyyssa has learned not to put Cinnamon and Bindi on kitchen duty at the same time.

'I got some takeaway,' I say. 'Here, I'll help with the rest of the drying. Cinnamon can leave if she wants.' I put down my backpack and grab a tea towel. Cinnamon throws down her tea towel and practically runs out of the kitchen and up the stairs to where Bindi is. If I didn't know better, I'd say those two were lezzo lovers.

There are only a few things left to dry, so I got some brownie points with practically no effort. Normally, I would watch some TV, but I feel tired. I try to read the ending of my book before I go to bed, but I can't concentrate.

It must be about eleven when I wake up. I feel dizzy. I'm going to be sick. I run to the bathroom and vomit into the toilet, but that's not the end of it. I keep heaving and heaving even though there's nothing left in my stomach. Then I start to cry. I've never felt so bad in my whole life. I want Daddy, but I don't know where he is. I hear Cinnamon stomp downstairs and pound on Lyyssa's door. 'Len's puking her guts out,' she yells, sounding annoyed. Then she stomps back to her room and closes the door.

'Len!' Lyyssa's in her bathrobe. She kneels beside me and rubs my back. I'm embarrassed about the vomit smell but Lyyssa doesn't seem to mind. She helps me rinse my mouth out. 'Here, let's get you back into bed.' I stagger back to my room, hanging onto Lyyssa for support. Lyyssa brings me some cherry-flavoured medicine and two cans of Coke.

'You poor thing. It must be the flu. I hope the rest of the kids don't come down with it.' Lyyssa puts the wastepaper basket next to the bed in case I have to be sick again.

'It's not the flu.' I've taken a few sips of Coke and I'm starting to feel a little better. 'It was the pizza.' Even though I know I should just keep my mouth shut, I tell Lyyssa about the pizza place and the Vietnamese kids and the guy lying in his own puke until the ambulance took him away.

'Well, it wasn't pizza that made him sick,' Lyyssa says, with a hardness in her voice I've never heard before.

'I know. It was heroin. I know all about that.'

Lyyssa is quiet for a good few seconds. 'Len, you've gone to a place specifically off limits. If the Foundation or DOCS hears about that, they might say I breached my duty of care. They might want to move you to another home. A place where you'd have less freedom.'

I start to feel sick again. They could send me to Ramsay. Or some foster home. I can imagine what happens to kids in foster homes.

'I know you didn't go to Kings Cross to get into any trouble. But in a place like Kings Cross, trouble can find you.' For once, one of Lyyssa's bumper-sticker sayings is right on the mark.

'I won't go back there,' I promise, and I mean it.

Lyyssa relaxes a bit. 'Good. I'll have to tell Renate Dunn to explain why you won't be at your lesson tomorrow. But I think our secret is safe with her.'

I don't know what Lyyssa tells the other kids about me being sick. She insists that I stay in bed on Monday. I read and she brings me my meals on a tray. And for some reason, Bindi and Cinnamon never tease me about the LeeLee Nelson song again.

Chapter 16

No sooner do I get over the food poisoning and convince Lyyssa not to take away my MyMulti pass than I manage to get into trouble over Scott the physio.

Scott clips the ultrasound film onto a light box and points at it with his pen. 'See that bit there? That's fluid in the sub deltoid bursa. You also have some inflammation in the tissue around the rotator cuff joint.' Scott yanks down the ultrasound, puts up another, and points at a fuzzy patch with his pen.

My left shoulder was starting to hurt even when I wasn't swimming. I couldn't even pick up a glass of water with my left hand. When I rolled onto my left shoulder at night, the pain would wake me up.

Scott stuffs the ultrasound films back into their envelope and looks at me, his mouth pursed into a line. 'Your condition is known as Swimmer's Shoulder. It's an overuse injury that can be caused by poor technique or overtraining. It appears that you deliberately pushed yourself too hard in the pool, in spite of my instructions to start out slowly.'

Scott's getting angry with me is starting to make me angry. I'm the one in pain, after all.

'Why can't you just tell me what to do about it and skip the lecture?'

Scott looks even more annoyed than he was before. 'Len, in addition to your physical problems, you have a serious attitude problem. If you'd followed my instructions in the first place, you wouldn't have a new injury that might well be permanent.'

Scott sighs and starts writing on a notepad. 'I conferred with Dr Mengers and he agreed that prescription anti-inflammatories are not appropriate. You can take Nurofen for the pain. The medication will be dispensed by Lyyssa or other Resident Counsellors.'

'I think I'm old enough to take it myself.'

Scott doesn't look up from his notepad. 'Serious athletes, especially stubborn ones like you, often exceed the recommended dosage in order to mask the pain and continue training at an inappropriate pace.'

Scott keeps writing. I look around the room. There's an anatomy chart of the human muscular system on the wall.

'Can I have a copy of that chart?'

'No,' Scott says sourly. He purses his mouth some more and keeps writing on his notepad.

I look at his strawberry blond hair, his pale

eyelashes. He's wearing khaki trousers, a pink polo shirt, and white New Balance cross-trainers without a single scuff mark on them.

'Are you gay?'

Scott smacks his pen down on the desk and rips the page from the notepad.

Ha. I knew he was gay.

'I want you to follow this regimen exactly. Swimming three times a week, max, supervised by Kelly or another qualified instructor. She can design a workout to maintain the strength in your legs without aggravating your shoulder. Stuff like aqua jogging and treading water with leg weights. Do *not* strain yourself. Ice your shoulder for twenty minutes afterwards.' Scott hands me the page of instructions, his hand shaking just a little. 'Make an appointment at the desk to come see me in a month. And when you come back, leave the 'tude at home.'

'Tude. That's American. Scott probably heard it on TV.

Chapter 17

Progress Report

Len Russell (AKA Samantha Patterson)

Len presented a subdued and quiet demeanour in the days following her recovery from a probable case of food poisoning. She seemed to deliberately avoid conflict with her fellow IWYR residents, and this non-confrontational attitude was reciprocated.

Approximately two weeks after Len's illness, she requested an appointment with physiotherapist Scott Nelson. Scott, in concert with Dr Mengers of St Stephen's Hospital, has developed a program to help Len recover from her injuries and maintain a healthy level of flexibility and muscle development. Since her first consultation with Scott, Len has shown extraordinary motivation to improve her fitness and achieved excellent results.

Len reported pain in her left shoulder and elbow. It is unusual for Len to admit pain. Len has never faked illness and is loath to admit any weakness. I immediately arranged an appointment with Scott at St Stephen's physiotherapy unit.

Before Len had returned to the shelter after her scheduled appointment, I received a phone call from Scott, who reported that Len had questioned his professional judgment and taunted him about his sexuality. Scott is married, but currently identifies as bisexual and has recently separated from his wife. Scott reported that as a result of Len's comments, he is taking two weeks stress leave.

I invited Len to my office for a conference as soon as she returned to IWYR. I explained that Scott had complained of her being rude, and emphasised that such behaviour jeopardises the arrangement in which IWYR residents get priority, high-level medical care from St Stephen's. Len seemed surprised at Scott's complaint and became indignant. Len produced the list of instructions that Scott had given her, and showed me that she had copied the instructions into her spiral notebook on the bus. I accepted this as an indicator that Len values Scott's professional judgment and plans to follow his instructions.

Len was considerably less cooperative in acknowledging that she had made unacceptable comments that caused offence to Scott. Len refused to address the issue of her own behaviour, and repeatedly tried to change the subject to times when she had felt offended by others. Len claimed to have been offended by the conduct of young Lebanese men, and said she had nightmares about them. Len's explanation was fractured and emotional, but she seemed to be referring to a well-publicised pack rape in which the alleged perpetrators were of Lebanese origin.

Len agreed to write a short note of apology to Scott, but flatly refused to participate in an exercise examining her negative stereotypes about ethnic people.

It is likely that Len is suffering confusion about her own sexual orientation. Len prefers unisex clothing and disdains cosmetics. Perhaps labelling Scott as 'gay' and lashing out at ethnic men for alleged sexual misconduct is Len's way of masking confusion about her own sexuality.

To prevent Len's prejudices toward people of ethnic background from becoming entrenched, I have arranged for next month's IWYR outing to be a dinner at a Lebanese restaurant in the suburb where the pack-rape occurred.

Chapter 18

A fortnight after I write an apology to Scott, I get a reply.

Dear Len,

I was very pleased to get your letter. I do accept your apology, and it means a lot to me that you offered it. As a result of personal stress, I was impatient with you during our consultation. I apologise for this.

My new partner and I have decided to relocate to Melbourne, where I have accepted a new job. I hope you will continue practising your swimming and tennis, but at a reasonable pace, please! Enclosed are some diagrams of exercises to improve the range of movement in your shoulders.

With best wishes,
Scott

After I've finished putting the diagrams up on my wall, I get a blue icepack for my shoulder from the freezer, then head into the lounge room. I'm in a good mood tonight. My homework is finished, so I can watch TV. And it's a Mrs Rowles weekend.

Twice a month, Lyyssa goes away for the weekend and a part-time social worker, Mrs Rowles, looks after us. She's not like Sky Morningstar or Jo. Mrs Rowles is about fifty-five, short and wiry. Mrs Rowles runs a newsagency with her husband, and just does the two weekends a month with us for the extra income. Mrs Rowles views herself as our custodian, not as our psychologist/parent/saviour. She pretty much leaves us alone, knitting and drinking tea in front of the small television set in the guest room, keeping her door open in case we need anything.

Tonight, the house is quiet, almost peaceful. Karen and Shane are asleep. Cinnamon and Bindi are upstairs trying on clothes and doing stuff with their hair. I've got the lounge room to myself.

I switch on the TV. On the 8:30 news bulletin, there's more about Lucy Grubb. They show a picture of her at a Hollywood party looking sexy and wild, then a snap of her walking down the street in New York City in a black jumper and trousers, her blonde hair blowing in the wind. I'm torn between feeling admiration for her glamorous lifestyle, and hatred that she can squash you like a bug if you piss her off.

Then they show a snippet from a press conference. Lucy is standing between two serious-looking men wearing dark suits. Lucy looks pale and upset, and cries as she says she wants the people who were hurt to know how *sorry* she is, how *awful* she feels.

In one *Clarissa Hobbs* episode, one of Clarissa's

clients was moaning about how sorry he was for embezzling money and how terrible he felt and how he'd give back the money in a second if he hadn't already spent it. Clarissa told him to cut the crap.

I wonder if Lucy Grubb's lawyers are going to tell her to 'cut the crap'.

I flick the TV to another channel. A horror movie is just starting. You can tell it's going to be a horror movie from the music.

I don't really like horror movies. I can't decide whether to watch it or not. But it doesn't matter anyway, because Bindi and Cinnamon pick this moment to do something stupid and interrupt my TV viewing. They come down the stairs wearing trampy-looking clothes and loads of makeup and try to head out the front door. Mrs Rowles is in front of them like a flash.

'And just where do you two think you're going, dressed like that?' Mrs Rowles demands.

'We're going to a party,' Bindi says rudely, trying to stare Mrs Rowles down.

'You're not going anywhere!' Mrs Rowles barks. 'You're both under curfew and you know it. Now go upstairs, wash that crap off your face, and don't come back downstairs until tomorrow morning.'

Bindi turns back, but just has to say 'Bitch!' over her shoulder. Cinnamon giggles and starts to follow Bindi. Mrs Rowles grabs Bindi's wrist and expertly yanks her off balance. Bindi totters on her high heels and falls backwards against the wall. Mrs Rowles stares at Bindi. 'You ever call me that again, miss, and I'll telephone your mother and tell her to come get you,' she says in a low voice. Then she lets Bindi go. Bindi, suddenly looking crumpled and cheap instead of flashy and seductive like she did half a minute ago, jerks away and stomps up the stairs. Cinnamon follows her without a word.

Mrs Rowles watches them go upstairs with her arms folded across her chest. Then she looks into the lounge room, gives me a half-smile and a wink, then goes back to the guestroom and picks up her knitting.

I look at the TV. The movie is one of those where they make it hard for you to tell what's real and what's an illusion. Since I've missed the first five minutes of it, I've got no chance of understanding it. I switch off the TV, say goodnight to Mrs Rowles, and head upstairs to my room with my icepack.

I bet Lucy Grubb has a TV that tapes everything automatically, so she never misses anything she wants to watch.

Chapter 19

I finally take *The Story of a Piece of Coal* out of the Refuge library. I've convinced myself that I'll be cursed if I don't read it. Also, I feel sorry for that tattered little book. Edward A Martin, FGS, went to all that trouble to write a book about coal, and now he's dead (he must be; if he were alive he'd be about a hundred-and-fifty years old) and maybe this copy is the only one left in the whole world. To be honest, I don't exactly read it. I just look at the drawings and run my eyes over the text before I go to bed. It helps me get to sleep.

At the end of my next lesson with Miss Dunn, I finally ask her.

'What does FGS mean?'

Miss Dunn narrows her eyes and frowns a little. She had just asked me if I had any questions, but since the lesson was about Australia's contribution to the Second World War, the question sounds totally irrelevant. 'FGS? In what context? I mean, where did you read or hear that?'

I tell her about *The Story of a Piece of Coal*, written

by Edward A Martin, FGS.

Miss Dunn thinks for a second. 'FGS . . . Ah, Fellow of the Geological Society, I'd say. That means your Mr Martin was a scholar, and he'd been recognised for having made significant contributions to his field.' Miss Dunn looks at me for a moment with that half-amused look she sometimes gets. 'Probably a fascinating book for someone who lived in dreary turn-of-the-century London, but what made you pick it up?'

I tell her about the library at the Refuge, about the Saddle Club books and *Too Rich, Too Famous* and *Bessie Bunton Joins the Circus* and the historical romance with the pirate pashing the Cinnamon clone on the cover.

Miss Dunn has been chuckling at my description of all the stupid books we've got, but at the mention of the historical romance, her mouth falls open and she flushes with anger. 'They've got *bodice-rippers* in the library of a *children's* refuge?' Miss Dunn rises from her desk and paces the room. 'That IDIOT Lyyssa!' she hisses under her breath, then clamps her hand over her mouth. 'You didn't hear that,' she says. I nod. Miss Dunn takes a deep breath to calm herself, then picks up her handbag and keys. 'Len, come with me. I'm going to show you a real library. You can leave your backpack here.'

When I leave Miss Dunn's office that day, I have a card that lets me take books out of the University library. In my backpack are two books that have to be returned in a fortnight, or I'll be in trouble. I'll have to hide them carefully so no one at the Refuge steals them or pours Coke on them or smears poo in between the pages just for the sake of being vile.

On the bus home I look at my library card. I imagine the books at the Refuge library crying, humiliated now that their shabbiness has been exposed. 'You'll never read me now,' sobs *The Story of a Piece of Coal*. 'My pages will never be turned again,' wails *Memoirs of a Midget*. 'No one will ever love me!'

'I still love you,' I say in my head to the Refuge books. 'I'll read you someday.'

I hope they believe me.

Chapter 20

I come back to the Refuge the back way, through the yard that has an old-fashioned gazebo that no one uses. Except today it is being used, by Bindi and a large, angry woman with masses of frizzy dark hair and a face like a bulldog.

It's Bindi's mother.

Normally Bindi glares at me whenever I pass her. Today, she's too busy glaring at her mother to even notice me walk past. Bindi's mother is hammering away at her with angry questions. 'So, what are you gonna do?' the woman barks. Bindi says nothing. 'Answer me!' Bindi's mother insists, her voice getting louder. 'Are you coming home or not?' Bindi is sitting with her arms tightly crossed and her mouth clamped shut. Only her bowed shoulders give her away – she's afraid of her mother.

I keep on walking. I've just about made it to the back door when all hell breaks loose.

'You little slut! You've always been a little slut!' Bindi's mother is screaming, then she and Bindi are fighting and clawing like two cats.

'Bindi! Mrs Peters!' Lyyssa cries and comes running from the kitchen, where she was hovering during this attempted mother/daughter reunion that was doomed before it even started. She doesn't get to the gazebo in time to keep Bindi's mum from landing a punch to Bindi's mouth, or keep Bindi from tearing out a fistful of her mother's black hair. I beat it back to my room, without even stopping in the kitchen for a glass of Milo. I want to keep out of the way until everything cools down.

I hear Mrs Peters roar off in whatever rust-bucket of a car brought her here. I hear Lyyssa try to be soothing and Bindi yelling, 'Leave me alone, bitch!' I hear Lyyssa sigh, or at least I imagine I do. I can tell by the noise of the door closing that she's retreated to her office. She can't change what just happened, but she can write a report about it and put it in Bindi's file.

I wait for about fifteen minutes, then I figure it's safe to go to the kitchen. On my way I pass the door to the bathroom, which is slightly ajar. And I stop dead in my tracks. Bindi is standing in front of the mirror, frantically plucking her eyebrows with tweezers. Except she's gone too far, and plucked her eyebrows out of existence. Now she has two reddened, puffy arches above her eyes. Her lip is swelling up where her mother split it open.

'You need some ice,' I say without thinking. Bindi's head snaps around, and in an instant she's pulled me into the bathroom and pinned me against the wall.

'You know what this is, runt?' Bindi puts her thumb on the inside of my forearm and presses, sending a flash of pain right to the bone. 'That's a pressure point,' she hisses, pressing even harder. I whimper and my knees give way. 'My boyfriend taught me how to kill people. I can kill you if I want.' Bindi lets me slide to the floor and walks out. I put my head against the cool tile floor and cry.

Chapter 21

The bruise on my arm is fading, but I can't stop thinking about Bindi and her awful mother. And Bindi's been watching me lately, watching me with narrowed eyes that seem to have turned an even more poisonous shade of green. It makes me more nervous than when she was being openly nasty to me.

I think she wants to kill me. She's trying to figure out how she can do it without getting caught.

What I need is something I can use against Bindi. A really nasty secret. Something that I can tell everyone about if she doesn't leave me alone. And as I'm tracing the fading outline of the yellowing bruise, I realise I know where to find what I need.

I keep myself awake until 2 am, when I'm sure that everyone will be asleep. I take my penlight from my desk, quietly leave my room and go to the kitchen, where I find a knife and a screwdriver. Then I make my way to the back wing where Lyyssa's office is, where all of our secrets are kept.

The door, of course, is locked.

I hear Daddy's voice in the back of my mind. 'What a loser,' the voice says. 'Does he think this Mickey Mouse lock is going to keep anyone out? Picking this kind of lock is easier than opening a bottle of Carlton Cold.'

I use the knife and the screwdriver to work the door open. I step inside the room and close the door softly behind me, then wait for a few minutes to allow my eyes to adjust to the darkness. Fortunately, there are no curtains on the windows and enough light comes in from the street. I look at the filing cabinet in the corner. In the top right-hand corner, a tiny silver key rests in the lock. Lyyssa hasn't even thought to take the key with her. Careful not to bump into any furniture, I cross the room and pull open the middle drawer.

D, E, F. I finger through the alphabet. I catch a phrase here and there from someone's file, from kids who used to live here. Obviously, they never throw anything out.

```
    . . . drop in the frequency of urges to
check. His score on the Maudesley Obsessive
Compulsive Inventory (MOCI) fell from 19
(pre-treatment) to 6 (post-treatment). At a
six month follow-up session, Anthony reported
that although he will still have a passing
urge to check that the door is locked, he
can easily resist it and most of the time he
```

doesn't even think of checking things twice anymore.

Whatever. So that kid liked to make sure the door was locked, so what? I hope Bindi's file is more interesting.

I keep flipping through the files. G, H, I, J, K. Kunkle, Karen Louise.

Case Summary

Karen Louise Kunkle

I never thought to ask Karen's last name. 'Kunkle' sounds exactly like Karen: fat, clumsy and stupid.

Ten-year-old female, eldest of three children, obese and suffering from diabetes insipidus, which causes frequent urination if left untreated. Removed from her home after visit by DOCS caseworkers who were alerted by school authorities.

Karen's mother, Gertrude Kunkle, is obese and developmentally disabled. Karen and her siblings are the result of consensual incest between Gertrude Kunkle and her own father. Karen's father/grandfather, Clarence 'Clarrie' Kunkle, is mentally normal, though illiterate and pathologically shy. Karen's grandmother is deceased.

Karen demonstrated poor academic performance at school, where she was also the victim of bullying because of her poor hygiene and local gossip surrounding the family. Karen was nicknamed 'the piss girl' by fellow students because the odour of urine clung to her. Ostracism and victimisation of Karen increased after she was rumoured to be the cause of an epidemic of head lice that swept the school. Fellow students called Karen 'Lousie', in a cruel misspelling of her middle name. Karen's teacher became alarmed after seeing red welts on Karen's arms. Karen's mother, Gertrude, admitted to investigating DOCS officers that she had whipped Karen with a belt because she blamed her for bringing lice into the family home.

On inspecting the child's home, investigating officers found conditions of nearly uncontrolled filth and disorder in every room except the kitchen. Karen's mother was deemed neglectful for giving Karen her diabetes medication only erratically — Gertrude admitted to caseworkers that when the medicine ran out and the family had no money to buy more, Karen was simply kept home from school or sent to school wearing loose clothing and an improvised nappy.

Caseworkers also determined that the child slept in the same bed with her mother and her father/grandfather. No evidence suggested that Karen had been sexually abused, but she was deemed at risk of such abuse and removed from the home, along with her two younger siblings, who were successfully placed in long-term foster care.

Karen has a passive attitude, demonstrates flat affect and is socially unskilled – not surprising in light of her dysfunctional family background. School results and aptitude tests administered since Karen was taken into care show that her intelligence is in the lower end of the normal range.

Also notable is that Karen has not processed the concept of having any internal locus of control: she views herself as helpless, entirely at the mercy of external circumstances, and having no power to change her eating habits, grooming or behaviour.

Karen does not understand that she and her siblings are the product of incest, and seems unaware that the incest taboo is one of the reasons for the ostracism she suffered in her home community. Karen regards the severe bullying she endured as a normal manifestation of the hostile world outside the home, not as a phenomenon caused by her and her family's inability to conform to social mores.

Rorschach and other tests reveal an obsession with food and television, which Karen views as the only reliable sources of comfort and reassurance. The one unifying activity engaged in by this family was the preparation, cooking, and eating of meals, in which all family members took part. After meals, the family watched television. Food was usually nutritious, but also high-fat, high-calorie, and eaten in binge quantities.

Karen remains at the Inner West Youth Refuge pending a decision by the Family Court about whether she may be returned to her mother's custody. As Gertrude Kunkle, since her relocation to a housing project in Goulburn, has drifted into alcoholism and promiscuity, this is seen as unlikely.

No wonder Karen's such a drop-kick. Her whole family are fat overeaters, her mother's a retarded slut, and her father is also her grandfather.

I yawn. But Karen isn't the real reason I'm in Lyyssa's office. I'm looking for Bindi's file. I keep flicking through the alphabet. L, M, N, O, P.

Peters, Belinda, typed on a label. *Bindi*, written alongside it in Lyyssa's sloppy cursive writing. I take the file into a corner and click on my penlight.

I stop reading after a few minutes because I'll vomit if I go on. I feel sick and polluted and ashamed of myself. My hands are shaking as I replace the folder.

I look at the rest of the files and slowly flick through them. P, Q, R. My fingers stop at R. No, I can't look at my own file. There isn't time. I have to get out of here.

I lock the cabinet and survey the room to make

sure I left everything the way I found it. I creep back to my room and lock the door behind me. Then I check the door again to make sure I locked it. I try to sleep, but I keep seeing horrible pictures of a four-year-old Bindi screaming. Pictures of Bindi's drunken mother turning up the TV so she wouldn't hear, pretending not to know what her own husband was doing to her own daughter. I try to force the pictures out of my mind by thinking of Daddy. I don't know my father's name, or where he is now. But I do know what Daddy would do to Bindi's rock-spider father if he ever met him.

Just before I finally manage to fall into an uneasy sleep, I wonder what was in my case file. Probably nothing interesting, just the medical stuff from the hospital. I bet my file is the slimmest one in the cabinet. After all, I haven't told them anything.

Chapter 22

Incident Report – Inner West Youth Refuge Officer - Lyyssa Morgan

At 8:00 am 8 June, Non-Resident Counsellor Sky Morningstar alerted me that the lock on the door of my office at the IWYR had been tampered with. On investigation, I discovered scrapes to the lock and to the surrounding woodwork, although the office was still locked. No other areas of the IWYR showed signs of forced entry, and none of the alarms covering the exits had sounded. Therefore, I believe that the person responsible for the break-in must be one of the juvenile residents at IWYR.

Nothing in my office was damaged, but the filing cabinet had been left unlocked. None of the files appeared missing, but two, those of Belinda Peters and Karen Kunkle, appeared to have been removed from the cabinet and replaced. No pages are missing from either file. There is a photocopier in my office, but an access code is required to operate it, so it is safe to assume that no sensitive information was copied.

It is verging on impossible that Karen Kunkle is the culprit, as she has neither the mechanical ability nor the initiative to accomplish such an act. In addition, Karen has shown no curiosity about the contents of her file.

Belinda Peters, by contrast, has extremely high intelligence and has in the past associated with criminals who may have taught her methods of breaking and entering. Recently, Belinda had an unpleasant visit with her biological mother that resulted in a physical altercation. Since that time, Belinda has exhibited anxiety and anger at the possibility of returning to her birth family.

As IWYR has a policy of openness, there was no need for Belinda to break into my office if she wished to view the contents of her file. Belinda is aware of this policy, but as her early life consisted of a brutal series of betrayals, Belinda may not have trusted me to honour it.

I consider that Belinda Peters was the most likely person responsible for the break-in, and that her probable motivation was to discover if DOCS and other authorities planned to return her to her birth family.

The motive for disturbing Karen Kunkle's file is unclear. Although Belinda has behaved in a rude and bullying manner toward Karen Kunkle, her attitude is one of self-centred defensiveness and aggression. Belinda demonstrates no curiosity about Karen or any other IWYR residents, and I cannot imagine Belinda having any interest in viewing Karen's file.

In the absence of definite proof that Belinda is responsible for the break-in, and in view of Belinda's fragile emotional state, I have chosen not to mention the incident to her or other residents of IWYR.

A funding request has been submitted to pay for a more sophisticated lock on the office door.

Chapter 23

For a couple of days I had what Clarissa Hobbs would call a moral dilemma. It's wrong to invade people's privacy. It's unethical to blackmail people by threatening to reveal damaging information. But on the other hand, I had every right to threaten Bindi with revealing her terrible secret, because if I didn't, Bindi would go ahead and kill me.

But a couple of days after I broke into Lyyssa's office, Bindi disappeared, and my moral dilemma disappeared along with her.

At first I worried for my own sake. Maybe Bindi was just getting me to drop my guard so she could come back in the middle of the night and slit my throat. Then I started to worry for Bindi's sake. Maybe she was on the street somewhere, knocking around with people who are worse arseholes than her mother and father. And then I stopped thinking about her much at all.

Lyyssa and Sky Morningstar tried to have one of their stupid 'rap sessions', where we were supposed to talk about how we felt about Bindi being gone, but no one wanted to say anything.

The only person who really cares is Cinnamon. Now she shuffles around with slumped shoulders and dull eyes, hardly says anything, and mumbles a reply if anyone speaks to her. Her sessions with Lyyssa must be even more excruciating than mine.

It's not just that Cinnamon misses her friend, it's that she has no personality of her own. Cinnamon is a follower, a hanger-on. She needs someone to tell her what to think and how to act. She was only ever nasty to me because Bindi was, not because she had any problem with me. In a way, I dislike her more than I ever disliked Bindi. At least Bindi made up her own mind about who she liked and didn't like.

Today, I'm making a vegetable stir-fry. The recipe calls for a wok, but we don't have one, so I'm using a plain old frying pan. I'm doing more cooking since Bindi isn't around, now that I don't have to schedule my kitchen time according to when she's is likely to come in and make trouble for me.

I make enough for two serves. One bowl I cover with plastic wrap and put in the fridge. I take a hair from my head and fold it into where the plastic wrap clings to the bowl, so that I can tell if anyone's tampered with it. What if Karen took off the plastic wrap and put her pissy-smelling finger into it? What if Bindi sneaked back and put poison into it? I'm not worried about anyone eating it, though. I must be the only person in the house except Lyyssa and Sky who actually likes vegetables.

The other bowl of stir-fry I take to the dining room and eat. I've just sat down at the dining table, at my usual place even though there's nothing to stop me from sitting at the head of the table or anywhere else, when I hear Lyyssa's voice coming from down the hall. She's in her office, talking on the phone with the door closed. I can barely hear what she's saying, but there's something about her tone of voice that makes me want to listen. I look down at my food. It's still steaming hot. I decide to eavesdrop on Lyyssa for a little while.

'But you said you were going to tell her last weekend!' Lyyssa cries. Silence for a minute or so, with Lyyssa making little noises of protest. 'Daniel, this isn't fair, not to me, and not to Bronwyn. You've got to tell her about us.'

A light bulb goes off above my head, just like in a cartoon. I get the picture. Poor stupid Lyyssa. As if a shelter full of problem kids isn't enough for her to deal with, she has to go and start a romance with somebody who's already taken. I start eating, catching just a phrase here and there about 'relationships' and 'agreements' and 'promises'. I finish eating and take my dirty dishes back to the kitchen to wash up. Lyyssa's always lecturing us kids about 'self-defeating behaviour cycles'. It sounds like she actually knows what she's talking about, for a change. But if Lyyssa can't stop herself from bonking a married man, how are the rest of us supposed to stop doing whatever it is we're not supposed to be doing?

I wash my dishes and put them away. Lyyssa is still talking on the phone as I leave the kitchen. 'So, next weekend, then?' she says, in a hopeful tone. Is next weekend a Mrs Rowles weekend? Lyyssa is probably planning a weekend away with Dickweed Daniel.

I climb the stairs to my room. Lyyssa can't work it out that getting a good screw isn't worth being screwed over. Hey, that's pretty clever, I think, as I open the door to my room. A good screw isn't worth being screwed over. That's really good. I'm proud of myself for thinking that up. Too bad I've got no one to share it with.

Chapter 24

It's after Easter, so everyone has money. Daddy bought a new motorcycle last week. We just went down to Coffs Harbour to get me some new clothes, and on the way back we stopped by Ernie's house.

Ernie's girlfriend Kerry is at his place, and she's brought her friend Brianna. They've just got back from Kmart, where Kerry spent some of Ernie's money and Brianna spent some of her cropper boyfriend's money. Kerry mostly bought clothes for herself, Brianna mostly bought things for the baby she's holding on her lap.

Kerry is cutting the tags off two pairs of jeans and some shirts.

'I have a pair just like that.' Brianna points at the pair of acid-wash jeans. Kerry holds them up to show the back, which has lacing like a corset. 'But I can't get into 'em since I had Jaidyn.' The baby on her lap drools and gurgles.

'You tried Herbalife?' Kerry asks. 'My mum lost heaps of weight on Herbalife.'

Kerry and Brianna start talking about weight loss pills, even though they're both really skinny anyway. Then Brianna takes Jaidyn into a bedroom to change him, and Kerry follows her so they can keep talking. Ernie gets two beers from the fridge and hands one to Daddy. He got a Coke for me as soon as we arrived.

'Gee, you're a nice guy,' Daddy says, nodding toward the sound of the chattering women.

'Got me arm up me back,' Ernie says in a low voice. Ernie means that since Kerry knows about his cropping, she has something over him. They sit in silence for a minute. 'At least she hasn't got herself preggers.'

'How long you think that's gonna last?' Daddy says. 'Better get the snip if you wanna protect yourself.'

Ernie looks appalled. 'Hey, that's me nuts you're talking about!'

Kerry and Brianna come out of the room with Jaidyn and go back to the couch. Kerry pulls a book out of one of the Kmart bags. 'See? They had this one marked down to twelve-ninety-five. It's about reincarnation and past life experiences.'

'I was Nefertiti in a former life,' Brianna says.

'So was I!' Kerry exclaims, surprised and pleased. 'Hey, Ernie, isn't that cool? Bree and I were both Nefertiti in our past lives!'

It's Daddy who answers them. 'You can't both have been the same person in a past life.' Usually, he starts sentences like this with 'Bullshit', but he doesn't this time because he's talking to a lady and he's in someone else's house.

'Why not?' Kerry blinks, surprised that anyone would disagree.

'Yeah, I think it could happen,' Brianna says, nodding.

Daddy waits a moment before replying. 'Have you ever noticed that everybody who says they had a past life always says they were Nefertiti or Cleopatra or Napoleon or Henry the Eighth? Nobody ever says they were a delivery boy or a garbage collector.'

Kerry shrugs. 'I guess those are the lives you don't remember.'

It's Saturday morning. I'm lying in bed, remembering those two stupid women surrounded by all the stupid stuff they'd spent Ernie's money on who were too stupid to understand that Daddy was telling them they were stupid.

When you think about it, stupid people usually win. There's strength in numbers, and there are lots more stupid people in this world than smart ones. Why are most TV shows stupid? Because stupid people want to watch stupid shows. TV network executives aren't smart, but they're smart enough to realise that most of their audience is stupid, and create stupid shows for them.

This line of thought is starting to confuse me. I get out of bed, grab my toiletries bag, and head to the bathroom. In the shower, I remember that this is a Mrs Rowles weekend. I'm looking forward to having Lyyssa out of my hair for a couple of days.

Since Bindi pissed off, this place has become a lot more tolerable. The feeling of something dangerous just waiting to happen has gone away. Still, before I leave my room, I always sit and listen to the house, trying to work out who's home, what room they're in, and what they're doing.

I sit on my bed in my underwear, my hair towel-dried, close my eyes, and listen.

Music down the hall. Cinnamon's in her room. Downstairs, Karen and Shane giggling and Mrs Rowles talking. Some clattering kitchen noises, then a squeal from Karen and Shane. Mrs Rowles has some sort of a trick flipping pancakes in the pan that kids like. No noise at all from Lyyssa's study. Sometimes Lyyssa hangs around after Mrs Rowles gets here, reminding Mrs Rowles about curfew times and fretting about Karen's medication, even after Mrs Rowles has pointedly told her, 'Very good, Lyyssa, we'll be just fine, enjoy your weekend.'

I look at my watch. Eight-thirty. Probably Mrs Rowles will be busy for the next half hour making pancakes for Karen and Shane and then doing the dishes. I'm hungry, but I've got a small bottle of long-life juice and a muesli bar, so I have that and read, keeping my ears tuned to the buzz of the house.

When I hear noisy cartoon sounds, I know that Karen and Shane, stuffed full of pancakes, have migrated to the lounge room and are pythonising in front of the TV. (Pythonising is a word of Daddy's. It means to lie around doing nothing after you've eaten a big meal.)

Daddy, Ernie, and Ernie's new girlfriend are pythonising in the lounge room. I'm lying on a camp bed on the back porch where it's cool. The porch is screened in, but I still have to light a mosquito coil to keep the mozzies away. Reggie is dozing on the floor next to me.

I'm supposed to be asleep, but Daddy and his friends are talking. They've forgotten I'm here. Daddy's in the armchair drinking a beer; Ernie and his girlfriend are sitting on the couch. The bong is on the coffee table. Ernie's girlfriend has a razor blade and is scraping white powder into a line on a mirror. Then she rolls up a hundred-dollar note and sniffs the powder up her nose.

Ernie is telling a funny story. The last time he came over, it was a funny story about his dog Lily, who had a litter of pups last year with our dog Reggie. Lily smelled banana cake cooking in the kitchen. Being a dog, Lily had no way of knowing that the banana cake had dope baked into it, so she sneaked into the kitchen and ate it when Ernie and his missus were gone. They came back home and found the banana cake gone and the dog out cold on the kitchen floor. Lily stayed stoned for two days – they had to carry her outside morning and night so she could go to the toilet.

Tonight, the funny story is about Ernie's ex-missus, who moved out and took his car with her. He saw her driving into town and ran her off the road.

'So the stupid bitch files an assault charge and I had to front up to the district court. This old goose of a judge is wearing a sheep's arse on his head and Dame Edna glasses.'

Ernie does an imitation of the judge. He picks up Daddy's sunnies and pushes them halfway down his nose like grandpa *glasses, and puts someone's beanie on his head like it's a wig. Then Ernie picks up the paper, screws up his mouth, and pretends he's the judge reading from some document.*

'He says to me, "Mr Antonelli, in this affadavit, the plaintiff has stated that in the course of this incident, you called her a – ahhhegggmmm – a 'dirty slut'. Did you in fact call Ms Gribble a – ahhegggmmm – a 'dirty slut'?"

'And I said to him, "No, Your Honour, that is a lie. Those are not my words. I did not call Tanya Gribble a dirty slut".

'So Old Beaky up there on his throne says, "Well, then, Mr Antonelli, will you please inform the court what you did say to Ms Gribble on this occasion?".

'And I said, "I called her a FAT dirty slut! I want that word FAT put on the record!".'

Daddy laughs himself limp; the blonde lady giggles hysterically until she has mascara tears running in black streaks down her face. Ernie takes off Daddy's sunnies and his beanie-wig. 'The bastard told me I was in contempt,' Ernie grumbles. 'Fined me eighty bucks.'

I put on my clothes and walk downstairs. Mrs Rowles is in the kitchen, scrubbing the frying pan clean with a piece of steel wool. The dishes have already been washed and put onto the drying rack. 'Good morning, Len,' Mrs Rowles says, looking over her shoulder as I come in.

'Good morning, Mrs Rowles.' I'm always polite and formal with Mrs Rowles. We both prefer it that way. I speak to Mrs Rowles the same way I would speak to Clarissa Hobbs, if I ever met her.

'I'm taking Shane and Karen to the zoo in about an hour. Would you like to come with us?'

The zoo. I would like to go to the zoo, but not if Shane and Karen are coming along.

'Actually, I have other plans for the day. But thank you for inviting me.'

Mrs Rowles could make me go along if she wanted to. But she knows I'm not going to get into any trouble on my own. Cinnamon, on the other hand, could get into plenty of trouble. But I guess that as long as Cinnamon is back inside by curfew, Mrs Rowles' arse is covered.

Mrs Rowles smiles a little. 'Not interested in the zoo? Well, I won't force you to go. But you know the rules. Back here before six-thirty.' She says this pleasantly, but firmly.

'I know,' I assure her. No sense in antagonising someone who's basically on my side.

Mrs Rowles takes off the rubber gloves she's been using to wash the dishes, then hangs them carefully from two pegs on the wall over the sink. 'I'm making chicken casserole for dinner. Will you be having some?'

I would like some of Mrs Rowles' casserole. She puts cooked chicken and broccoli in a big pan, then covers it with a mushroom sauce and cheddar cheese. She usually makes roasted potatoes and salad to go with it. So why is my first instinct to say no, thank you, I'll make myself a vegetarian stir-fry?

'Yes. Yes, I will, please,' I manage to say.

Mrs Rowles tries not to smile. 'Good. Dinner's on the table at seven. I'll expect you to help with the dishes afterward.'

Fair enough.

It takes Mrs Rowles about an hour to get those two morons Shane and Karen out the door to go the zoo. Shane took forever deciding which T-shirt to wear, then Mrs Rowles made him change because it was the one with a picture of a pro wrestler giving the middle finger, then Karen cried because Mrs Rowles told her she had to wear proper shoes, not her pink flip-flops. Then she cried some more because she couldn't find bobbles for her hair that matched her outfit. 'Both of you go to the front door and stand next to it while I go to the ladies!' Mrs Rowles yells, muttering under her breath as she passes by the lounge room on her way to the toilet. I'm channel surfing. Nothing much interesting is on.

In a few minutes, Mrs Rowles comes back calm, powdered and lipsticked. 'We're going in my car,' she announces. Karen makes a whining noise. 'NOW!' Mrs Rowles barks. The door closes firmly, and Karen whimpers about something. 'I *told* you, your medicine is in my handbag!' Mrs Rowles says, exasperated. How she's going to put up with Karen all afternoon is beyond me. I hear Mrs Rowles start up the car and drive off. I breathe a sigh of relief.

My relief quickly turns to boredom.

Everything on TV is crap, so I switch it off. I notice the picture hanging on the wall, some awful piece of donated 'art', is crooked, but I can't be bothered straightening it. I look at the painting on the other wall. This one was obviously done by some kid who used to live here. It's just a bunch of words painted in black on a red canvas.

A SHELTER is someplace
you can feel SAFE.
A SHELTER is someplace
where you are PROTECTED.

Woohoo, IWYR has talent. That's just sooo good. I bet whatever idiot painted that ended up going to art school.

They used to call this place the Inner West Youth Shelter, but then someone decided that 'Shelter' sounded 'pejorative', like someplace people dump stray dogs and cats, so they changed it to 'Refuge'. Now some of the dickheads that Lyyssa talks to are starting to say that 'Refuge' sounds pejorative and want to change it to 'Home', but some other dickheads say that's pejorative because it implies that the kids here don't have homes, and that it should be called the Inner West Youth Sanctuary, but the first group of dickheads says that 'Sanctuary' is pejorative because it sounds like a place for endangered animals, and it's also discriminatory because 'Sanctuary' has religious connotations.

Pe-jor-a-tive. I couldn't find that word in the dictionary because I thought it was *per*-jorative, so I asked Miss Dunn.

I look at that dumb painting again. A SHELTER is someplace where you are BORED OUT OF YOUR BRAIN is what I'd paint.

I don't want to read. I don't want to study. I look out the window. It's a fine day, but I can't think of where I'd go except to the zoo.

The zoo. The zoo. The zoo.

Two hours and about twenty dollars later, I'm inside the zoo. If I'd gone with Mrs Rowles she would have paid, but then I would have had to put up with Shane and Karen. At least I remembered to bring bottled water and put on sunblock before I left. The sun must be more bitey here than anywhere else in Sydney.

I take the cable car to the top. At first I'm annoyed because I have to share with three other people, but it turns out they're tourists and they start talking in German. On the way to the top, we see an orangutan or baboon sitting in a tree house with his shaggy back to us.

After an hour of walking around, I realise why that ape won't come down from his tree.

Children with sticky ice-cream faces run around screaming at nothing. Mums push enormous prams loaded with bags of oranges and boxes of disposable nappies and boxes of muesli bars and cans of drink and enough Tele-Tubbies to stock a toy store. Asians take photos. Some clown takes off his Akubra and puts it on the head of a wombat that's acting more like a pet dog than a wombat. Some kid pats a wallaby that's lying in the sun like a lazy old cat. The wallaby has a chunk missing from its ear, like it had a tag there but it got ripped out. People pay to have their picture taken next to a mangy koala that's sitting too low in a fake tree. There's a miniature farm-zoo and some granny is squawking at her grandkids to come look at a stock saddle and an old tin of saddle soap locked up in a glass case.

A tiny burning twinge hits the back of my neck. I forgot to put sunblock there. You can get skin cancer forty years from now if you get sunburnt as a kid. I read that in a pamphlet at the Community Centre. I find a gift shop, but I don't want to pay for sunblock when we get it for free at the Refuge. I need a hat. The only one that fits me and that I have enough money for is lime green, with the zoo logo and glow-in-the-dark tiger eyes on the front, and flaps hanging from the back brim to protect your neck. Okay, it's dorky, but since everyone else here is a dork, I don't reckon that's a problem. I pay for it and ask the cashier to cut the tags off.

I'm too hot and tired to pay attention to the signs marking out the trails. I'm just trudging along hoping to see something that will make this trip worthwhile. Then I come to a place where you can see the harbour, and the city across the water. Ferries make their way steadily toward the Quay, or away from it. Sailboats skate in lazy, aimless arcs. The office buildings probably aren't as tall as the ones in LA, but I bet people like Clarissa Hobbs work in them. I can't see far enough to where the Refuge is, but I can see Woolloomooloo, and kind of guess where Kings Cross is, where I got sick on that pizza. *My Sydney, my Sydney, my Sydney . . .*

'I caaan't!' The whine jolts me out of the only happy moment I've had all day. I blink and look down. Beneath the trail I'm on, there's an observation point and a telescope. Mrs Rowles is trying to get Karen to look through it. Karen is wriggling her arms and stomping her feet in a stupid little tantrum dance. Shane is looking inside a plastic gift shop bag, staring at whatever he bought. Like he won't have time enough to do that once he gets back to the Refuge.

'Karen, CLOSE one eye and LOOK through the other!' Mrs Rowles is trying to be patient. I turn and hurry along the trail until I'm sure they can't see me. I should have been more discreet. Why didn't it occur to me that I might run into Karen and Shane and Mrs Rowles? I guess I thought the zoo was big enough so that wouldn't happen.

I sit down on a rock in the shade and try to work out what I'm going to do. Mrs Rowles drove here with Shane and Karen. That means they'll be leaving by the top entrance, not by the ferry. I look at my Casio watch. 4:30. The zoo closes in half an hour, so Mrs Rowles will be getting the two junior dickheads out of here soon, unless she decides to feed them to the lions.

I manage to stay at the zoo an hour past closing time by answering 'yes' every time a zoo employee asks me if I'm going to the concert. Yeah, right. The people going to the concert are all fiftyish, smartly dressed, and carrying camp chairs, blankets and expensive-looking wicker hampers that probably have bottles of champagne and real glasses in them. The zoo is somehow more interesting after it's shut. I watch a couple of sea lions lolling around in the water and blowing out blasts of rotten fish breath. I find an aviary full of pretty parrots. Finally one of the employees sees me twice, twigs to what I'm up to, and escorts me to the ferry. Fortunately, it's twenty minutes before the next boat comes, so I can look at the harbour.

I'm on the ferry and halfway across the harbour before I realise that I can't possibly get back to the Refuge in time.

As soon as the ferry pulls into Circular Quay, I find a payphone to call the Refuge, but it's broken. So I walk another two blocks and find another phone that's broken, too. I walk back to the bus stop, and the first two buses that are supposed to be there never show up. Then I get on a bus that goes down University Road instead of Enmore Road, so I have to get off and walk back to Newtown Station to catch the correct bus.

Everyone's already at the dinner table by the time I run through the front door, half an hour past curfew. I start gabbling that I know I'm late and I'm sorry and the bus didn't come when it was supposed to and none of the phones worked. Karen and Shane stare. Cinnamon smirks, figuring that Mrs Rowles will say I can't watch TV or assign extra chores or report me to Lyyssa.

Mrs Rowles is spooning out casserole onto plates and passing them around. She looks at me calmly. 'I'm sure there's a good reason why you were late. I won't need to mention it to Lyyssa unless you make a habit of breaking curfew. Now go wash your hands and join us for dinner.'

Cinnamon's mouth falls open and she clenches her knife like she wants to stab someone with it. 'You let that little bitch get away with everything!'

Mrs Rowles pauses, the serving spoon dripping sauce and melted cheddar back into the casserole dish.

'We saw you at the zoo,' Shane says.

'How much did that hat cost?' Karen asks. I feel that stupid green hat burning a hole through my backpack, sending a flashing beacon like a lighthouse.

Cinnamon's face changes from angry to delighted. 'You didn't have anything better to do than follow those losers around?' she squeals, then claps her hand over her mouth. 'And you spent your own pocket money, too!' she screams. 'Ha ha ha ha ha ha ha!'

Mrs Rowles waits until Cinnamon has stopped laughing, then puts the serving spoon into the dish. 'A *bitch*, Cinnamon, is a woman who is intentionally malicious toward others and takes pleasure in their misfortune. Someone like Bindi. Maybe even a bit like you.'

Cinnamon's face scrunches and she looks at her plate. Oh, dear. Mrs Rowles has *damaged Cinnamon's self-esteem*.

'Len, I asked you to go wash your hands.' Mrs Rowles spoons some casserole onto a plate and sets it at my place at the table.

After dinner, I'm helping Mrs Rowles with the dishes, taking extra care to make sure everything's clean. Music drifts down the stairs from Cinnamon's room; TV noises come from the lounge room where Karen and Shane have parked themselves. Mrs Rowles and I work without speaking. Mrs Rowles isn't the sort of person you have to talk to.

'Well,' she finally says, 'how much *did* that hat cost you?'

My shoulders tense and my cheeks feel hot. 'Ten dollars,' I mumble.

'Wipe down the counters, would you? I'll be right back.'

Mrs Rowles leaves the room and goes into Lyyssa's office. I hear a filing cabinet open and shut. Mrs

Rowles comes back with two twenty-dollar notes and hands them to me. 'There was forty dollars set aside for each kid who wanted to go to the zoo. You didn't have to spend your pocket money.'

'Thank you,' I say, stuffing the money into my back pocket. I'm starting to feel better. The day isn't a complete write-off now. Still, it'll be a long time before I wear that stupid hat again.

'It's not easy when you've got no one to talk to,' Mrs Rowles says after a while, wiping a dish. 'I grew up on a property near Broken Hill. My mother died when I was a baby. I was the youngest of six, and the only girl.' Mrs Rowles sets the dried dish on the counter and picks up another wet one from the draining rack. 'There were some romance novels that belonged to my mother. I read every single one of them. Stories about beautiful young English girls who lived in castles and married dukes and earls.'

Cade and Riana. But without the disgusting bits about having your virginity forced.

'I used to dream about what it would be like to sleep on satin sheets, and wear silk gowns, and dance minuets, and have a tiny waist, porcelain complexion, long, flaxen hair and slender, delicate fingers.' Mrs Rowles laughs quietly. 'My hands were always rough and red from washing dishes and doing laundry by hand. My waist wasn't tiny, even as a girl. And my *complexion* was sunburnt and freckled.'

Mrs Rowles stacks the dish on top of the first one,

and starts drying a third. 'I met Mr Rowles when I was sixteen. He sold farm equipment to people like my father. We didn't have a proper wedding, just a little ceremony at the registry office. Nobody danced any minuets.

'Mr Rowles quit his job and brought me to Sydney. He bought a mixed business with the money he'd saved and we ran it for thirty-odd years. Sometimes we stocked novels like the ones my mother left behind, but I never read them. I didn't have time.' One more dish stacked, another picked up.

'Boys must run in my family. Both my children were boys, and I was thankful for that. Boys don't care about silk gowns or cry because their hair isn't flaxen.' Another dish stacked. 'Mr Rowles and I fostered over a dozen children after our sons left home. All boys. I told Social Services not to send us any girls. I wouldn't have known how to raise a girl.'

I rinse out the sponge and put it on the rack to dry.

Mrs Rowles puts the stack of dishes into the cupboard and surveys the kitchen. 'Thanks for your help this evening, Len. I think this kitchen is about as clean as we can make it.'

Chapter 25

Mrs Rowles says she doesn't know how to raise girls. She seems to do all right around here, but I guess she's not really raising us.

Lyyssa doesn't know jack about raising boys *or* girls.

I'm not sure Daddy knew how to raise me. How do you raise a girl? What if I have a kid someday and I don't know how to raise it? I think about that until I'm tired and fall asleep.

Daddy is gone for a few days. Holly looks after me. Most ladies have brown or black hair that they make blonde. Holly has yellow hair but she dyes it black. She says 'Blessed be' instead of 'G'day' or 'Hello'. All of Holly's clothes are black. She has a tattoo on her arm called a pentacle. Holly likes our house because it's at the junction of two rivers. She sings outside at night when there's a full moon. Sometimes she drives into town while I watch television.

One time when Holly is gone I get hungry and eat some corn chips and sour cream dip, then get a bad stomachache. Holly comes back and sees me crying 'cause my tummy hurts. 'You dag,' she says, looking at the sour cream dip container. 'It's past the use-by date.' She puts some coloured stones in a circle around me and says she's casting a spell but the stomach ache doesn't go away.

Holly gets mad that I'm still crying and asking for Daddy. She takes a pill from her purse, gets me a glass of water, says, 'Here, just swallow this.' Then I get very sleepy, and my stomach still hurts but I don't care. When I wake up I'm still on the couch, but it's the next day and Hi-Five is on the TV instead of Seventh Heaven.

I hear a car pull into the driveway and the sound of a car door slamming. Daddy is home. Holly is talking to him out front. I want to run out and see him, but my legs won't hold me up. I fall into the coffee table and knock over the bowl of corn chips. My hands are shaky but I manage to clean up the mess before Daddy sees it.

'I got ripped off, that's what happened,' Daddy says as he comes in the front door.

'The whole crop?' Holly says, sounding madder than when her spell didn't fix my stomachache. 'You didn't let them get all of it, did you?'

'Just shut up and get me a beer, would ya?'

Holly stomps into the kitchen and Daddy drops his leather jacket on the couch. 'Hey, Poss,' he says in a tired voice.

'Blessed be, Daddy.'

The slap hits me across the face and knocks me across the room. 'Mick!' Holly gasps, but Daddy punches her in the face before she can say any more. I run to my room and hide in the closet.

'You taught her to say that, you filthy bitch! You keep your goddamn witchcraft away from my kid!'

Outside, Reggie is barking and pulling at his chain.

Finally the screaming stops and the house is quiet. Holly is gone. I hear Daddy go into his room and fall onto the bed. He groans, like he has a stomach ache. I stay perfectly still and quiet until I hear him start to snore.

If Daddy sees me before tomorrow, he'll still be mad and everything will be wrong. If he doesn't see me or hear me until tomorrow, then we can both pretend that he never went away and that Holly was never here and that he never hit me, and everything will be all right.

Chapter 26

I'm sitting at my desk, trying to figure out what answers to write on the quiz that Lyyssa gave me. 'It'll be something for us to talk about during our next session,' Lyyssa said, taking the pages off her printer and handing them to me along with a new biro. 'I'll do the quiz, too, and we can compare our answers.'

I can't blame Lyyssa for trying to get me to talk. She's supposed to counsel me, but I never want to talk in our sessions. Still, I can't get the point of these goofy questions.

1. There's no school today. I would like to:

2. My wardrobe is mostly made up of:

A month ago, Lyyssa taught me some self-hypnosis techniques, to see if I could bring back memories of my life before the accident. Of course I didn't bother trying self-hypnosis, but I told Lyyssa that I had, and that it didn't work. I told Lyyssa that I still couldn't remember anything.

The more I remember, the less I want to talk to Lyyssa or anyone else.

I remember a ginger-haired man, white-trash women, a dog, drugs being sold and used and stolen.

I may have had amnesia six months ago, but I don't anymore. The ginger-haired man was my father, and the white-trash women were his girlfriends. The dog was our pet, but he was also meant to protect us from being robbed or hurt. I remember that my father made drugs and sold drugs but didn't use drugs himself and didn't want me to use them, either.

But if I were totally cured of my amnesia, wouldn't I remember something about my mother? I must have a mother somewhere. And wouldn't I have some idea of where my father is now?

I can't concentrate. Sky and Jo are helping a new girl move into the next room and they've left the door open. They're moving furniture and talking.

I take another look at the quiz. It's a real *Glamour Girl* sort of quiz. There was a copy of the magazine in the dentist's office last month, which I only picked up because there was nothing else remotely interesting to read. The dentist saw me reading it and thought it was a huge joke to call me *Glamour Girl* all the way through the consultation. I wanted to bite his rubber-gloved finger off.

    3. My ULTIMATE DREAM job would be:
    4. Which celebrity would you want as your best friend?

5. One beauty product I can't leave home without is:
6. My best buds would describe me as:
7. I would ABSOLUTELY NEVER go to the beach without:
8. What exercise is best to get a TOTALLY bodacious bod?

I flip my new biro around in my hand. These questions piss me off. Nobody calls their friends 'best buds' or refers to their body as 'bodacious'. I'm reading real, grown-up books from our library and from the University library, and Lyyssa thinks she can trick me into talking with some retarded quiz.

9. My FAVE piece of jewellery is:
10. Which male celebrity would you LOVE to go out on a date with?

This pink-tinted putrescence can't possibly come from anywhere else but *Glamour Girl*. And who reads that trash? Karen.

I look at my watch. Karen and Shane are downstairs watching some stupid TV show about a boy detective and his pet chimpanzee. Cinnamon's in her room with the door shut, and Lyyssa's in her office. I walk quietly down the hall, looking into the new girl's room as I pass. Sky and Jo are moving the bed. The new girl has her back to me. I stop, looking for a moment at her perfect blonde ponytail, skinny arms sticking out of a T-shirt, jeans, and scuffed trainers. She's putting posters of horses on her wall, very carefully pressing each corner to make the Blu-Tack stick. The posters are kind of tatty-looking, like they've been unfolded and folded back up again lots of times. But the horses are all impossibly beautiful. One is a glossy black Arab rearing up on his hind legs. Another is a black and white Gypsy Vanner with huge feathers on his hooves prancing through a meadow.

Something in my chest twists when I look at the horses on the wall. I quickly turn away before anyone sees me, make my way to Karen's room, open the door, and flick on the light.

Welcome to Obese Dorksville. Pink fake fur rug, pink beanbag chair. Two boxes of Maltesers and a bag of jellies on the night table. Closet full of fat girl clothes. Desk just like mine, except it's got retard schoolbooks and colouring books scattered all over it, along with a huge plastic bucket full of crayons and coloured pencils. Stupid drawings Blu-Tacked to the wall – Karen's drawn pictures of a red-haired princess, a red-haired mermaid, and a red-haired ballerina. A poster of LeeLee Nelson wearing ripped hipster jeans with a white leather belt and a bikini top that shows most of her boobs. Dream on, Karen. You couldn't pull those skinny jeans past your fat ankles.

The copy of *Glamour Girl* is next to the beanbag

chair, underneath a dirty plate that Karen's left in her room. *Pig.* The Refuge has a rule about not leaving dirty things in your room. I pull the magazine out by the edges so I don't have to touch the dirty plate, but the plate turns over anyway, spilling crumbs onto the carpet. Well, it's not my fault. The plate wasn't supposed to be there in the first place.

The cover of the magazine looks pretty much the same as the time I read it in the dentist's, except this time it's lime green and aqua instead of purple. There's a picture of LeeLee Nelson on the cover, wearing a white dress and looking cute, not trashy like she does on the poster. I scan the headlines. *Lila-Rose & LeeLee: How to Tell Them Apart!* Glamour Girl *Guide to Totally Awesome Fashion. Model Comp: Are YOU Our Next Cover Girl??? Special Quiz: What Kind of Glamour Girl Are You?*

I flick through the pages until I come to the quiz.

Lyyssa did lift her questions from *Glamour Girl*. It's a quiz to find out whether you're an Earth Goddess, Beach Babe or Rock Chick. It's multiple choice, so you can circle A, B or C for each one, then count up your answers. Which Karen has done.

I leaf through the magazine to find the quiz answers. Karen has circled 'mostly C's' – Karen is a *Rock Chick*! Each *Glamour Girl* type has a paragraph with fashion recommendations, dating advice, and info about celebrity soulmates, but I'm laughing too hard to read it. I let the magazine drop to the floor and run out of the room, flicking off the light before I shut the door. Karen's too dumb to notice that the magazine and dirty plate aren't where she left them.

After washing my hands in the bathroom – the cover was sticky with jam or butter or something greasy – I go back to that stupid quiz that Lyyssa plagiarised. Miss Dunn told me about plagiarism when she showed me how to write a report. Plagiarism is when you copy stuff from other people's books or magazine articles.

1. There's no school today. I would like to: *make Karen clean her room, then take her to the hospital to get her stomach stapled.*
2. My wardrobe is mostly made up of: *jeans and T-shirts – duh!*
3. My ULTIMATE DREAM job would be: *lawyer.*
4. Which celebrity would you want as your best friend? *Celebrities suck.*
5. One beauty product I can't leave home without is: *bottled water. Beauty comes from hydrated skin.*
6. My best buds would describe me as: *I don't have any 'best buds', dickhead.*
7. I would ABSOLUTELY NEVER go to the beach without: *I don't go to the beach, dickhead.*

8. What exercise is best to get a TOTALLY bodacious bod? *Tennis, swimming, and yoga improve your cardiovascular fitness, muscular strength, and flexibility. 'Bodacious' is a stupid word. So is TOTALLY.*
9. My FAVE piece of jewellery is: *I don't wear jewellery, dickhead.*
10. Which male celebrity would you LOVE to go out on a date with? *I told you, celebrities suck.*

I look at what I wrote. I can't show this to Lyyssa, and I've written it in pen, so I can't erase it. I crumple it up and throw it in the bin. I'll tell Lyyssa that I lost it, and make up the answers during our session.

We meet the new girl at dinner. Her name's Anna, and she's twelve. She looks like she might be okay. Unfortunately, Karen got to her first and it looks like they're best buds already.

'Anna's got loads of horse posters in her room,' Karen tells Lyyssa, as if it matters.

'Oh really? Do you like horses, Anna?' Lyyssa asks.

'Yeah,' says Anna, dropping her eyes to her plate.

'Anna Montana,' Cinnamon snipes. She starts to hum the theme song to *Hannah Montana* and does a little dance in her chair, like Miley Cyrus does during the opening sequence. Anna looks up from her plate and stares at Cinnamon, her eyes narrowing a little.

Lyyssa ignores Cinnamon and persists with Anna. 'Did you ride horses with your foster family?'

It turns out that Anna has never ridden a horse in her life. And her foster family were at Silverwater, which makes Cinnamon start laughing because Silverwater's a dump and they have a gaol there.

So, it's a typical new kid arrival day. Someone's mean to the new kid at dinner and gets sent to the kitchen to clean up for violating the Refuge's Mutual Respect policy.

Anna only lasts a fortnight. I don't know where she goes next. Karen cries when she leaves, and puts up a poster in her room of Lila-Rose and LeeLee riding matching white horses.

Chapter 27

Lucy Grubb was in the news again. It's getting close to her trial date, and some news commentator is talking about the 'class resentment' that this case has exposed. In America, the working classes are getting tired of waiting on and being abused by the snotty upper classes. People are wearing shirts that say 'White Trash', with the imprint of a tyre tread printed over the top. Someone started a website called www.nukethehamptons.com, because The Hamptons is where rich people like Lucy Grubb go on holiday when they feel like tearing around in their four-wheel drives and running over people for a laugh. Somebody else started a website that has a computer game of Lucy driving a car. You get points for each pedestrian that you run over.

How can I check out this website?

Lyyssa has the internet in her office, but she wouldn't be game to let me use it unless she watched over my shoulder. And even if they got us new computers and hooked up the internet, they'd install Net Nanny or find some way to spy on what sites we'd visited. There are internet cafés, but there's other stuff I'd rather spend my pocket money on.

The computers in the library are crap. They used to work even though they were old, but then some kid named Dirk who's not here anymore went postal because Lyyssa caught him getting into gay porn sites and banned him from the computer room. I heard Bindi and Cinnamon talking about it one day in the kitchen; I was reading in the dining room and they didn't know I was listening. Dirk broke the lock on the door to the library and started kicking towers and throwing monitors around. Supposedly this Dirk was in the Refuge because they caught him living with some bent priest who was molesting him. You'd think gay porn would be the last thing he'd want to see. Anyway, Lyyssa called the police and the do-gooder squad, and Dirk was taken away.

'So now he's right back where he was, renting his arse at the Wall,' Cinnamon laughed. 'I saw him on my way to perform at a bucks' night.' Cinnamon's full of it. She's been under curfew ever since she's been here, so how would she see Dirk at the Wall?

'No *way*. Dirk isn't renting *his* pretty little arse at the Wall anymore,' Bindi said, all full of herself at knowing something Cinnamon didn't. 'He's eighteen now. He camped at some old fag's place, bought some clothes, started going to the gym and now he's a high-class rent boy.'

Bindi's full of it, too. How would she know this?

'It's *so* unfair that I'm stuck here when I could be making five hundred bucks an hour, easy. They can shove their pocket money.'

Cinnamon mumbled something in agreement and the two of them headed upstairs, and I was left sitting alone at the dining room table with my plate of McVitie's digestive biscuits, glass of milk, and my English homework that I couldn't concentrate on anymore.

I hope I never see Bindi again. Lucy Grubb's someone I only see on TV. Cinnamon's too stupid to pay any attention to. I decide right then and there that I'm not going to bother myself about any of them. People who waste time on www.nukethehamptons.com are people who should get a life. I've got better things to do.

But I might ask Miss Dunn if I can use the internet at the University. After all, I might need it for my schoolwork.

Chapter 28

Jo's brother came down from Queensland to visit their mum. He brought a big crate of mangoes to the Refuge, big sweet mangoes that would cost six dollars apiece in Sydney. There are heaps more than we can eat, and Karen won't eat fruit anyway, so nobody minds that I take half a dozen of them and put them on a tray in my room. I have a mango every morning for breakfast, and one after dinner. I bring some more from the crate. They're starting to go a bit spotty, but I like the smell.

Until the smell reminds me of something I don't really want to remember.

There are two canvas bags in the boot. One has the stuff. The one that doesn't matter has some old clothes and a rock to make it heavy. Daddy takes the one that doesn't matter. We'll be back for the other one. But this one first.

'You sure she shouldn't wait in the car?'

Daddy and I are going to a block of flats in Marrickville. A guy named Terry is with us. Terry is younger than Daddy, with a dirty-blond mullet haircut. I don't like Terry, and I don't think Daddy really likes him, either. Terry doesn't take much notice of me. And he never refers to me by name, it's always 'she' this or 'she' that.

Daddy doesn't bother answering Terry. 'You done business with this guy before?'

I don't know why Daddy's asking Terry that. We wouldn't be here if Daddy didn't know that already.

'Yeah, he's a mate of mine. He's all right. He's up on the second floor.'

We stop at a milk bar on the corner. Daddy buys four hamburgers and four cans of Coke. The man we're going to see is a block away.

There isn't a lift, so we walk up two flights of stairs. Terry knocks on a door and a skinny man with stringy hair answers.

'Have any trouble parking?'

Terry starts to say something, but Daddy cuts him off. 'No.'

'Good. Can be hard round here. Close by?'

Daddy gives him a quick, direct look. The man shouldn't be asking this. 'Don't worry about where we're parked, it's close enough.'

You never want anyone to know where your car is.

'What about the kid?' The man looks at me doubtfully as we go inside.

'She's too young to know what's going on,' Daddy says. Daddy knows this is a lie, so do I, so does Terry and so does the man, but we all understand that we have to pretend that it's the truth. If we don't, what needs to be done won't get done.

We step inside. 'Nice place,' Daddy says. 'Wanna show me around?' Daddy needs to make sure no one else is there. Once

Daddy has looked into every room, we sit in front of the TV and eat our hamburgers.

'Let's have a look at the stuff,' the man says.

'In a while,' Daddy says.

We have to wait for half an hour. Daddy, Terry, and the stringy-haired man watch TV and I read Black Beauty.

'Right,' Daddy says finally. 'I'll go get the stuff.'

The man looks at the bag. 'What's that right there?'

'Just some other stuff. I'll get the stuff you're after.'

You can tell by the look on Terry's face that he didn't know there wasn't anything worth having in that bag.

Daddy takes me with him. Daddy puts the fake bag in the boot and takes the real one back to the flat.

'So, let's have a look,' the man says.

Daddy pulls a heavy plastic garbage bag from the larger canvas tradesman's bag.

Daddy puts the bag on the floor and pulls another bag out of that bag, and a bag out of the second bag, and a bag out of the third bag. The top of each bag is twisted and the top folded back over itself, sitting upside down into the next bag so it's airtight. Unwinding them takes a bit of time. The last bag is a fertiliser bag. You get it from the agricultural supply store. Daddy opens the last bag and takes a step back. The room smells sweet and sticky, almost like mangoes. He nods at the man, who steps forward and has a look.

'Lotta kif in that,' the man says without conviction.

Kif is little pieces of twigs and sticks and stalks and leaf. Kif isn't worth anything.

'Crap,' Daddy says, like he knows he's right.

The man pulls out a handful and sniffs. 'Pretty green. Bit wet, too.'

Dope that's green hasn't been dried thoroughly, so the moisture content makes it artificially heavy. Dope is sold by weight, so low-life growers with no principles just don't dry their stuff properly so they can get more money .

'Crap,' Daddy says again. 'Look, don't worry about it. We'll get rid of it someplace else.' Daddy bends down and starts doing the bags up. Terry looks nervously at the man.

'He means this, you know,' Terry says to the man.

The man takes a step forward. 'Maybe it's not that bad.'

Daddy looks up and gives the man a foul look. 'I don't grow or sell bad stuff.'

The man shrugs. 'I guess I could move it on. Twenty pound, you say. Must be pretty squashed up.'

'Yeah, twenty elbow.'

The man picks up the bag. 'Doesn't feel like twenty elbow to me.'

Daddy is starting to get cranky. 'Well, we'll have to sort this out. Where's your scales?'

The man opens a cupboard and takes out a scale, but it's a grotty old bathroom scale that shows the weight with a red needle against black numbers. This guy's dumber than I am, and I'm only twelve. I want to laugh, but I can't let on that I know that using a cheap bathroom scale to weigh dope is a stupid thing to do.

Daddy knows weights and measures in English and metric and can estimate the weight of anything without needing a scale. So can most other people he does business with. But the scale is like manners. You have to have a scale in such a situation, and you have to have the right kind. It can be an old-fashioned kind with brass weights, or a kitchen scale with a digital readout. Otherwise, it's like inviting someone to dinner and not serving any food, or serving dinner and not giving them a knife and fork to eat it with. What this man has done is embarrassing.

'Mate, what's this?' Daddy points at the scale.

Terry is getting more nervous. He's looking from Daddy to the man, back and forth.

The man looks up, open-mouthed. 'You said weigh it.'

'Not on a Mickey Mouse scale, I didn't. Don't you know those things are unreliable? Haven't you got an electronic one?'

The man looks confused. 'Well, it's the only scale I got.' He stands with his hands hanging at his sides.

'There's twenty pound there, believe me,' Terry says, trying to sound confident. 'Why don't you just put it on that scale and see what it says.'

Daddy looks at Terry. 'I'll do this bit of the talking. Leave it to me.' What Daddy means is, butt out, we're talking eighty thousand dollars here, don't screw it up.

The man picks it up and puts it on the scale and the scale goes closer to twenty-one than twenty.

'Did you zero that first?' Daddy says.

'Yeah,' the man says in a pathetic whimper. This guy is really a loser.

'Well, mate, you better get yourself a new scale, 'cause this one's costing you money. There isn't twenty-one pound in that bag, there's twenty. If you trusted that thing, I'd be taking four

thousand bucks out of your pocket that I shouldn't be getting. You can't do business like this. Now I said twenty, and there is twenty. Agreed?'

'Yeah, looks like it, okay.'

'Right. Now for Chrissake, close that bag up and get it inside two other bags before we stink up the whole neighbourhood.'

'Yeah, I s'pose.' The Loser's voice is getting smaller all the time. He tries to close the bags, but he's not doing it properly. Daddy doesn't say anything. He just steps forward and looks at the Loser, and the Loser steps back and lets Daddy take over.

Daddy bends down to close the bags up, twirling, folding, and locking each bag as he goes.

'How do I know the weight of the bag?' the Loser says.

Daddy stops what he's doing instantly, looks up and says, 'For Chrissake, mate, I just stopped you from skinning yourself to the tune of four thousand bucks. And now you're asking me about the weight of the bag?'

Daddy goes back to what he was doing. 'The bag would be lucky to weigh three ounces. Seems to me you don't know when you're on a good thing.' Daddy twirls another bag, folds it back onto itself.

Daddy rocks back on his heels and stands up when he's finished wrapping up the bags. 'Right. Let's count out the cash.'

The Loser disappears into a room and comes back out with a white plastic shopping bag. There's nine or ten rolls of fifties with an elastic band around each one. He says each one is five thousand.

'Let's start counting,' Daddy says.

'You want to count it out?' the Loser says.

'Yep. Every fifty.'

Daddy and the Loser move to the table and get on with counting the money. Terry has been moving backward one step at a time.

'Will I make a cup of coffee while you blokes are doing that?'

'I'll make the coffee,' the Loser says.

'No you won't,' Daddy says. 'You'll sit here with me and we'll watch each other do this. That way there's no argument from either side.'

Terry looks at the Loser. 'Milk? Sugar?'

Daddy looks up at Terry for half a second. You can see it in Daddy's eyes. Terry doesn't know how the Loser takes his coffee. He hasn't been doing business with this guy for years.

'White and one. Ta.'

Terry brings back the coffee.

'Got anything for my kid,' Daddy says without looking up.

Terry gets me a Coke from the fridge.

The counting takes about twenty minutes.

'Let me have that rug rolled up and put in that bag so it looks like I'm carrying out what I carried in. Terry can bring it back to you.'

'Terry? Bring it back? When?' the Loser says.

Daddy looks straight at Terry. But all he says is, 'He'll bring it back.'

We leave and walk down the street a bit.

'Where did you meet that idiot? Where did you hear about him?' Daddy asks Terry in a low voice.

'Hey, he's my mate, I told ya . . .'

'You don't know how he takes his coffee,' Daddy says. 'I don't know who put you onto him, but I never want to do business with him again. Or see him.'

'Well, you got your money,' Terry says.

'Yeah, and that was a bloody struggle.'

We get in the car and Terry starts spouting some crap. Daddy cuts him off.

'Don't take me near that bloke again and don't lie to me.'

I think Terry takes his point.

Chapter 29

Daddy, Terry, the Loser, and the mango smell. That memory hums in my brain for a few days, then dims as the remaining mangoes spoil and have to be thrown out.

A few weeks later, it comes back to me. Not as a mango smell, but as a scared, tight feeling in my ribcage.

It happens when we're in the van, going to the Westgardens Metro. Lyyssa is driving down the street. I'm in the front seat next to Lyyssa because I made it to the car before Cinnamon. Cinnamon is sitting behind me, staring angrily at the back of my head. Karen and Shane are sitting in the very back seat, playing some stupid game with a neon yellow rubber ball that they keep throwing back and forth. 'Careful with that ball, kids!' Lyyssa calls, turning around and craning her neck to look at them, which causes her to cross the centre line, which makes another driver swerve to avoid her and sound his horn. Karen and Shane start screaming 'Eeee! Eeee!' pretending that we've actually had a wreck.

'Ohhh . . . Shhhugar!' Lyyssa exclaims, her cheeks flushing, conscious of having Set a Bad Example. I turn to look at Cinnamon. She glares back at me and rolls her eyes, like she's embarrassed to be seen with all of us.

I'm not the sort of person you'd be embarrassed to be seen with, but Karen and Shane are. Karen's wearing a pair of hot pink shorts that are a size too small. Her fat white thighs spill out of them like disgusting, overstuffed sausages that have split their casings. As if that wasn't bad enough, she's wearing a frilly white midriff top, and flip-flops on her enormous feet.

Shane is wearing his usual jeans and three T-shirts, despite the thirty-eight-degree heat. The outermost T-shirt is the one Mrs Rowles wouldn't let Shane wear that day they went to the zoo, the one with the bald wrestler who's giving the finger with both hands.

Lyyssa is the sort of person who likes everything to go according to plan, so when we come up to where the street is being torn up and we have to follow a detour, she gets all flustered. There's a big orange sign marking the next turn, but Lyyssa drives right past it, biting her lip, her face tense with worry. I saw her miss the turn, and I'm sure Cinnamon did, too, but neither of us says anything. It's hopeless trying to distract Lyyssa once she's got a certain idea in her head. The minute Lyyssa saw that street being torn up, our shopping trip was immediately classified in her mind as a 'disaster', something that she had to save us from, something requiring a messy and complicated solution. That's why she missed those huge, obvious signs pointing which way to go — she was too busy frantically trying to remember if there were any emergency flares or tinned food rations in the glove box in case we ended up stranded all night in darkest Marrickville.

Lyyssa turns right for no reason, follows the street for a while, then turns left for no reason. Then she stops the car and makes a fake cheery announcement about 'stopping for a breather', and pulls a street directory out of the glove box. As she's paging though it, trying to figure out where the hell we are, I look out the window and notice something.

We're across the street from a three-storey, red brick building. Not pretty dark red brick, ugly bright red brick, like that stuff that is made to look like brick, but really peels back from the side of the shabby building like some weird kind of exterior wallpaper. I get a funny feeling as I stare at the building. Then I remember — I've been here. Daddy brought me here. There was a man with stringy hair. A man Daddy didn't like. A loser.

'Of course!' Lyyssa shouts, startling me. 'Yes, yes, I know where we are, nothing to worry about kids, we'll be there in no time.' Nobody's paying any attention. Cinnamon's in a sullen daydream, Shane and Karen are playing with the rubber ball, and I'm staring at the entrance of that ugly brick building.

We drive off to the Metro, Lyyssa finds a parking space, and we go in. Cinnamon buys lip gloss, mascara and semi-permanent home hair colour from the chemist. Karen buys a huge box of Maltesers from the grocery, a yo-yo and blow-up plastic pillow from the toy store, and a battery-operated pen that lights up from the Two Dollar Shop. That's Karen for you. Maximum goofiness for the minimum amount of money.

Shane spends all his money on one thing – a heavy-duty rechargeable flashlight that he finds in the camping section of the sporting goods store. Kind of a weird choice for an eight-year-old kid, but at least he picked something that's good quality.

We're milling around trying to decide where to go next when I notice the kitchen supply place. Something about the shiny display of pots in the store window catches my eye, but just at that moment, Karen starts whining that she has to go to the toilet.

'Lyyssa, I'll just be in that store over there. I'll stand outside and wait when I'm done.' I take off before Lyyssa has the chance to object, leaving her to find a ladies' room before Karen whizzes her pants.

I go into the store, hoping the clerk didn't see me with the rest of the Refuge kids. The clerk, or maybe she's the manager, is a slim, dark-haired woman.

She's wearing a navy blue apron over a white shirt. She smiles at me, then goes back to checking figures on a sheet of paper.

I walk through the shop, careful of breakables like coffee mugs and glass bowls. I think of Clarissa Hobbs' kitchen, which is filled with gleaming pots and pans. In *Clarissa Hobbs, Attorney at Law*, you occasionally see Clarissa cooking, but you never see a dirty-looking pot. Maybe you're supposed to assume that Clarissa's cleaning lady deals with the mess. Does anybody have a kitchen like that in real life?

Daddy never cared about kitchen stuff; I guess most men don't. At the Refuge, we have drawers full of bent, mismatched cutlery, and a whole cupboard full of plastic containers with no lids and plastic lids with no containers. Some of our dishes are plastic, some are china, and all of them are ugly. There's a frying pan coated with a layer of cooked-on grease that won't come off no matter how hard you scrub. I won't use that frying pan because one day I opened up the cupboard and saw a cockroach sitting in it. The cutting board is a scarred plastic rectangle. And of course, all of our knives are dull.

I walk over to the displays of knives. You can get the whole set that comes in a wooden block, if you have two hundred dollars to spare. I look at the ones that are sold individually. They're kept locked behind a glass case. There's a brand that is made out of a single piece of steel that I like the looks of. The larger-sized knives are too expensive, but the smaller paring knife is thirty-five dollars. Exactly the amount I have with me.

'Excuse me.'

The manager looks up from her stack of invoices.

'Could I see that paring knife, please?'

The manager hesitates, then comes from behind the front counter with a ring of keys. 'I'm certainly happy to show them to you,' she says carefully, 'but do you know that we're not allowed to sell a knife to anyone under sixteen?'

'Not even a kitchen knife?'

The manager shakes her head regretfully. 'It's the law. But I can take one out and let you have a look if you like.'

I look at the knives – sharp, ordered and perfect – out of my reach. 'No, that's okay,' I tell her. If I touched them, then I'd only want them more. I look around the shop. There's a stack of stainless steel woks.

'How much are those?'

The manager turns to look. 'The woks? Thirty-nine ninety-five. They have a nice, heavy base. Normally, they go for fifty dollars.'

'Oh.'

The manager looks at me for a moment. 'Are you a bit short?'

I nod.

'How much money do you have?'

'Thirty-five.'

She smiles. 'I can let you have it for thirty-five. We have too many of them. That's why we marked them down.'

The manager takes a wok from the top of the stack, and I follow her to the cash register. She carefully wraps the wok in paper and puts it inside a large plastic bag. 'You need to season a wok with oil before you use it,' she tells me. 'There's a little pamphlet stuck to the label explaining how to do it.' She hands me the bag. 'Not many young people are interested in nice things. I'm sorry I can't sell you that knife.'

I come out of the store just in time to see Lyyssa walking toward the store with the rest of the Refuge crowd. At least they didn't make it inside and embarrass me in front of the manager who liked me.

'My, that's a big bag, Len!' Lyyssa says brightly.

'Yeah,' I say.

'What did you buy?' she persists.

'A wok.'

Lyyssa blinks. 'Well, that's an interesting thing to buy.' She turns around. 'Is everyone ready to go?'

We walk through the shopping centre back to the car park. Karen catches up to me. 'Can I see what you bought?'

'No,' I tell her. 'And you're not allowed to use it, touch it, or think about it, either.' I run ahead toward the van.

When we get home, everyone goes back to their room to hide what they bought, then comes downstairs for dinner. After dinner, everyone goes up to their room to play with the stuff they got. Shane locks himself in his room, turns the light out, and switches the flashlight off and on repeatedly. Karen blows up her plastic pillow, stuffs herself with Maltesers, and doodles on a pad with her new pen that lights up. Cinnamon heads to the showers with two towels and her burgundy hair rinse. I don't want to season my wok with anybody else around, so I go into the lounge room and turn on *Clarissa Hobbs*.

Chapter 30

When I wake up the next morning, the first thing I see is the shopping bag with the wok inside. I remember the Westgardens Metro. I remember the ugly red brick block of flats.

The problem with living in this place is you can't follow things to their natural conclusion. Yesterday, when I saw that block of flats that I recognised, the logical thing to do would have been to get out of the van and take a closer look. But I couldn't do it, because I would have had to explain to Lyyssa why I wanted to look at a block of flats that's especially ugly, and because it would have interrupted our shopping trip, and because Karen probably would have pissed her pants.

Actually, that would have been funny. We could have knocked on the door of the stringy-haired Loser and asked if Karen could use his toilet. Then she could weigh herself on that stupid Mickey Mouse scale of his, then the scale would break because Karen's so fat, then Karen would cry, then Lyyssa would apologise profusely, and invite the Loser to hop in the van with us to come to the Westgardens Metro, where she'd buy him a new scale. And then I could say, 'Excuse me, Lyyssa, but perhaps the man would prefer a kitchen scale instead of a bathroom scale. You never know what he uses it for.'

My imagination's running away with me. I'm going to find that building.

It's not that far to Marrickville, but once I get there I can't exactly remember where the block of flats was. I end up on the main shopping street, which is a lot more interesting than the Westgardens Metro. There's an aquarium shop that sells goldfish for $2.50 and fish that look like miniature sharks for $49.95. There are lots of smelly butcher shops, with lights shining on the meat to make it look even redder. There are Asian supermarkets selling fish balls and bunches of leafy cabbage and stuff that you can't even tell what it is with Chinese writing on the packet. There are two-dollar shops selling clothes pegs and storage containers and cheap clocks and a battery-operated red and gold cat that waves its paw at you and fake jewels to paste on your fingernails and plastic ice cubes that light up and flash blue, red or green when you put them in a glass of something cold. There's a doctor's surgery with no-hopers going in and coming out. There are stern warnings posted in the window of the surgery about how you must bring your Health Care card with you, and that no drugs of addiction or money are kept on the premises. There's a curtain store. I can hear the lady inside talking on the phone.

There's a Target. I ignore it. There's a McDonald's. I ignore that, too. I go off into a daydream and somehow end up at a supermarket called Banana Joe's, where I go in to buy a bottled water and maybe a muesli bar or yogurt. Elvis is playing on the sound system. After I've been in the store for ten minutes, I wish they'd play something else. But as Clarissa Hobbs says, you should be careful what you wish for. When 'Blue Hawaii' finishes, the music changes to Paul McCartney and Wings. I buy a muesli bar and a bottled water and get the hell out of there before 'Live and Let Die' gets stuck on a repeating loop in my head. At least the bottled water was only two dollars fifty.

I've just about finished my muesli bar and almost remembered that I came to Marrickville for a reason, but something distracts me.

Two Asian men are chatting in Chinese or Korean next to a car. A nice new car – nothing flashy, but not a rust-bucket, either. One of them is taking out his keys to unlock the door. An Aboriginal man coming down the street sees them. 'Hey!' he yells. 'Hey!' You can tell by the way he's walking that he's drunk.

The Asians look at him. How stupid. The first rule with obnoxious drunks is that you don't make eye contact.

'HEY!' The Aboriginal guy yells, even louder.

'What are you doin' here? Yellow bastards!'

The Asians screw up their faces, blinking, perplexed. I don't think they understand a word of English. They look at each other, then look at the Aboriginal guy. *How stupid are you? Aren't Asians supposed to be smart? Just ignore him, get in the car, and drive off.*

'YELLOW BASTARDS!' the Aboriginal guy bellows. 'Get off my land! I OWN THE LAND!'

Finally, those two Asian thickos get in the car and drive away, like they should have had the sense to do in the first place. The Aborigine stares after them. 'Yellow bastards,' he says, to no audience except me. Then he starts walking down the footpath. 'And me?' he raises his voice again. 'I'm a bastard, too! I'M A BLAAACK BASTARD!' he yells, loud enough that you could hear him three postcodes away.

I start to laugh and run in the other direction. I laugh until there are tears running down my cheeks and my sides ache and I can't run anymore and I have to sit on the front step of a house belonging to somebody I don't even know, and laugh until I can't laugh anymore. That Aboriginal guy is so funny he ought to be on television. Too bad Clarissa Hobbs doesn't really exist. She'd know a TV executive and introduce him.

That running made me tired. I've lost interest in finding that red brick building. I get up and head back toward the Refuge.

Once I get back to University Road, I stop to look in the window of a store. The Sun of Life, it's called. The window display shows a couple of mannequins in dresses. A couple of Daddy's girlfriends had dresses like that, with flowing sleeves and lace. Around the mannequins are piles of pillows, displays of incense burners, crystals, books about Feng Shui. 'Crap, all of it,' I hear Daddy say. I move on.

Further down the street I see a little old man coming toward me, walking the littlest dog I've ever seen. The man has short grey hair, and bright blue eyes behind steel-rimmed glasses. He's incredibly skinny – I bet he weighs less than I do. The dog is black and brown.

'What a cute little dog,' I say to the old man, in spite of myself. I don't usually talk to people I don't know.

'He's a very good dog,' the man says. 'His name's Harvey. He's going to see his girlfriend.' The old man has a funny way of speaking, like a cartoon character. His voice is kind of raspy, and he talks fast.

'Can I pat him?' I ask. Daddy always said that you should never touch another person's dog without asking, because you never know if they bite.

'Oh, yes, he loves pats,' the old man says.

I crouch down and let the dog sniff my hand, then I pat him and his little tail goes crazy. The old man is talking about how Harvey's a happy boy because he got sausages for breakfast. Then the little dog jumps up and balances both his front paws on my knee. When I go to pat him on the head again, the dog licks my hand.

Something hurts me deep inside, like when I was looking at the posters of horses in that girl Anna's room. I straighten up, quickly say goodbye to the man, and start walking.

'You be good,' the old man calls after me.

I don't want to be rude, so I turn halfway around, force a smile, and wave.

I keep walking past the shops selling flowers and CDs and Indian jewellery and clothes, past a piercing salon, past Chinese and Thai restaurants. Then I come to a Turkish restaurant. A sign says it's not open until five. In the window, there's a display of gleaming tea and coffee pots, and things that look like grinders for coffee beans.

A memory, a hundredth of a second long, flits through my mind. The lights are low, and there's a candle on the table. I'm sitting very straight in my chair, careful not to spill any food on my velvet dress. Daddy is wearing a dress shirt and trousers. A lady with silky blonde hair sitting across from me is looking at me and smiling. *Ah, Mick, look at your little princess.*

A bus roars past and I'm suddenly confused. I stare at the teapots, trying to remember more about that restaurant I visited with my father. But I can't, so I take another swallow of my mineral water and decide to head back to the Refuge.

I take a slightly different route back, leaving University Road sooner than usual so I can walk down a different side street. The houses in this street are mostly shabby terraces, except for one. The walls are a creamy yellow, and the cast-iron lace is painted a deep, intense blue. The little garden is edged in mondo grass, and has clumps of blue flowers alternating with small bushes and pretty stepping stones. There are a couple of Japanese-looking stone lanterns. Then I notice the plaque by the door. *Nohant*, the house is named. Just like the house Georges Sand grew up in. I only read the first few chapters of that book about Georges Sand that I tea-leafed from the Refuge library, but I remember that much. I start to wonder what sort of people live there. Maybe it's a married couple who are both French teachers or professors.

A window bangs open; I look up, surprised. A lady is staring at me. She's maybe fifty, with a flushed, blotchy complexion, bleached hair, and a mean, pinched mouth. 'Is there something I can help you with?' she snaps.

Nohant. Georges Sand. Is there something I can help you with?

I shake my head, turn away, and slowly walk back to the Refuge.

Chapter 31

The burgundy rinse that Cinnamon put through her hair did look over-the-top right after she did it, but that was a couple of weeks ago. Now, her hair just has discreet purpley glints in it.

After Bindi left, Cinnamon's personality sort of collapsed. She's always been dumb, but when Bindi shot through, she went from just plain dumb to positively docile. She never cared about school except as an opportunity to chat up boys, then after Bindi left she wasn't even interested in boys anymore and refused to go to school until Lyyssa, Major Heath, and some dork from DOCS cajoled, reasoned, and finally forced her to go back. When Bindi was still around, she listened to Bindi's music. With Bindi gone, Cinnamon rarely listens to music. Her room went from rebelliously messy to a complete pigsty, and her fashion sense went from 'Look at my boobs' to 'I don't give a rat's arse'. She went from flaunting her big tits in halter tops and exposing her bum cleavage in hipster jeans to skulking around in track suits. For a while, she didn't even bother to shower every day. She never got smelly like Shane, though.

The hair dye changed everything.

Cinnamon started fooling around with her hair again, giving it conditioning treatments and fiddling around with curling tongs for hours on end. She bought a couple of hairstyle magazines and tried to duplicate all the ones in the 'long' section. I had a look at that magazine when she left it in the TV room one day. Some of the styles in the 'avant-garde' section were so ridiculous they made me laugh. Anyway, my hairstyle is what you'd call a chin-length bob, and no amount of extensions or fancy colours would do anything for me.

Then her dress sense changed. Cinnamon bought some fashion magazines, including an Italian one that cost fifteen dollars that she couldn't even read. She studied these magazines for a week. Then she stopped dressing like a slob, but didn't go back to the flashy moll look. She came up with a style that's not Designer Chic or Sporty or Classic or New Age Gypsy or any other 'style' that you see in a magazine. It's her own style, and nobody else's.

She put her track suits away, and threw the tarty tops and skin-tight jeans into the storage room with all the other cast-off clothes. She used some clothing vouchers to buy some black jeans, and scored a pair of practically new Doc Martens when Major Heath brought over some clothing donations to let us have first pick before they went to the Op Shop. With her pocket money, she bought some T-shirts at Jay Jay's on University Road.

Then she made herself a necklace.

All those fashion magazines Cinnamon bought have ads for pearl necklaces that cost thousands of dollars and diamond necklaces that cost a million dollars. None of them looks as good as the necklace that Cinnamon put together from a leather string with a clasp and a handful of beads. And there's not another one like it in the world.

For a long time, Cinnamon's room was silent. Lyyssa asked Cinnamon if she wanted the CDs that Bindi left behind. Cinnamon said yes, but she never listened to them, and before too long she chucked them all in the storage room. Then, three weeks after the hair dye and a week after the wardrobe transformation, music began to drift down the hall from Cinnamon's room.

She flitted between radio stations. One day it would be middle-of-the-road pop, the next day oldies from the sixties and seventies, then some weird alternative station run by students at some university who sometimes forgot that the music was due to finish and broadcast silence for five minutes before someone realised what was going on, then the gay station with non-stop dance music and cheesy stuff from the fifties that you're meant to laugh at, then the Arabic-language station, then the Spanish-language station. I really couldn't believe it when

I heard Cinnamon's radio set to a classical music station, all dazzling piano cascades and screeching opera. After sampling radio stations for a couple of weeks, Cinnamon came home with a few CDs. Then Sky Morningstar burned her a copy of a Portishead CD, which she keeps playing.

There isn't really a name for the kind of music Cinnamon settled on, or if there is, I don't know it.

The music drifting down the hall is slow, moody, hypnotic. It's music to dance to, music to have sex to, music to smoke dope to. Music that announces you're too old for a Refuge full of kids that no one knows what to do with.

I know Cinnamon won't be with us for much longer. She won't run off like Bindi did, though. Cinnamon's music tells me that she'll pick her moment more carefully.

I lie in bed thinking about Cinnamon's hair, how it shines when the light hits it.

Daddy's got business down in Sydney, so Reggie and I are staying at Ernie's for a couple of days. The first day I'm there, a Kombi comes up Ernie's drive. It's yellow, with peace signs painted on the side.

'Shit,' Ernie says. 'Coupla jerks from Sydney.' He looks at me and bites his lip.

'It's okay, Ernie,' I tell him. 'I know what they're here for.'
'Yeah?' Ernie says. 'You're not supposed to.'
'Do you think I'm stupid?'

Ernie sighs. 'I'll get rid of 'em before sundown. Make yourself scarce when we're talking business.'

The Kombi door on the passenger side opens and a petite lady steps out, gingerly placing a Doc Marten into the mud. She's wearing a long denim skirt and a tie-dyed tank top. She's kind of pretty, with a little brunette doll's head on a short neck. A young man with long legs and black hair gets out of the driver's side carrying a six-pack.

Reggie growls. 'Quiet,' I tell him.

'Hellooo!' the lady sings out. 'Hey, doggie!' She goes for Reggie. He runs under the house.

Ernie walks out to greet them. 'Shannon. Dylan. Good to see you.'

'We just happened to be driving through. We thought we'd stop by on the way to Byron.'

Wankers. They haven't 'just happened' to drive here. They've left the Pacific Highway and driven a hundred kliks inland to someplace that isn't even on the map.

Shannon talks all the way up the stairs, down the hall and into the lounge room. Shannon's an artist. She's also a psychic. Dylan doesn't say anything. His eyes don't focus on anything. He's on his third beer by the time Shannon stops talking about what she's going to paint at Byron and how she makes fourteen dollars an hour plus commission for giving tarot readings on a 1300 number.

'Oh my God, Dylan, would you look at this view? I could sooo paint this view, it is sooo awesome.'

Dylan ambles onto the back verandah and sucks on his beer.

'Ernie, you are sooo lucky to have a place like this. Dylan

and I are paying five-eighty a week for our flat in Fairlight.'

'Luck's got nothing to do with it, Darl.' Ernie never calls any woman he likes Darl. 'Nobody handed me this property on a silver platter.'

Shannon turns back to face Ernie. 'Oh, but you are lucky! You've even got a vegetable garden! Just think, Dylan, if we moved up here, we could have a baby, and grow fresh veggies, and I could make my own jam.'

Dylan carries his empty bottle into the kitchen and comes out with a fresh one.

Shannon is wandering around the room looking at things while she talks. She starts going through Ernie's CDs. 'Oh my God, I love Portishead.' She puts the CD on without even asking Ernie.

Ernie hates Portishead. Ernie likes Cold Chisel. Kaydee must have forgotten to take the Portishead CD when Ernie threw her out for borrowing his new leather jacket without asking and losing it someplace.

Shannon does a few slow ballet twirls around the room. Ernie gets up, crosses the room, and turns the music down.

'Ernie, you should paint,' Shannon says.

'Paint?' Ernie says. 'I can't paint. I never went to no art school.'

'But Ernie, you're a Scorpio. You're intense, you don't need training. It's cool as long as you're creatively creating what you want to create.'

Ernie turns to Dylan. 'How's the removals business?'

'Mad,' Dylan says.

'We're going to Spain next year,' Shannon says.

Suddenly, it goes quiet. Shannon looks at me, smiles vacantly, and then looks at Ernie. Ernie looks at me.

'I think I'll take Reggie for a walk,' I announce, and walk out the front door. How lame. Nobody takes their dog for a walk in the country. And Reggie won't come out from under the house, so I walk down the front drive kicking stones.

Those two showing up here is so uncool. I start kicking a stone for every stupid thing Ernie has done.

He got too drunk to watch his mouth. Kick.

He told somebody that he grows dope. Kick.

He used his real name. Kick.

He told somebody where he lives. Kick.

He told somebody exactly where he lives, right down to the dirt road with no name. Kick.

He was probably trying to get into Shannon's knickers. Kick.

He was so keen to get into Shannon's knickers that he told her his astrological sign. Kick.

He didn't put the brakes on the situation before those two morons got in the house. Kick.

After kicking all those stones, I feel pretty good. I'm not wearing a watch, but I reckon they've had enough time. I head back inside.

'What do you mean it shouldn't be legalised?' Shannon is squealing.

'Some of the most beautiful experiences of my life happened when I was on drugs,' Dylan says. He's staring at Ernie like Ernie just farted in church. 'Shannon's brother is halfway through a ten-year sentence. And for what?' He shakes his head and looks at Ernie like he thinks Ernie is a real retard.

'And just think, the police wouldn't hassle you or anybody else.' Shannon nods vigorously.

'Yeah, I'd be laughing if the price dropped to ten bucks a kilo.' Ernie's hands are balling into fists.

He let it slip that he grows commercially, not for personal use. And he let it slip to a motormouth who might let it slip to her stupid friends, who might let it slip to their stupid friends. Kick, kick, kick.

I'm kicking the Portishead CD case across the wood floor with the side of my foot. Ernie looks at me. I pick it up and put it on the entertainment unit.

'Grow your own mull, grow your own veggies, milk your own cows. Utopia.' Shannon smiles dreamily.

Ernie stands up. He's smiling dangerously. These people don't know he used to be a boxer. *'You want to be on your way before it gets dark.'*

We sit on the verandah and watch the Kombi drive away. Reggie comes out from under the house. Ernie knows what I'm thinking. I don't even have to say it.

'Met 'em at a party in Sydney,' he explains wearily, and shuffles inside.

Chapter 32

Tonight's *Clarissa Hobbs* episode is about racehorses. Clarissa's accountant has told her that she needs to lose some money for tax purposes. He says that owning a racehorse is a good way to lose money, so Clarissa goes to an auction and buys herself a thoroughbred horse.

The episode ends with Clarissa's horse winning a big race at Del Mar. As the credits roll, Clarissa is in the Winner's Circle, dressed in a yellow linen suit and wide-brimmed hat. Clarissa smiles for the photographers as she holds the big silver trophy, then poses next to the horse, holding his bridle and patting him even though he's prancing and tossing his head.

I turn off the TV, grab a couple of muesli bars from the pantry and a Gatorade from the fridge, and climb the stairs. Cinnamon's music is a little more mainstream than normal tonight. She's back to playing Portishead. I can still hear the music after I go into my room and close the door, but I don't mind.

I keep a carafe of water in my room, and a spare

glass. I dilute the Gatorade to quarter-strength, and sip it while I'm doing my yoga routine. The sequence came from an old book with a damaged cover, so I figured there wasn't any harm in cutting out the pictures I wanted and putting them on my walls with Blu-Tack. It's not like anybody else wanted that book.

After I've finished my yoga and most of the diluted Gatorade, I go down the hall to pee before I go to bed.

Portishead is still playing and Cinnamon is singing along as I drift off to sleep.

It's raining and we're standing next to the fence in the upper paddock. Daddy's wearing his Driza-Bone and a hat. I'm wearing my hooded yellow raincoat and gumboots. My feet got wet anyway and my socks are squelching around. Reggie isn't with us because he's a wuss about going out in the rain.

'Looks like Holly's dumped another horse that she couldn't be arsed looking after,' Daddy grumbles. Holly doesn't visit us anymore, not after what happened. When we see each other in town, she and Daddy ignore each other.

There's a new horse in the paddock. He's chestnut, with a white face. He's made friends with the others already. There's an old grey gelding that's blind, and an old chestnut gelding that wobbles because he had a stroke. There's a fat little yellow Galloway mare, and a funny little Appaloosa gelding with a short neck who thinks he's boss of the paddock. These are the horses that Daddy agreed to take, because the people who had them were going to shoot them otherwise. They don't get fed or rugged up. They seem to do okay looking after themselves.

Word got around that Daddy was a soft touch, so after the fourth horse, Daddy started saying no to people who were looking to unload a horse they didn't want anymore. 'I've already got four, I can't take another,' Daddy would say firmly.

Horse number five, Queen of Cups, appeared in the paddock after Daddy and Holly had the fight. Holly went to Byron Bay to stay with some friends for a while, and couldn't be bothered making arrangements for someone to look after Queen of Cups, so she dumped her in our paddock. When Holly came back to Riggs Crossing, she didn't come to get Queen of Cups. She just got herself another horse.

'Probably got him 'cause she liked his white face,' Daddy comments, watching the horse canter around the paddock. 'Wonder why she's thrown him away after three months.'

Daddy hears from Ernie who heard from someone else that the new horse is named Aghamore. When Holly named Queen of Cups, she was into tarot cards. When Holly named Aghamore, she was into Celtic things.

Daddy sends word back via Ernie and on through the feral grapevine that if Holly dumps one more horse on his property, she'll get all three of them back as dog meat.

The next time we go to the upper paddock it's raining again and Ernie's with us.

'Aghamore,' Ernie snorts, looking at the horse. 'How pretentious is that?'

'Possum calls him "Aggie".'

'Yeah? He used to be a racehorse, or so they say, I dunno. Holly come off him when he spooked. That's when she decided

she didn't want him anymore.'

'Useless bitch. If she can't ride properly and can't be arsed learning, she should forget about horses and start raising guinea pigs or get herself a goddam worm farm.'

Daddy never uses language like that in front of me. Except when he's talking about Holly.

'I reckon Holly's lost interest in horses. She's got other stuff to keep herself busy. Bree seen her in town picking up an old crib and a pram from Stevie Jackson and his missus.'

Daddy's mouth falls open. 'How far along is she?'

Ernie laughs. 'Coupla months. Don't worry, you're sweet.'

Daddy looks relieved. 'Whaddaya reckon she dumps the kid in the paddock when she gets tired of it?' Daddy doesn't usually say mean things about other people, but when Holly's name comes up in conversation, he can't seem to stop himself.

'Naaah. Kids get you more dole money. That's why all those feral chicks get themselves up the duff in the first place, they've worked out that being a single mother's a good bludge.'

Aggie is furrier than the last time we saw him. He's a nice horse. He grooms all the other horses except for the two mares. Whenever Aggie tries to go near the mares, the little Appaloosa charges him.

'Useless little runt,' Ernie laughs. 'Like he could do anything with those mares anyway.'

'Daddy, can I ride Aggie?'

Daddy looks at me sharply. 'No, you may not. Horses are very dangerous animals. One bite can take your finger off, one kick can kill you. If you're not a stockman or a grazier or a jockey, you've got no business riding a horse.'

'But Aggie's a nice horse. He wouldn't bite me or kick me.'

Daddy takes my hand and leads me down the hill back toward the house. 'Poss, any horse can bite or kick. It's their nature.'

Ernie follows behind us, grumbling about how he thinks he's got a leech in his boot.

Chapter 33

I took the wrong bus, so I'm late getting to the Randwick Racecourse. I guess it's just as well I'm late, otherwise I'd have to pay admission. I didn't realise they charged just to get through the gates.

Nobody knows I'm here. I thought that Lyyssa might not want me to go to the racetrack for some reason, so I didn't bother asking permission. I just wrote 'gone shopping on University Road' on the whiteboard. On the way back, I'll buy something from a shop on University Road, even if it's only an ice-cream, so it won't really be a lie.

I don't know where to go or what to do, so I just walk in the general direction everybody else is going. As we get closer to the big stadium entrance, the crowd gets thicker and I kind of fall in step with everyone else.

I don't really know why I'm here. Daddy always said horseracing was a mug's game. But that *Clarissa Hobbs* episode about her horse winning the race started whirring around in my head. Then the ads for the Autumn Racing Carnival started: models wearing floaty dresses, strappy shoes, and wide-brimmed, flowered hats; gleaming blacks and bays thundering across the finish line, tastefully dressed couples toasting their wins with champagne.

Maybe I went to the wrong racecourse. The people here are nothing like the elegant, laughing people in the ads on TV. I start getting the same uncomfortable feeling I get whenever I have to go out in public with Lyyssa and the other Refuge kids: These people aren't the sort of people I want to be around.

Like the couple in front of me. They're maybe nineteen or twenty. The girl is wearing a shimmery pink halter top that shows the rose tattoo on her right shoulder blade, a crotch-length leopard-print miniskirt, red fishnet stockings that end at the ankle, red spike-heeled shoes, and a cheap gold chain around her right ankle. She's really skinny and pale.

'I saw this outfit at Dotti that I might buy, and a rose gold bracelet at Proud's . . .' she's saying in a nasal voice. She's holding hands with a guy who's wearing a lavender nylon shirt, lime green synthetic trousers, and thongs.

I speed up and pass them, looking over my shoulder discreetly. The view from the front isn't any better. He's got spots and she's wearing way too much eyeliner.

I peel off from the crowd and head to the women's loo, nearly bumping into the back of a girl in a purple lace dress who's stopped abruptly just at the entrance to the toilet block.

'Hallooo, you gorgeous thing!' she squeals at a girl wearing a tight white tube dress and fifteen bangles on her arm coming out of the ladies, and they air-kiss each other. They're both wearing silly feathered hats and really high heels. The girl in the lace dress loses her balance and grabs the tube dress girl; they both think this is really funny and start shrieking with laughter.

'Soozanne's?' Tube Dress asks Lace Dress, pointing at her hat. 'Me too!' More shrieks and giggles.

Soozanne's. That's almost as classy as Dotti.

'Excuse me, could I get through?'

They both look at me like I've passed wind, then put their noses in the air and move away. 'You've got something on the back of your dress,' I say over my shoulder to the girl in the tube dress. She does, too, chocolate or something.

After I come out of the toilet block I try not to look at the crowd around me as I'm walking. How do I get close to the horses? At least I'm closer to the main action.

There's a big stadium entrance that everyone's going into. There are stalls everywhere selling food and drink.

'Gentlemen, collect your reward,' someone says loudly.

I bring my eyes back to earth. It's a very young man, soft and pink-faced, handing cans of Jim Beam and cola to his mates. They're all wearing grey suits with waistcoats and proper shoes. There's something annoying about the stuck-up way he's smiling.

Gentlemen. Ladies. *You gorgeous thing!*

I'm getting a headache. I find a place out of the sun and get two aspirin from my backpack. Two painkillers and half a Gatorade later, I feel ready to press on.

There's a dark-haired woman wearing a red jacket with a badge who looks to be some sort of guide. She sees me coming and smiles.

'Excuse me. Can you tell me what's up there?' I'm pointing toward the highest place in the stands. I have no idea what's behind that tinted glass, but I think it's probably the best place to see the race.

'Those are the private and corporate boxes,' the guide explains.

In other words, people like me and the girl with the rose tattoo and those two girls in their silly feathered hats aren't allowed there. That bothers me. I wonder if it bothers them.

'Oh. Well, where is the closest I can get to the horses?'

The guide points straight ahead. 'If you walk

straight through the Betting Auditorium, you can see the horses being walked in the Winner's Circle before the race. You'll be close enough to get a good look at them.'

I thank her and start walking.

The Betting Auditorium. Punters. If these are punters, I don't ever want to be one.

One fat man stands with his glazed eyes glued to a TV monitor displaying odds. A drop of sweat rolls down his bald head. He's too fixated on the screen to mop his brow. His mouth turns down at the corners.

No one seems to move in the Betting Auditorium, except the people behind the counters. Even the air doesn't seem to move. It's like a garden of sad, breathing statues. I hurry through without looking at anybody else. Just before I escape I see a sign, something about a Gambling Addiction Hotline on a free 1800 number. Yeah, right. Like any of the sad statues are going to stop pissing away money on the ponies and take up lawn bowls instead.

When I leave the Betting Auditorium, I exhale all that horrid sick sorrow and breathe in some fresh air. Some horses are being led out and paraded in a circle. I'm almost close enough to touch them. There's plenty of room at the railing. Why don't any of the sad statues want to come and have a look at the horses they're blowing their wages on?

I'm so busy watching the horses that I don't notice the jockeys coming out. All of a sudden, there's a person to the side of each horse who throws each jockey into the saddle, like he weighs nothing.

'Oooh!' I hear myself squeal, and feel embarrassed. But it doesn't matter. No one's paying attention to me.

There's a TV crew behind me and to the left. A reporter is asking someone about which is his favourite to win, but it's pretty boring so I don't listen.

I drift off into a daydream where I'm in a private box with Clarissa Hobbs and Wade, wearing a silk dress, sipping champagne and watching the race from up high. When I snap out of it, the horses are gone. I follow everybody else's eyes to where the starting gate is.

There's suddenly less room at the railing. My elbows are being pressed on both sides. To my right are two Westie boys; to my left is a stumpy little man wearing a bowling shirt and polyester trousers. He's carrying a little radio tuned to the racing channel.

The next couple of minutes makes me wonder what's wrong with everybody here. Or is there something wrong with me?

'Racing!' someone calls.

You can't really see what's going on from where we are, and all the horses look alike at a distance, anyway. But some people must be able to tell what's going on, the ones listening to the radio or the ones up in the stands watching through binoculars.

The guy with the radio squints at the track. The

two Westie boys are yelling 'Go, Go, Yes, YES!'

A roar erupts in the stands; shouts and cheers ring out around me.

'Kingston Rain!' the radio voice announces triumphantly. 'Kingston Rain by a nose!'

'NOOO!' one of the Westie boys howls, turning away and burying his head in his hands. The other one just closes his eyes and groans like someone hit him in the stomach.

The jockeys canter the horses around a bit, then slow to a trot before bringing them back to the Winner's Circle at a walk. Then only three horses are left, and the jockeys dismount and people come to hold each horse.

The winning jockey is really young, with blond hair and a smooth, pink face. He looks really happy, but I guess you would be if you just won a race, even a small-time one. He's also a lot taller than the other two jockeys.

'A real achievement for an apprentice jockey to win a race like this, up against veteran jockeys like Steve Moran and John Price,' an announcer says.

Those must be the two guys who came in second and third. They don't look very happy. In fact, they look like they'd like to kill that baby-faced kid who beat them. They also look like they haven't had a decent feed since they were about twelve. Their heads are too big for their bodies, and their faces look old and lined. They probably hate that apprentice jockey 'cause he won the race without starving himself and taking speed.

The Racing Queen gives the blond apprentice jockey his medal. Her hair is bleached a uniform colour of blond, ironed straight, and fixed at the ends with some kind of styling wax. Her makeup must be for the TV – thick foundation and heavy eyeliner. She's wearing high heels that make it difficult to walk in the grass, and a flowered dress with a little black lace shawl that keeps slipping off her shoulders. The black lace shawl is part of the 'Italian Widow' look that's in this season. Probably you can buy the whole ensemble at Soozanne's.

I look around and sure enough, the Soozanne's pink logo is one of the signs fighting for attention with all the other logos on display.

I don't know why I'm having such nasty thoughts about the Racing Queen. It's not like she gets a say in what clothes or makeup she wears.

After she's presented the jockeys with their medals, she wobbles over to a table and picks up a trophy. It isn't anything like the one Clarissa Hobbs got, made from real silver. This trophy is a sort of clear plastic egg glued to a particleboard base.

The Racing Queen steps carefully over to a clutch of people who are wearing suits and fancy dresses and looking bemused. They don't seem to notice that Kingston Rain is getting stroppy, in spite of the two handlers trying to keep him in line, and is close enough to kick them. Who are these stupid people?

Oh, they're the syndicate that owns the horse. The Racing Queen figures out which one of them to give the Plastic Egg on Fake Wood to. The syndicate people chatter and mill around on the grass until two older men in dark suits round them up and escort them to a door that says Members Only. Then the handlers lead Kingston Rain off to wherever he's going. Before they get him out of the Winner's Circle, Kingston Rain aims a little kick at a track employee who's crouched down to pick up a flag or something that's fallen on the grass. The kick didn't come anywhere close to connecting, but the track employee stops what he's doing and gives Kingston Rain and his handlers a long look.

There's one more race after this, but I think I've had enough.

I follow the crowd leaving the Winner's Circle and manage to wander into a pub that's four storeys high. No one stops me, despite the signs with the stern warnings about how no one under the age of eighteen blah-de-blah-de-blah. There's a guy wearing a shirt that says 'Free Dick' with an arrow pointing downwards. He stops talking to his mates and stares at me. I turn and walk back down the stairs.

I don't know where I'm headed anymore. I go through a tunnel where people are travelling in little motorised carts. One of them is carrying a little girl with long curly dark hair sitting in between her two quietly dressed parents. 'Hello, people!' she yells to me and some of the other walkers as the cart whizzes past us.

'Emma!' her mother scolds.

'That's showing off,' her father tells her, with an embarrassed smile in my direction.

I think they're the closest to ladies and gentlemen that I'm going to see here.

When I get to the end of the tunnel, there's nothing but a big car park and someone collecting for the Salvation Army. I say hello to the Salvation Army man, then turn and walk back.

The races are over and lots of people are leaving, so there's a bit of a bottleneck happening close to the gate. Some people are happy and loud, some people are aggro and loud. I keep getting jostled. Something is going to . . .

'GRONK!'

. . . happen.

A bottle smashes. 'WHAT'D YOU CALL ME?' In between the shoulders and handbags I see an angry, bug-eyed, young-old face on top of steroid shoulders. 'STEV-IE!' a fat chick whines, but he still throws a punch and men wearing orange vests come running and I'm being pushed forward by people who want to see the fight.

I turn and run back against the crowd, bumping into people. Some of the people I bump into don't notice, some look surprised, some look concerned, and some mean girls yell at me to 'WATCH IT.' I run until it's not crowded anymore and I can't hear the fight. I don't realise until I slow to a walk that I've been crying.

I wipe my face and stop next to some sort of building. There's a fence that has a sign saying 'Members Only' past this point. A large, happy-seeming woman holding a long pole with a copper pan on the end of it is leading a horse toward the building. I think it's the horse that won that last race. Kingston Rain. He's calmed down now.

'Excuse me.'

The woman looks in my direction and smiles.

'What's that pan for?'

'It's to collect his urine. All the horses have to have urine tests.'

Oh. For drugs and stuff. 'What if he won't wee?'

'He's got an hour to have a wee. They almost always do. But if he doesn't, the vet takes a blood test.'

'Can I watch?' Kingston Rain turns his head toward me like he understood what I said and thinks it's funny.

The woman shakes her head apologetically. 'Sorry, love. It's members only in the swabbing room. Come on, boy,' she says to Kingston Rain, and they disappear into the building.

Members Only. I bet Clarissa Hobbs is a member

of anything that's worth being a member of. I'm not a member of anything.

The crowds have thinned enough for me to get out of the racecourse, but there are still long queues for the buses. I start walking along the footpath in the opposite direction, up a hill, and come to a piece of land that has a little house that doesn't seem to quite belong there. I don't think anyone lives there anymore, but just to be safe I keep away from it as I walk past.

At the foot of the hill away from the street, the grass turns to dirt. It's the old stables, with maybe sixty or so stalls. The wood is grey and weather-beaten, but I doubt these stables were anything flash even when they were new. There are horseshoes lying around all over the place. I pick one up. What horse wore this shoe? Did he win his race? Where is he now?

'Stupid donkey!' Ernie yells at the TV, banging the armrests of the chair, his face purple. He's choking back all the words he can't use in front of me. 'Damn that horse and damn Aaron for his goddam hot tip! Bloody thing belongs in a Pal can!'

I let the horseshoe fall into the dirt. Some people say horseshoes and rabbits' feet are lucky. Tell that to the horse. Tell that to the rabbit.

'There was movement at the station, for the word had passed around, that the colt from old Regret had got away,' Daddy reads, with me sitting on his lap.

There's a lot of old regret here. But I guess it's less ugly than the new regret I just left.

I walk back up the hill and queue for the buses with the crowds of noisy people. I have to, or I won't get back to the Refuge by curfew. For the next quarter hour, I'm stuck amidst loud, drunken bogans, praying that another fight doesn't break out and feeling like everyone's staring at me 'cause I'm here alone. By the time I'm crammed into the aisle of the bus, thirsty and tired and pressed against the back of some girl in a pink nylon dress who smells of cheap perfume and beer, I know Daddy was right. Horse racing is for mugs, and right now, I'm feeling like one myself.

When we've finished our geography lesson on Monday, Miss Dunn makes a pot of tea and asks what I did on the weekend. I tell her about the races, about the jockeys with the big heads on tiny bodies, about the tattooed Westie chick and the screeching girls with their silly hats, about the sad statues and the horse that smiled at me before he was taken away to wee into a pan. I don't tell her about the guy with the shirt that said 'Free Dick', or mention that I went into the pub.

'I didn't like the kind of people I saw there.' What I mean is that I was hoping to see people like Clarissa Hobbs or the girls in the Racing Carnival ads, but I don't say this. I still feel embarrassed for caring so much about a TV show.

Miss Dunn arranges two cups on a tray. 'You didn't tell Lyyssa where you were going, did you?'

'Um, no.'

Miss Dunn pours the tea and gets that look on her face when she's about to say something that she knows she really shouldn't say to someone my age. 'Len, people who go to the racetrack aren't the best sort. If they'd been alive five hundred years ago, they would have gone to see a bear baiting.'

Bear baiting. I don't even want to know what that means.

'Anyway,' Miss Dunn says, 'if you like horses, or animals in general, you should stay right away from the racetrack. You don't want to know what they do to those horses to make them run fast. Or what happens to them when their racing careers are over. They end up as dog food.'

Aggie prances around in the paddock, pawing the ground, shaking his head. I slam that part of my mind shut.

'Len,' Miss Dunn says, a bit loudly. She's been talking to me. I snap out of my Aggie daydream.

'Do you like horses?' she repeats.

I like Aggie. I miss Aggie.

'Len, do you like horses??'

'I hate girls who "like horses",' I snap back. 'There was a stupid girl at the Refuge who had pictures of horses all over her room, and she'd never even seen one, except on TV. There are nice horses and mean horses and pretty horses and ugly horses. It doesn't make sense to say that you "like horses". You have to know the horse before you know if you like it or not. And you're wrong about them all ending up as dog food. Some of them end up as pets. My dad had horses.' I feel my nose burn like it does before I start to cry. 'You think you know everything.'

Miss Dunn gives me a long look. 'Critical thinking skills. That's what I'm trying to teach you. It's fine for you to point out a flaw in my logic, but I don't appreciate your tone.' She takes another sip of tea without taking her eyes off me. 'And speaking of people who think they know everything, is there anybody else in the Refuge you *don't* think is stupid?'

I drop my eyes.

'The reason I asked if you like horses is that I know a very talented horse trainer. He doesn't normally give riding lessons to children, but he *might* agree to give you a lesson a week, provided you help him with mucking out boxes and such. Are you interested?'

I can't look up. 'Yes.' I'm still mad at her for telling me off.

'Right. I'll call him. His name's Reynaldo. But I want you to understand that we are asking a big favour from someone who is a master of his craft. Ray won't tolerate any rudeness or laziness on your part, and neither will I.'

Daddy used to tell me off if I was lazy or rude. I

can't stand being told off by a woman. All Daddy's girlfriends *were* stupid. I look up. I don't know what to say to Miss Dunn or how to say it.

Miss Dunn looks at the clock. 'Our time is up. Maybe you could talk to Lyyssa about your father's horses.'

I have to form the words in my head and push them through my mouth. 'I don't want to talk to Lyyssa about my father. Please don't tell her what I said. I want to help with your friend's horses. I won't be rude or lazy.' I shove my books into my backpack. 'Thanks,' I say, then walk out of Miss Dunn's office, tripping over my own feet.

Chapter 34

Reynaldo looks sort of Asian, but not entirely. You can't tell where he comes from by the way he talks. His skin is a golden colour. He has black, almond-shaped eyes and would have black hair if he didn't shave his head. He has a scar running across his left cheekbone, a deep gouge. Miss Dunn said he used to live in Los Angeles and worked in the film industry.

So what's he doing in Sydney, mucking out boxes for rich people who can't be arsed looking after their own horses? I don't even know how or why Miss Dunn knows him. To ask Reynaldo where he comes from or how he got his scar or why he's doing menial work or how Miss Dunn knows him would be rude, but that's not why I don't ask. Reynaldo is a quiet person. To ask him these questions would be *breaking the quiet*.

Breaking the quiet is an idea I thought up. I only think that idea around Reynaldo. Most people are full of pointless noise. Even if they're not noisy, it wouldn't necessarily be a bad thing to ask them something. But with Reynaldo, you just know that if it's not about horses, you shouldn't ask him.

I talked about him to Lyyssa without telling her who I meant. Maybe she figured out who I meant but didn't let on. Anyway, Lyyssa said it was good that I understood that with certain people, some topics were off-limits.

Off-limits isn't the same thing as *breaking the quiet*. But it's close enough.

Reynaldo never asks me where I come from, or how I like the Refuge, or anything except what I'm doing with the horses. He knows not to break the quiet with me, either.

Reynaldo shows me how to muck out a box, wash down a horse, pick out its hooves, curry its coat and brush the mane and tail, clean the tack, put on the saddle and bridle. He tells me how to tell if a horse is angry or annoyed, what it means when they swish their tail or pin their ears back. After a few weeks, he tells me I can start learning how to ride.

I'd almost forgotten that's what I was there for.

I liked looking after the horses so much that I didn't particularly care about riding them. I like it when Dolly leans down and sniffs my back when I'm drying her feet so she doesn't get greasy heel. I like it when Buster closes his eyes and leans into the sponge when I'm washing his face.

'Len, would you like to have your first lesson today?' Reynaldo repeats. I'm standing there with a head stall and lead rope in my hand. I was off in a daydream. Reynaldo speaking to me makes me forget which horse I'm attending to.

'Um, yes. Which horse was I supposed to shampoo?'

'You can shampoo Buster after our lesson. You're riding Dex.'

On the bus on the way home, I decide I'm not going to talk to anyone about Dex. No one who doesn't know horses would understand. Anybody who does know horses doesn't need to be told about him. Another variation of *not breaking the quiet*.

Chapter 35

Progress Report

Patient: Len Russell/Samantha Patterson

Caseworker: Lyyssa Morgan

An enormous improvement has occurred in Len's conduct during psychotherapy sessions. She is now actively participating rather than displaying passive-aggression through monosyllabic responses or silence. Len still claims not to remember events prior to her accident, and continues to parry any question or remark that she perceives as an intrusion on her privacy or autonomy. Nevertheless, Len is now willing to share certain observations and feelings. This transformation seemed to coincide with Len's work experience with horses under the supervision of Reynaldo Klaas, a renowned horse trainer. Although Reynaldo Klaas has no tertiary qualifications in psychotherapy or social work, he has successfully worked with young offenders in the juvenile justice system on a volunteer basis.

Len enjoys talking about the horses she is being trained to care for, ascribing distinct personalities to each animal. She also enjoys giving detailed, almost technical descriptions of how to saddle, bridle, bathe and ride horses. Unsurprisingly, in view of her intelligence and her lack of interest in books and entertainment aimed at younger teenagers, Len has requested an expensive colouring book intended for students of equine anatomy. The book is a series of line drawings mapping out the various bones, tendons and ligaments of the horse. Funding for this book cannot be requested through the Department, as it falls outside the guidelines for required educational materials, but the Salvation Army has agreed to purchase the book and accompanying text.

Although Len has mentioned that she would like to become a horse trainer, it is to be hoped that she will choose another career path, one that offers greater security and is more in keeping with her academic potential. I have requested that Renate Dunn, Len's tutor, introduce her to the idea of a career in veterinary medicine.

Perhaps the greatest observable improvement in Len since the start of her work experience with Reynaldo Klaas has been the improvement in her conduct toward others. She is less critical of her peers and less suspicious of those in positions of authority, myself included. I am optimistic that Len will continue to transfer the concepts of mutual respect that she has learnt to situations outside of the stables and in her future life.

Chapter 36

Tonight's episode of *Clarissa Hobbs* is about how Clarissa deals with Hamish, a lawyer at the firm who's having an affair with Susannah, who's still in law school and working for the summer as a clerk. Everybody knows what they're up to, but nobody says anything. It's an open secret.

'It's disgusting, the way Hamish is using that young girl,' Clarissa fumes to her friend Barbara as they lunch at a pricey restaurant.

'Oh, Clarissa, don't be naive.' Barbara takes a drag of her cigarette and looks amused. 'Office romances are nothing new.'

Clarissa and Barbara argue about whether it's immoral or unethical for a boss to have an affair with his secretary or clerk. After the commercials, the scene has changed to the law offices. Clarissa is walking purposefully down the hall. She's got that half-smile on her face, the one she gets when she's figured out the solution to a particularly difficult problem.

'Nooo!' screams Lyyssa from her office, as all the

lights go out, Cinnamon's stereo goes quiet, the TV goes dark, Shane starts to scream and Karen starts to howl.

'What happened?' Cinnamon stomps down the stairs in her bathrobe with wet hair, then whirls around and yells back up the staircase at Shane and Karen. 'SHUT UP, both of you!' And they do. Like someone flicked an OFF switch. Cinnamon goes straight to Lyyssa's office. 'What did you do?'

'I just switched on the air conditioner.'

'Look at how many things you've got turned on in here! EVERYBODY knows you don't use that many appliances at once! You'll overload the switchboard! Where's the fuse box?'

'Cinnamon, I can't allow you to try to fix this. I'll call the handyman. Electricity is dangerous.'

'It's only dangerous if you don't know what you're doing,' Cinnamon says coldly. 'My step-dad's an electrician. Now where's the fuse box?'

The show's over by the time Cinnamon does what she needs to, the power comes back on and the TV comes back to life. As the credits roll, I glimpse the title of tonight's episode: 'An Open Secret'.

The rest of this week is going to be like having an itch that you can't scratch.

I get myself a Gatorade from the refrigerator and take it upstairs. I lie on my bed, trying to work out what happened after Clarissa and Barbara's lunch. I stare at the moulding around the light fixture. A spider has started building a web. I'll have to get a broom tomorrow and get rid of it.

Open Secrets.

Riggs Crossing was full of open secrets. Lots of people were cropping or dealing. People were sleeping with each other's wives or girlfriends. Women had babies that came from men who weren't their husbands or boyfriends.

One day when he was in town, Daddy saw a girl from the commune wheeling around a baby that everyone knew didn't come from her boyfriend. I heard him tell Ernie about it. But since the girl's boyfriend was an arsehole, Daddy thought it was funny. And what made it even funnier was that the real father of that baby was the husband of Vera the postmistress, who knew about the baby and was furious about it. So to get even, Vera had it off with the girl's boyfriend, even though she didn't like him any more than anyone else did.

Another open secret was how real croppers and dealers dealt with wannabe croppers and dealers. Kids wearing Doc Martens blew in from Sydney on motorcycles, or in big hotted-up V8 Coke-bottle Fords. They camped at the commune, or in some rented shack. They'd be mouthing off in the bottom pub, bragging about 'contacts' and 'drops' and 'elbows' and 'short croppers' and 'hydro' and other stuff you're not supposed to talk about in public. Someone would hear. He'd catch the eye of someone else who heard, then look around to see who else was listening. Four or five men would simply look at each other, then go back to their beers. Nothing was ever said. A few days later, Wonder Boy just up from Sydney would disappear. In a rainforest, there are lots of places you can disappear.

You can't have some brash young kid mouthing off and attracting attention, bringing the heat in. Nobody felt good about these young boys disappearing. But nobody felt bad about it, either. They brought it on themselves.

There was one open secret that everybody did feel bad about.

A man lived further down the road, in a little shack Daddy never took me to. A man they called the Scoutmaster. In his shack, there were phrases in Thai on pieces of paper tacked up all over the walls. What time does the boat leave? Which way to the station? May I have some tea?

'How much for that little boy?' *Ernie says sarcastically, crunching an empty beer can in his fist. He's just come from the Scoutmaster's place. He opens another can of beer. It's summer, and I'm on the back verandah, pretending to be asleep.* 'Mate, it was all I could do not to knock his teeth out, the dirty bastard. I know what he gets up to in Thailand, rock spider that he is.' *Ernie's shoulders are tight. He's drinking a lot of beer. I know he's not getting along with his missus. She'd better have the sense to keep out of his way tonight, otherwise she'll cop the hiding Ernie wanted to give the Scoutmaster.*

'Save yourself the trouble,' *Daddy says in a low voice.*

The Scoutmaster did get a hiding, but not for having sex with little boys in Thailand. He shot at a police helicopter that was hovering over his crop in the thick forest. The helicopter didn't crash, but it flew away. The Scoutmaster thought he was pretty clever, shooting from underneath bracken where the police in the helicopter couldn't see him. But some other croppers heard where the shots were coming from and showed up at his place an hour and a half later. They felt his rifle. It was still warm. They beat the crap out of him for doing something stupid that might bring the heat in.

The Scoutmaster got his nose and several of his ribs broken. But it didn't matter. He recovered, sold his crop, and went to Thailand after Easter.

Chapter 37

I'm not so much into *Clarissa Hobbs* anymore, but I still watch it. Recently, the episodes seem to focus more on Clarissa's personal life and gloss over her work. Maybe they've changed the writers, or maybe the producers have told the writers to do something different. They don't show her much in court anymore, they just show her leaving her law office for the day, going off to do something glamorous and exciting. In the last episode, Clarissa was shopping in an exclusive boutique, trying to choose a dress for the Charity Ball. Her friend Barbara helps her choose a Vera Wang dress.

Do they even sell Vera Wang dresses in Sydney?

After my lesson with Miss Dunn, I usually go back to the Refuge after walking down University Road. But today, I take a bus into the city. I don't know why I've never done this before. It's not that far away.

The bus follows City Road, turns right onto Broadway, and trundles up the hill past the old Brewery on the right, then UTS on the left. Further up the hill, we go through the very edge of

Chinatown, with neon signs in Chinese lighting the entrances to jewellery stores and noodle shops. Then comes Town Hall: cinemas, game parlours, Baskin Robbins, KFC. When the bus stops in front of the Queen Victoria Building, I know we're getting close. I get off at the next stop, walk up half a block and turn right, walking toward Hyde Park. When I come to Llewellyn's, I stop to study the window display. It's summer and boiling hot, but the mannequins are dressed in wool skirts and jumpers. 'Autumn Attractions', the sign says. I pull open one of the heavy doors and go in.

A blast of air conditioning makes me shiver in my T-shirt. I can feel the sweat under my arms congealing – I hope I don't smell bad to the clerks who've been working inside where it's cool all day.

I try not to worry – after all, the other shoppers have been out in the heat, just like me. I walk past the rows of scarves and the display cases of watches, past the hosiery section, to the cosmetics department, then ride the escalator up to Designer Collections, on the third floor.

I walk around the floor. Simona. Trent Nathan. Moschino. Akira Isogawa. Covers. Dolce & Gabbana. Aquascutum. Max Mara. Colette Dinnigan. Carla Zampatti.

Floral prints seem to be in this season. I stop to look at a dress that has a pretty pattern of lilies all over it.

'It looks like a muu-muu.'

The voice comes from behind me. It's a young guy who looks like he paints houses for a living. He's got paint splatters over his shorts and he's wearing thongs. His girlfriend, skinny, blonde, and wearing heavy black eyeliner, is holding up a different floral dress against herself to show him what it will look like on.

'Kev!'

'Yeah, that's what it looks like, a muu-muu!' the painter guy says. He seems a nice guy, but he's talking a bit too loud and his accent is full-on Westie. 'A really fat lady lived across the street from us in St Mary's and she used to wear 'em all summer. You know how you do this with your T-shirt to cool yourself down when it's really hot?' He flaps the hem of his T-shirt to demonstrate. 'Well, that's what this lady would do with her muu-muu.' The blonde girl groans and puts the dress back on the rack. I move on.

I get bored looking at dresses and ride the lift to Level 7. The door opens onto an expanse of quiet. No one's talking about muu-muus up here. The only noise is the whir of hair dryers and muted conversations from the hair salon on the opposite side of the floor.

I see a few names up here that I didn't downstairs – Donna Karan, Valentino, Norma Kamali, Calvin Klein, Vivienne Westwood, Yves Saint Laurent, Ralph Lauren – but they don't seem to have very much stuff by any one designer. I see one dress that I think is pretty, but they only have just the one in a size 10. Also, a lot of the clothes look like they've been tried on a million times. They're a bit grubby around the edges and don't stay on the hangers properly. I find one blue dress that wasn't anything special to begin with, has a loose button and a lipstick smear on the neck, but still costs nine hundred dollars.

It's a good thing there aren't any clerks around. I'd be embarrassed if anyone heard me laughing because I imagined that blue dress showing up at the Refuge in a box of donated clothes.

There's some exhibition going on – ballet costumes done by Australian fashion designers. I decide to forget about the clothes and have a look at the tutus. One is a tutu made out of lots of ballet shoes. Each shoe has a ballet dancer's name written on it. Intelligent and imaginative, but not wearable, Clarissa Hobbs would say. She was one of the judges of a fashion design contest in one episode. She would have said the same thing about the one that had all these wires with discs hanging off them. Imagine dancing ballet in that. You'd impale yourself if you did a jump and landed wrong.

The Akira Isogawa one isn't pretty like his dresses and skirts downstairs, but his tutu costume definitely has an attitude about it that I like.

It's the Collette Dinnigan tutu that makes the ride up to the seventh floor worthwhile. It has a bodice with lots of black beadwork and sequins, and a long, lacy skirt. I mentally squeeze my thick waist and chunky thighs into the tutu. I will my legs to grow longer and slimmer. Is it too late for me to start learning ballet? Bouquets of roses are thrown onto the stage, cries of 'Encore!' and 'Bravo!' echo through the Opera House as I bow, having performed for an audience of thousands wearing the famous Colette Dinnigan tutu . . .

A scream jerks me out of my stupid fantasy.

'GET OUT!' A large blond man wearing black trousers and a white shirt is standing near the entrance to the hair salon, pointing a finger out the door. A younger, slim, dark-haired man strides angrily toward him.

'Fine! I WILL leave!' the younger man shouts, throwing a towel onto the front counter.

'Your behaviour is totally unprofessional!' The blond man has his hands on his hips.

'What's unprofessional is YOU and the FASCIST way you run this salon. You STEAL my clients, you DON'T pay me the bonuses I'm entitled to, and you INTENTIONALLY give me bad shifts! I'm SICK of you! You're JEALOUS of me!'

The blond man splutters. 'JEALOUS?' he screeches. 'Of YOU? You're a non-talented suburban hairdresser! I only hired you because Ian asked me to.'

'Well, if we're going to talk about "non-talented

suburban hairdressers" we might start with Ian, mightn't we?' the younger man smirks, craning his neck and aiming his voice toward the back of the salon. 'We all know why you keep HIM on!'

'LEAVE NOW OR I'LL CALL SECURITY!'

The younger dark-haired man flounces toward the lift, trying to look triumphant, but I can see that he's about to cry. Without stopping to think, I run after him and we go into the lift together. He punches 'G' savagely and the doors of the lift close.

I look at his nametag. 'Derrykk'. Yep, two r's, two k's, and a y.

I remember Scott, the physiotherapist. Like I do whenever I feel a little twinge in my shoulder.

Fortunately, no one gets in the lift on our journey down. As we whoosh down seven floors, Derrykk starts to cry silently, tears rolling down his cheeks. 'Are you all right?' I ask him, just as the lift arrives at ground level and the doors open.

Derrykk looks down at me, manages a smile, and pats me on the shoulder. 'Don't go into hairdressing, Little One,' he chokes. 'It'll break your heart.' Then he runs for the Elizabeth Street exit, breaking into a wail of sorrow that makes people turn and look as he heads through the door.

The doors of the lift shut by themselves. I'm standing in the lift wondering what to do, then I remember that I wanted to check out Level 2 for some casual clothes. I find a black long-sleeved T-shirt marked down to $19.99 on the sale rack.

Chapter 38

I leave Llewellyn's by the Castlereagh Street exit, making sure I catch the bus in time to get back to the Refuge before dinner. We have to sign out and sign back in, and if you don't come back when you're supposed to, Lyyssa has to keep a closer eye on you. I don't like anyone keeping me on a lead, so it's easier just to follow the rules.

On the bus, I remove the tags from the shirt and despite the heat I put it on over the T-shirt I'm wearing. When I get off the bus, I find a rubbish bin and throw away the tags. The Llewellyn's shopping bag is folded neatly inside my backpack, where I can get it up to my room without anyone seeing it and then use it as a dirty clothes bag.

I check my reflection in the window before I open the front door. I hope no one notices I'm wearing a new shirt.

'. . . and I just told him, "I've only done *that* twice in my whole life, so don't you lay *that* on me".'

I don't know this voice. I don't want to know this

voice. It's a whiny, reedy, nasty, ill-bred voice.

'And he says some rubbish about stuff that some other girl did and I got blamed for, and *that's* when I picked up the chair and threw it at him.'

I stop at the entrance to the lounge room. Karen is sitting on the couch, staring at the new girl with her mouth open. Shane is sitting next to Karen, staring with his mouth closed and a worried look in his eyes. Cinnamon is sitting in the lounge chair, watching the new girl with barely suppressed contempt.

The new girl is perched on the edge of Clementine, swollen with pride at her recital of whacking some juvenile justice officer or dickhead social worker with a chair. She's about my age, with mousey hair, teeth with spaces in between them, and mean little blue eyes.

Lyyssa is standing rigidly next to the TV, a smile frozen on her face, obviously wondering what the hell to do with this loud, stupid nutcase. I can hear Jo in the dining room, tapping away on her laptop.

'Len!' Lyyssa cries, like she's drowning and I'm the surf lifesaver. 'We have a new member of the household. Allie is explaining why she came to live with us.'

'Sounds real interesting. Sorry I missed it.' This comes out before I've had a chance to think it over. Karen and Shane just keep staring. Cinnamon lets out a tiny snort of laughter.

'They put me in Seggro for three days,' Allie says

proudly. *Seggro?* This trashy little Allie is a wanker. Even I know that Seggro only happens in real jails, not kiddie detention centres or group homes. It's short for 'segregation', and means they put you in a cell by yourself because you're violent or uncontrollable.

'I'll put you in Seggro if you ever sit on my couch again.'

'Len!' Lyyssa gasps. Allie's mouth snaps shut. Cinnamon hides her face in her hands, her shoulders shaking with laughter. Karen and Shane have dimly realised that something's up and are giggling vaguely, even though they haven't really understood what's funny. Jo comes to the doorway and stares.

'Len,' Lyyssa repeats sternly. 'That couch is for everyone's use. And that's no way to speak to a newcomer. I'd like you to apologise to Allie.' She looks around. 'Cinnamon, Karen, Shane, can you please help me in the kitchen? Allie and Len, please come join us in the dining room in five minutes.'

Lyyssa walks briskly from the room and Jo retreats with her, followed by Karen and Shane, both of whom can't stop laughing and will probably keep laughing all the way through dinner. Cinnamon doesn't look at me as she leaves the room, but her face has just a trace of a smile on it, something I haven't seen since Bindi left.

That leaves me standing in the middle of the room and Allie sitting on Clementine. I shop at Llewellyn's. I'm not sharing Clementine with some ugly little mutt who might have crabs. I ball my hands into fists and take a step closer to Allie.

Allie leans forward and looks me up and down. Her mean little eyes sharpen onto my new shirt. 'Nice shirt. What size is it?'

What she means is, I'm going to take your shirt.

'My size,' I say in a low voice, taking another step toward her. 'Now get off my couch and don't ever go near it again.'

Allie is out of the room in a flash.

Chapter 39

Nothing happened during dinner. Allie was seated across the table from me, and I stared her down every time she looked at my way. I'll keep doing this for a couple of days, then ease off. But every once in a while, I'll stare her down again.

I'm in my room, sitting on my bed. I've decorated it as much as I can in Leo colours, orange and gold. At the Westgardens Metro I bought a couple of gold candle holders, and put peppermint-scented candles in them. There's a rule about not lighting candles or cigarettes or joints or bushfires in the Refuge, but Lyyssa and I have an agreement that I am allowed to light candles provided that I never light more than two and never set them next to anything flammable or put them any place they might be knocked over. I've put the candles on the mantelpiece above where the fireplace used to be.

I used to have my books on the mantelpiece. Now I put them in a small bookshelf that I found in someone's garbage and spray-painted a saffron colour. And at a fabric store at the Westgardens

Metro, I found four metres of sheer orange fabric threaded through with gold. It was on the remnant table and only cost $12.99. I draped it over the fixtures that hold the window blinds, so that the fabric hangs like a curtain.

'I'M NOT WEARING ANY PYJAMAS! I SLEEP IN MY CLOTHES, YOU STUPID COW!' Allie screams at Lyyssa.

Whoever decided Allie should come to the Refuge made a blue. She's way too crazy for this place. I don't think even Major Heath will be able to do anything with her.

I lie down on my bed and look at the ceiling. Yes, I'll have to do something a little bit mean to Allie once a week. Otherwise, she'll get stroppy.

It's all right to be mean to people, even to hit people, if they really need to be taught a lesson.

I close my eyes.

Daddy drives us into town. We stop at the Post Office and get the package with the books Daddy ordered for me. The package comes from Sydney. Once we're in the car again I take Daddy's bowie knife from the glove compartment and cut the strong tape so I can open the package. There are some books that I asked him to get me, and the next volume of Self-paced Mathematics *that Daddy says I have to finish before I can have a 50cc motorbike. There's also* The Rise and Fall of the Third Reich *for Daddy, which weighs more than all of my books put together. Every once in a while Daddy gets one thick book and spends the rest of the year reading it.*

We park outside the bottle shop and I leave the books on the car seat.

'G'day,' the man behind the counter says. He's reading a girlie magazine, the kind that shows ladies with huge, perfectly round boobs that Daddy says are really fake and ugly.

I follow Daddy as he heads toward the back of the store to get a slab of VB. We've reached the coolers when the bell on the door tinkles and another customer walks in.

'Small bottle of Johnny Walker Red, thanks.'

It's Terry. The blond mullet bloke we went down to Sydney with, the one who introduced Daddy to that loser with the bathroom scale.

Daddy cut Terry dead after that, and so did Ernie and so did some other people in Riggs Crossing. Then, a big patch of Daddy's crop got ripped. It wasn't too hard to work out who stole it. Terry's car ran a lot better and had two new front tyres the week after Daddy's patch got ripped. And the work on Terry's car hadn't been done in Riggs Crossing. How did Terry get the money to get those repairs done? And why didn't he have the repairs done at Murphy the Mechanic's in town? It stuck out like dog's balls.

Daddy stops dead in his tracks when he hears Terry's voice. 'Stay here,' he says to me, then strides to the front of the shop.

I don't move an inch from where Daddy told me to stay, but I step onto a box so I can see over the cardboard display with a fake palm tree advertising a free glass with each bottle of Kokomo's coconut liqueur.

'Terry,' Daddy says loudly.

Terry turns white when he sees Daddy. 'Hey, Mick!' He forces a smile. 'Long time no see!'

Daddy grabs Terry by his jacket and throws him into the palm tree display, sending some bottles crashing to the floor. They roll around, but none of them breaks. The clerk looks up from his magazine, annoyed. 'Hey, mind the stock!' he says.

'Never mind the stock. I'll pay for whatever his head breaks,' Daddy yells. He boots Terry in the ribs, pulls him up, punches him in the mouth, then drags him to the door and tosses him out onto the pavement. I creep toward the front of the shop so I can see them. Daddy is crouching over Terry as he lies groaning on the footpath. 'You rip my patch again, you're dead meat,' Daddy hisses.

The clerk puts the Johnny Walker in a paper bag and takes it outside. 'Um, that's seventeen dollars for the whiskey,' he says to Terry.

'It's on me,' Daddy says, reaching for his wallet. 'Best seventeen bucks I ever spent.'

I open my eyes and look at the ceiling for a minute. I wonder if Lyyssa would let me paint the ceiling gold. If she says yes, how would I paint it so that the paint doesn't drip onto the floor?

'I TOLD YOU I'M NOT WEARING ANY PYJAMAS! TAKE YOUR PINK POOFTER PYJAMAS AND SHOVE THEM UP YOUR ARSE!'

Allie's door slams, then Lyyssa and Jo try to talk

to Allie through the door before they give up and go back downstairs.

Allie's not really angry. She's just working out how far she can push Lyyssa.

I turn onto my side and stare into the flame of one candle. Yes, Allie will need to be taught a lesson regularly. But her ribs won't get broken, like four of Terry's did.

Chapter 40

I'm the only one at home when Cinnamon leaves.

Even without Bindi's bad influence, Cinnamon still isn't doing well at school and wants to drop out. The principal, DOCS, Lyyssa, and what's left of Cinnamon's family all agree that Cinnamon is mature enough to quit high school, providing that she does some TAFE course to ensure that she learns some way of making a living without going back to the stripping and petty theft she was into before she was brought to the Refuge. It's arranged that she'll study hairdressing at TAFE and live with her elderly auntie, one of the few members of her family she can stand to be around.

How do I know all this? Cinnamon doesn't bother talking to me, and Lyyssa would never violate someone's privacy by telling me. I haven't been doing any more snooping in Lyyssa's office, either. In a place like this, you just breathe in knowledge like this, like you breathe in air or someone else's fart smell, whether you want to or not. You can hold your nose, but you've still got to breathe the same air in through your mouth.

Where I lived with Daddy, it was the same. Everybody's private business was an open secret. Everybody knew who was growing, selling, or dealing marijuana or other stuff, but no one said anything.

Selling and dealing aren't the same thing, by the way. If you have a large amount of marijuana that you've grown yourself and you sell it, then you're a seller. But a dealer is something totally different. A dealer buys drugs from lots of different sellers and then re-sells them to whoever he can. You'd never want to be a dealer, because too many people, hundreds of people, know what you're doing. Most dealers are sleazy people with no ethics. They'll cheat you, or give you up to the cops in a minute to save their own skin. And a ripper is even worse. A ripper is someone who steals someone else's crop. A ripper is probably the lowest form of life on the planet, except for a rock spider.

The day Cinnamon leaves, I'm in the lounge room watching some trash TV before I get started on my homework. Karen is at retard school, Allie is at Junior Crim school, and Lyyssa is with Shane at the doctor's. Cinnamon is waiting in the front hall, sitting on top of her largest suitcase. She's managed to assemble a collection of old leather suitcases, some brown, some black. She's wearing her necklace, a short-sleeved black T-shirt with lace at the sleeves and neck, a long flowered skirt, and Doc Martens. Since Lyyssa isn't home, she lights a cigarette and flicks the ash out the window into a shrub. After a while, I hear a car coming, so I get up and look out the window. A young man in a new Gemini has pulled up in front of the Refuge. He's good-looking, dressed in a flannelette shirt and tight black jeans.

Cinnamon opens the door for him. 'Hey, Gazza,' I hear her say, without much enthusiasm.

'Hey, Sis,' Gazza says, in the same tone. 'I'll get your bags.'

They load up the car, and then Cinnamon comes back in and goes upstairs to check her room, just in case she forgot anything. She comes back down with a bottle of styling gel and a black beaded purse. She glances into the lounge room and sees me watching her. 'Bye,' she says gracelessly, and leaves without waiting for me to reply.

Chapter 41

The Refuge feels wrong with Cinnamon gone. I listen for her music but it's not there. Shane and Karen's stupid kiddie music and TV shows irritate me even more than usual. I look at the way people dress on the street and they're always wearing an ugly colour or awful shoes. Even posh women look like they're trying too hard with their clothes and jewellery and handbags. Cinnamon could do better than any of them on bugger-all pocket money and stuff picked out of Salvation Army donations.

Cinnamon wasn't my friend.

I used to have friends.

Avril's driving one of the commune's cars even though she's only fifteen. Megan's in the front seat and I'm in the back with Kevvie.

I was sleeping over at Megan's. Her dad had to take the dog to the vet, because he was cutting bracken with a brush hook and nicked the dog by accident. Mr Wilson looked about to cry. He lifted poor Bluey into the front of the truck like a baby and roared down the dirt road.

Avril is Megan's friend from school. She heard Mr Wilson's truck going past the commune and called Megan. A bunch of parents at the commune went off for a two-day trail ride, so the kids are having a party. 'Sweet,' *Megan said.* 'Dad won't be back for hours, he'll get pissed at the pub after he gets Bluey fixed up.'

'Hey,' *Avril says to me.* 'Haven't seen you at school.'

'I'm home-schooled,' *I say.*

'We've known each other since kindy,' *Kevvie grins.* 'What's your old man up to these days?'

I shrug. Kevvie knows what my old man is up to, the same as his old man.

'That necklace is so cool,' *Avril says.*

I feel myself blush. 'Thanks.' *It's a silver chain, with small charms hanging from it. A heart, a peace sign, a unicorn, a cross, a star. Daddy's girlfriend Aleta makes necklaces. She made this one specially for me before she left for Sydney to sell them at the markets. The charms are all supposed to bring good luck, but the unicorn is special to me. When I want something really badly, I hold onto him and make a wish.*

Kevvie's got taller since I saw him last year. He smells like freshly mown grass and Lynx body spray.

Avril and Megan chatter about school all the way to the commune. Kevvie and I just listen. We drive down the mountain, turn onto another dirt road. Kemboja, the wooden sign by the broken-down gate reads.

'Kemboja,' *Daddy snorts every time he drives me here for a birthday party or something.* 'That's Aboriginal for "place of many bludgers".'

When the road forks we turn to the right, drive for ten minutes, and stop at the third shack. It's the kind of place Daddy hates, the kind of place I'm not allowed to go if there's a sleepover. They're tree-worshippers and haven't cleared the land around the house, which makes it dangerous if there's a bushfire. They've also left sacks of fertiliser lying around, which means they're too stupid to hide the fact that they're growing dope. And a bag of garbage torn open by a dog or possum hasn't been cleaned up, showing that they don't have any house pride.

We park and a girl opens the front door. She smiles, hugs Avril, and yells over the music for us to come in. 'My mum came off her horse,' the girl shouts. 'She'll be in hospital two nights, how cool is that?'

The girl starts introducing us around, but it's hard to hear and I get confused and start forgetting names after the fifth person I've met. The girl and Avril push ahead into the kitchen, but Kevvie steers me onto a couch.

'You like the music?'

'Yeah.' I do. I've never heard the song that's playing before. The CD case is on the side table. Kevvie shows it to me.

'That song,' I say. 'It sounds like "Spirit in the Sky".'

Kevvie laughs. 'Your dad's still into hippie music. Just like mine.'

The girl comes back. 'What are you drinking?'

'Um . . .'

'A couple of Breezers would be good,' Kevvie tells her. 'So, what's been happening at your place?'

I tell him about the goat. A mate of Daddy's had some

business down in Sydney, so he left his pet goat and her kid with us. He chained them to stakes in the yard, but their chains kept getting twisted together. So Daddy built a little A-frame shelter for each of them, just far enough away from each other so the kid, at the end of his chain, could nurse from his mother at the end of her chain.

But Reggie got it into his head that the kid belonged under his shelter. Every time the kid went to nurse, Reggie would drag the kid back under the shelter. Daddy didn't figure out what was going on until he found pink dog teeth marks in the kid's neck. The skin wasn't broken, Reggie was being very careful with the kid. Daddy stood on the verandah very quietly and waited. Reggie was hiding under the house. He came shooting out like a rocket every time the kid poked his face out from underneath his little shelter and bleated.

Not a smack on the nose or a boot in the ribs would stop Reggie from keeping the kid safe where he belonged in his little shelter. Daddy gave up and chained Reggie up out the back, grumbling that he'd paid for a staffie, not a goddam border collie.

'Pretty funny,' Kevvie says.

The girl brings us two Breezers.

I can't think of anything to say and neither can Kevvie. So we drink.

'Hey!' Megan's shaking me. 'We have to get back.'

I sit up but I feel ratshit. My mouth tastes awful and every heartbeat sends a flash of pain through my head.

Megan's across the room trying to wake up Avril, but she's

in even worse shape than I am. I reach for my necklace to make a wish on my unicorn but he's not there. My necklace is gone.

'Megs, owww,' Avril groans, turning over on the couch. She looks even worse than I feel.

Megan's mouth is trembling as she looks around the room. The party has got larger all of a sudden. It's full of people we don't know, older kids dressed like they're from Sydney. I feel young and stupid as I stumble across the room, bumping into people.

'Are you all right?' one girl asks.

'Fresh off the farm,' another girl laughs.

'Megan, my necklace is gone.'

'Look, we've gotta find someone to drive us back, now.'

'But my necklace . . .'

'Forget your necklace, my dad's gonna kill me.' Megan pushes through the crowd and I follow her, trying not to cry and looking at every girl's neck. I know it didn't just fall off. Someone took it, and that makes it worse.

We pass the bathroom and I duck in, grab some toothpaste and run it around my mouth with my index finger, then rinse my mouth out. Someone giggles – there's a couple in the bathtub behind the shower curtain. Screw you, I think angrily, open the medicine cabinet and find the Panadeine Fortes. I take two for my head, wipe my mouth on my T-shirt and go to find Megan. She's standing in the front room next to Kevvie.

'Come on!' she hisses at me, and we head out the door.

Kevvie drives us back in someone else's car, even though he won't have his L plates for another two years. It's late, we *haven't got Buckley's of Mr Wilson still being at the pub. Megan's in the back seat, trying frantically to text on her mobile. Of course all her messages fail – there are only three or four places on the mountain where you get reception. She was so proud of that phone when she got it for her birthday, even though there's practically no place in Riggs Crossing where she can use it.*

The lights are on in the lounge room and Mr Wilson's squinting out the front window into the darkness. And Daddy's truck is there.

Megan gets out of the car first. She slams the rear door and walks quickly toward the house, her hands balled up into fists.

'Thanks for getting us back,' I say to Kevvie. I move to get out of the car, but my seatbelt holds me in. I didn't even know I had it fastened. It's totally uncool to wear a seatbelt. Nobody in Riggs Crossing bothers with seat belts, except little kids whose parents make them. My face burns as I fumble with the belt. The strap is twisted around.

'Here.' Kevvie leans forward, then pulls me to him and presses his mouth on mine, pushes his tongue into my mouth. Then he releases the seatbelt. I can't look back as I stumble out of the car and run toward the house.

Kevvie drives away and Mr Wilson opens the door. 'Go to your room,' he says to Megan. Megan runs up the stairs, her head down. Mr Wilson turns to me. 'Your father's in the lounge room.'

Kevvie's kiss is still burning on my mouth. Daddy's sitting in a chair, leaning forward with his hands clasped and his elbows resting on his knees. He gives me a long, steady look and slowly rises to his feet. He and Mr Wilson shake hands, then we go out to the truck.

I don't know what's going to happen next.

Daddy starts the truck and stares at the steering wheel while the engine idles. 'I can't keep moving farther up the mountain to keep you safe.'

'Someone stole Aleta's necklace.' My eyes start to burn. 'The one with my lucky unicorn.'

'It won't be lucky for whoever stole it,' Daddy says, and throws the truck into gear.

I reach to my neck, feel my collarbone. I haven't worn a necklace since Aleta's was stolen from me. That's what my world feels like, with Cinnamon gone. Like I'm missing a necklace.

Kevvie. Megan. Ernie. Daddy. Was I stolen from them, or were they stolen from me? I stare at the carpet, my chest tightening.

I hear the van pull up, then the sound of Lyyssa's key in the lock. I turn on the TV and pretend I'm watching.

Chapter 42

The past couple of weeks have been pretty depressing here at the Inner West Youth Refuge. It seems like the whole world is getting ready to celebrate Christmas and New Year, except us. Lyyssa will probably engineer some sort of carefully non-religious celebration, which will just end up making us feel even worse about not having families, or having families that can't or won't take care of us.

Fortunately, Lyyssa hasn't been paying too much attention to me lately. She's had to deal with four new kids in the past month, none of whom lasted more than a week. Either they acted up and got sent to kiddie gaol, or whatever was going on with their families resolved or they went home.

Lyyssa and Major Heath did ask me what I wanted for Christmas, and I told them I wanted to paint the ceiling in my room gold. They both looked surprised and said they weren't sure I could do that, and asked me to think about other things I might like instead. But a few days later, a professional painter came and painted the ceiling for me. He showed me some pieces of cardboard on them with different shades of gold, and let me pick the one I liked. I think he belongs to the Salvation Army church and did the work for free. Probably someone gave him the money for the paint.

Aside from looking at my new gold ceiling, about the only thing I have to look forward to in the holidays is the season finale of *Clarissa Hobbs, Attorney at Law*.

Tonight is the Christmas episode, even though we have a few more days left before Christmas. A few minutes before nine, I go to the kitchen to make some popcorn.

Down the hall, I can hear Lyyssa in her office, working on her computer. I can hear the sound of the keys clicking on the keyboard. That's the way I like Lyyssa the best – out of sight, out of my face, but there if I need her.

We have an oil popper, but I always use the air popper. At the community centre, I picked up some leaflets about nutrition. Fats and oils should be used sparingly. As the popcorn is popping, I melt one teaspoon of butter and get the salt shaker out. Then I carefully drizzle the melted butter over the popped corn.

'That looks good.' I look up, annoyed. It's Karen. The noise of the popcorn popper masked the sound of her clomping down the hall, so I didn't hear her coming.

I don't bother to reply. I put just three shakes of

salt onto the popcorn and put the salt away. Salt makes you retain water.

Karen stands there watching, like the sight of me making popcorn is the most interesting thing she's ever seen. 'My mum makes popcorn in a pot. With oil and lots of butter. Sometimes she puts cheese on top.'

No wonder you're so fat, I think. 'Air popping is *low-fat*,' I say pointedly.

Karen inches closer. 'Can I have some?' Then, without waiting for me to answer, she reaches her chubby, grubby, pee-smelling hand toward the popcorn bowl.

I grab her hand, twist it behind her back, and push her out into the hall.

'You know what this is, you stinky fatso?' I press my thumb into the place on Karen's forearm where Bindi hurt me. 'This is a *pressure point*,' I hiss into Karen's ear. Karen whimpers. 'My dad taught me how to kill people. I can kill you if I want.' I let Karen go and she goes wailing down the hall, crashing across the floorboards on her size eleven feet, then locks herself in her room. I can't make myself feel sorry for her. I've tried to let her know often enough that I want her to leave me alone, but she never takes the hint.

I listen for the sound of Lyyssa coming down the hall to see what the fuss is about, but there isn't a break in her typing. Tap-tap-tap-tap-tap-tap . . . tap-tap-tap-tap-tap. I feel a little put out that Lyyssa hasn't come to check on us, but at least I'm spared the trouble of making up a story.

Thanks to Karen interrupting, I miss the first five minutes of the show. When I finally make it to the lounge room, turn on the TV, and settle into Clementine with my bowl of popcorn, Clarissa is driving to her daughter Jenny's house for Christmas dinner.

Jenny lives in a nice suburb, but it's nothing like the posh neighbourhood that Clarissa lives in. You can tell by the way Clarissa is looking out the window that she's not impressed, and not looking forward to Christmas with her daughter. Clarissa parks in front of the house, takes a bagful of packages from the boot of the car and carries them to the front door, then pastes a smile on her face and rings the doorbell.

Then the action jumps forward an hour or so. Clarissa is angrily striding out the front door of Jenny's house. Jenny, who's fat and wearing an apron with reindeers on it, is screeching after her that Clarissa is the worst mother in the world. 'Nothing I did was ever, ever good enough for you!' Jenny shrieks from the doorway, tears running down her red, puffy face.

Clarissa turns, stares at her daughter coldly for a moment, then gets into her Mercedes and locks the door. She drives off, stopping at a liquor store and getting a bottle of their best champagne. The clerk is wearing a Santa Claus hat. 'On your way to Christmas dinner with the family?' he asks her, smiling.

'Yes, indeed,' Clarissa says, blinking back tears. She drives to the ocean and parks her car. Then she opens the boot, removes one wine glass from a wicker hamper, and walks down to the water. She drinks champagne and stares at the ocean for a while, then lies on her back and gazes at the night sky. 'Momma and Daddy,' she says, 'I know you're out there somewhere. I've done my best. I hope you're proud of me. Merry Christmas.' Then the credits start to roll.

So rich, beautiful Clarissa Hobbs is having a crap Christmas, too. That wasn't the sort of Christmas episode I was expecting. I switch off the TV, take the popcorn bowl back to the kitchen, wash it and put it back where it belongs, then climb the stairs. No noise coming from any of the junior dickheads' rooms. I don't even want to think about what Christmas was like with any of their families.

I lie on my bed and look at my gold ceiling. I'm not tired of it yet.

There's a box on the floor wrapped in red and green paper. Something's inside it, scratching and whimpering.

'Open the box, Poss,' Daddy says.

I lift the top off the box and a puppy jumps out, wagging his tail and licking my face like he loves me more than anybody in the world. He has a red bow tied around his neck. Daddy lifts me and the puppy onto the couch. The puppy squirms all over the place, pawing the front of my T-shirt because he's so excited.

Daddy kisses me on top of my head. 'Merry Christmas, Poss. His name's Reggie.'

I turn onto my side and stare at my schoolbooks lined up on my desk. Christmas.

I wish it would just be over.

Chapter 43

I get a break from my lessons the same time as school holidays.

Miss Dunn went to Melbourne to visit her family. She sent me a postcard with a picture of a tram on it.

I'm lying in bed trying to figure out what to do with myself. I look at the clock radio. Nine-thirty and I can already tell it's going to be a stinking hot day. I can hear the cleaners downstairs; I'd better take a shower before they want to start on the bathroom. I grab my robe and bag with all my toiletries and head down the hall.

Once I get back to my room, I throw some clothes on and pack an extra T-shirt in my backpack, because I know I'll sweat through the first one. I don't like walking around feeling sweaty and stinky. Before I learned to keep my mouth shut, I mentioned this to Lyyssa in a counselling session. She got all excited and started talking about obsessive-compulsive disorder. What's obsessive or compulsive about not wanting to smell bad?

I decide to go up to University Road and have a

look through that huge bookstore, then maybe catch a bus into the city and see the Opera House, or even go over the Harbour Bridge. I know there are posh neighbourhoods on the north side of the bridge, but aside from that, I don't really know much about what's on the other side of the harbour, except for the zoo.

I stop into the kitchen for a quick glass of orange juice. Major Heath is in the lounge room, reading a story to Karen and Shane. Lyyssa is on the phone, so I write 'going for a walk – back before dinner' on the whiteboard and scoot out the door.

Our street is shaded by trees, so the heat isn't so bad until I come to Canterbury Road, where I have to walk with the sun burning a hole in the top of my head. I won't wear a hat – not after that day at the zoo. I put on sunscreen before I left the Refuge. When I reach Enmore Road, it's not so bad, because there are shops with awnings that block out the sun.

Once again, I've managed to get myself onto University Road without a bottle of water. That means that I have to buy one, for sixty cents more than I normally pay, at the 7-Eleven.

I've just about made it to the refrigerators at the back of the store when that shrill beep announces that someone has come through the door. 'Packet'a Winnie Reds, thanks.'

Small bottle of Johnny Walker Red, thanks.

Daddy isn't here to tell me to stay where I am and

not move. I turn and walk back toward that voice that I remember.

He's still got a blond mullet, and still wears acid-wash jeans. It's hot, so he's wearing a singlet, not a flannelette shirt like he was the day Daddy gave him a hiding in the bottle shop. Terry.

I feel kind of numb and sick, so I'm not really looking where I'm going. I bump against a rack stocked with potato chips, and one of the bags makes a crunching, crackly sound. *Hey, mind the stock!*

Terry looks toward the noise and sees me. He's reaching for his wallet, and stops, his hand frozen an inch away from his back pocket. His usual facial expression used to reflect a weird combination of slyness and stupidity. Not the brightest bulb in the chandelier, but cunning as a rat, was how Daddy described him. Now, Terry's face is leaner, harder, meaner.

'Your pack-et of Win-fields, sir,' the Indian clerk says, sounding slightly alarmed. God knows why. Terry's just standing there, staring at me. Surely the Indian clerk sees far weirder behaviour like that, running a shop on University Road. Once, I saw a man shuffling down University Road with no pants on, not even any underpants.

Terry stares at me for a fraction of a second more, then snaps out of it. 'Yeah, thanks.' He pushes a twenty across the counter, takes the smokes and his change, and walks out of the store too fast. He's itching to look at me again, but doesn't.

I turn around and get my bottle of Mount Franklin, then take my time pretending to scan the covers of the magazines before going to pay. 'And how are you to-day, miss?' the Indian clerk beams. He obviously hasn't made any connection between me and Terry. I tell him I'm fine, we talk a little about the weather, then I leave the store. I look up and down the street, but see no trace of Terry. Just to be on the safe side, I cross the street and hop on a bus bound for Leichhardt, to throw Terry off my trail just in case he's watching me from someplace I can't see.

I get off at Norton Street. I'm confident that no one's following me, so I start to relax. Across the street, there's a place selling gelato, so I go over and get a double scoop of Vanilla Bean. Walking while you're eating is kind of tacky, but you see people doing it all the time, so it mustn't really matter. I walk down Norton Street, eating my gelato and looking at the restaurants and bookstores and coffee shops.

There's a cinema where they're having an Italian movie festival. Two very pretty dark-haired girls are talking to the ticket seller. 'But we're with our aunt!' one of them says, protesting. A middle-aged woman in an expensive-looking dress and high-heeled shoes is standing behind them. She's wearing sunglasses with heavy gold trim and carrying a Louis Vuitton handbag. Her hair doesn't move – it's been teased and sprayed.

'All the films have R-ratings,' a voice says from behind the Plexiglas.

The girls turn back to their aunt in disappointment. 'They won't let us in 'cause we're only sixteen.' Their aunt murmurs something and the three of them walk off.

I cross the street and look into the window of a shop that sells shoes imported from Spain. There are three pairs of black riding boots in the window.

I'm walking away from the shop imagining myself in black tall boots, teamed with tan jodhpurs and a black velvet riding coat, when I see something wrong, someone out of place, someone who drags me back into my dreary everyday life. It's Lyyssa, sitting at one of the outside tables at a café.

Lyyssa has on a lightweight purple blazer with shoulder pads over a scoop-neck T-shirt. She's pulled back her hair into an unsuccessful chignon that looks as if it might come loose at any moment. She's sipping a cappuccino or something, darting her eyes from side to side, self-conscious at being alone in the midst of chic-looking couples. Then she very discreetly checks her watch. Looks like Lyyssa has been stood up by Dickhead Daniel.

Fortunately, a waiter comes to Lyyssa's table, blocking her view of the footpath. I pick up the pace and walk as fast as I can to Parramatta Road, and hop on the first bus that comes without looking to see where it's bound.

Parramatta Road is kind of weird. On the bus, an illogical stream of businesses flashes past. Bridal couture, kitchen supplies, pine furniture, fireplace grates, pole-dancing lessons, outdoor equipment, McDonald's, car radios, more pine furniture. If you go far enough, you go past the morgue. I ride the bus for a few minutes, then get off at a servo near the Irregular Jeans Warehouse, one of the places Lyyssa or Major Heath takes us when we need new clothes.

I cross the road to Australia Street. There's a car lot on the corner with huge banners announcing the prices of cars: $39,990. Some people wouldn't make that much in a year.

It's a long walk up Australia Street. Most of the houses are nice terraces that have been renovated, although a few have peeling paint or a front garden choked with weeds. About halfway to University Road, I see a little white car come to a stop and a very large redheaded lady struggle out. Her face is flushed and her mouth is tight with anger. 'Ruby, get out of the car!' she shouts.

The door on the passenger side opens and a fat redheaded girl gets out. Her red hair is long, carrot-coloured and curly, not short and auburn like her mother's. She looks a couple of years younger than me, but she's crying like a baby, tears rolling down her chubby cheeks. 'Muuummeee!' Ruby wails. 'You PROMISED to buy me tap shoes today! I'll NEVER grow up to be a dancer if you won't buy me tap shoes! Annhhh-hanh-hanh-hanh!' she sobs.

Tap shoes? Did I hear that right? How could that blimp of a kid tap dance? She'd look like a dancing hippo.

A rush of angry embarrassment comes over me as I remember that a fortnight ago at Llewellyn's, I was fantasising about being a ballet dancer in a Colette Dinnigan tutu. And that an hour ago I was fantasising about being a tall, elegant dressage competitor in jodhpurs and expensive boots. It isn't fair that Fat Ruby has a better chance of getting the tap shoes she wants than I have of getting those riding boots. Or a Colette Dinnigan tutu.

'We're not buying anything today!' her mother barks. She's having trouble breathing. 'Now come help me with these groceries!'

'I'm not helping you do anything today!' Ruby shrieks, loud enough for the whole street to hear her. She runs across the street and waits by the front door, blubbering angrily. It's one of the houses on the street that hasn't been renovated. They've got two garbage bins in their front garden, a letterbox painted a faded red, and a mountain of junk hiding the two front windows. There's a broken pram, a broken desk, a broken chair, two broken lamps, a rusty child's bicycle with flat tyres and a deflated basketball. There's also some trash that passersby have thrown there – styrofoam coffee cups, Macca's wrappers, junk mail – that they haven't bothered to pick up.

'Ruby!' the woman yells, puffing for breath. 'Come help me!'

Ruby slides down the door and collapses onto the front step, her mouth open in a grotesque scream. 'NOOO!' she bawls.

That kid needs a boot up the arse so hard, she doesn't hit the ground till Armidale, I can hear Daddy say.

Ruby's mother mutters something under her breath, opens the little car's back hatch, and lifts the plastic bags out. She waddles across the street, gasping for breath. 'Ruby, at least use your key and open the door for me!'

'I'm not doing anything for you because you're so MEEEAN!' Ruby screeches.

I can't watch any more of this real-life icky TV show without stopping and staring, so I keep walking. Is this the way 'normal' people live? Awful Ruby and her mother living in a house where the garden is filled with junk. Is there a Mr FatGuts? Does he have red hair, too?

Ruby is still wailing and her mother is still yelling at her when I reach the corner, where three council workers have set up some orange witch's hats around a big hole they've broken through the concrete. Two of the council workers are looking at Ruby's mother.

'Jeezuuus,' one of them says. 'How'd you like to have to climb aboard that?'

Climb aboard. It takes me a minute to work out what he means. Going down the street, I start to notice the bright pink fliers stuffed into all the mailboxes. I know it's illegal to look in someone else's mailbox, but fortunately one of those pink flyers has been dropped on the footpath. I pick it up.

LOSE TWENTY KILOS A MONTH!
Tried fad diets?
Tried exercise?
Tried every weight loss pill on the market?
Stop suffering and start living!
Marcia Moore's patented program combines
sensible eating with light exercise and one delicious
lo-cal shake per day.
Results guaranteed! First week free!

There's a mobile and a landline phone number given.

I look up and down the street. There are no bright pink flyers in the mailboxes on the opposite side of the street. It looks like whoever was stuffing these flyers into the mailboxes ran out or just got lazy. That means Ruby and her mother didn't get one, which is really unfair. They probably need it more than anybody else on this street.

I turn around and go back toward Ruby's house. The construction workers have gone. If Ruby's mother signs up for this diet program and it works, people will stop making nasty jokes about 'climbing aboard'. And if it works for Ruby, nobody at school will rag on her for being a fat chick.

I don't think I'll try it, though. It would cost too much money. Also, I'm not really fat, I'm a mesomorph. The physiotherapist said so.

I cross the street to Ruby and her mother's house, carefully fold the flyer in half, and slip it into the red mailbox. Feeling pleased with myself, I head back up the street. I don't get as far as the corner before a shout stops me dead in my tracks.

'HEY!'

I slowly turn around. It's Ruby's mother, clutching the pink weight-loss flyer. Her face has turned the same shade of bright pink as the flyer.

'YOU COME BACK HERE THIS INSTANT!'

I can't move.

Ruby's mother takes a deep breath and lowers her voice. 'Would you please come here. I'd like to have a word with you.' A tear rolls down the side of her face.

I slowly walk toward her.

Ruby's mother and I stand looking at each other and now she's really crying. 'I won't ask you inside,' she says hoarsely. 'A girl your age shouldn't go into a stranger's house. I've warned my daughter never to go off with someone she doesn't know.'

She motions me toward one of the two camp chairs that are sitting to one side of the pile of broken-down junk. We sit down. I have no idea what's coming next.

'I saw you watching us when Ruby and I came home,' she says, a little calmer.

I am *so* busted.

'I suppose you're the perfect daughter? You've never misbehaved, never given your parents any trouble?'

Daddy would have booted me up the backside if I had. I shrug and look down.

'Never been rude?'

Rude. I don't have an answer for that one.

Ruby's mother looks at the weight-loss flyer. 'Putting this . . . *thing* in my mailbox was really rude. Why did you do it?'

I mumble something about how her side of the street didn't get any.

Ruby's mother crumples the flyer, throws it into the rubbish heap. It lands on the seat of the broken pram. Ruby's mother sighs. 'I've tried every weight-loss programme there is. The fact is, some people are born fat and there's nothing they can do about it. My parents were both overweight. So were three of my grandparents. There wasn't much chance of me or my daughter turning out like Kate Moss. And in any case, it's *none of your business*. How would you like it if a girl at school was mean to you because she's skinny and you're not?'

Mesomorph!

My head has dropped so that I'm staring at my

thunder thighs. 'Two girls called me fat.' It comes out almost as a whisper. 'But I'm not fat. I'm a mesomorph.'

Ruby's mother gives a sad chuckle. 'Pleased to meet you, mesomorph. I'd introduce myself according to my body type, but I think I've morphed right off the scale. I believe the clinical term is *obese*.' Ruby's mother is quiet for a few seconds. 'But that really isn't the point, is it?'

'I guess not.' My head has dropped a bit lower.

Ruby's mother clears her throat. 'The point is that it is wrong to judge people on their appearance. It is also rude to tell someone that they ought to lose weight, and that's what you did when you put that flyer in my letterbox.'

'Mummy!' a voice wails from upstairs. 'Can I watch TV now?'

Ruby's mother looks up. 'I sent Ruby to her room because she threw a tantrum.' She struggles to her feet. 'I don't know what your parents are like, but I should think they'd be a bit worried about you. It will be getting dark soon.' Ruby's mother lumbers to the front door and goes inside.

I sit there for a while, listening. Ruby says she's sorry, then runs down the stairs. Someone turns the TV on. Pots and pans are clattering – probably Ruby's mother is making dinner. Then the phone rings and Ruby's mother calls out, 'Ruby, it's Vanessa!' Then Ruby is chattering away on the phone. I get up and walk slowly down the street.

It's another ten minutes before I reach University Road, and another twenty before I get back to the Refuge. There was probably a quicker way to get home if I took some shortcuts, but I didn't want to risk getting lost.

I look up and down the street before going back into the Refuge. No sign of Terry, so I pull open the front door. A blast of warm air and the smell of roasting lamb washes over me.

Lyyssa's in the kitchen preparing dinner for us. 'Hello Len,' Lyyssa says. I'm surprised to see Lyyssa back at the Refuge so soon; then I remember that she has a car and the drive from Leichhardt wouldn't have taken her ten minutes. She's changed out of her purple blazer, released her hair from that silly chignon, and washed off her makeup. 'What have you been up to?'

Enough to fill up a month of therapy sessions, and nothing I can tell to Lyyssa. I push Terry's mean face out of my thoughts, along with Ruby and her mother.

'I went up to University Road and got an ice-cream,' I reply, trying to sound casual. 'What about you?'

Lyyssa's smile wobbles a fraction. 'Oh, I had coffee in Leichhardt with a friend,' she says brightly, and goes back to peeling the potatoes.

Not exactly a lie. In fact, much less of a lie than what I said.

Chapter 44

It's a week before I realise that 'season finale' means there aren't going to be any more episodes of *Clarissa Hobbs* for three months. I watch the repeats, but watching repeats is sort of like drinking Diet Coke instead of regular Coke. It's a diluted pleasure.

January has blurred into February. Country New South Wales is having a drought. Sydney is hot and dry. The outer suburbs burn in bush fires, and the smoke turns the late afternoon sky a neon pink.

The stables are full of bratty rich Pony Club bitches that don't have anything else to do during school holidays. They hang around the club rooms at the different riding schools, bragging about the ski holidays they're going to take in the winter and making nasty comments about other girls. One of them said 'povvo' in a loud voice when I walked past one day. I wanted to rub her face in a big pile of manure, but then I'd be banned from the stables and she'd have the last laugh.

All the riding instructors are out of patience and

short-tempered. I pity the horses, being worked in this heat. Ray looks tired all the time. He says even less than usual.

I lie awake at night, afraid to go to sleep because I might have a dream about my father.

Why should I be afraid of finding out what happened to Daddy? I might as well find out the truth and get it over with. But that's not how I feel. At night, I feel my past catching up to me, spiralling out of control, mutating into something horrible. I want to escape it.

That's why I liked *Clarissa Hobbs, Attorney at Law* so much. There are problems in every episode, the show would be boring without problems, but Clarissa always manages to solve them, or at least deal with them.

The thing that I'm trying not to fall asleep and dream about is the end of my past life's episode. Something really bad happened to me, and to Daddy, and to my dog Reggie. There isn't going to be any bright, upbeat ending to the story of my life before the Refuge. Whatever happened to us would make people want to turn off the TV and forget they ever saw the Len Russell show.

I'm the sort of person that people want to forget about. They might feel sorry for me, but there's nothing they can really to do help me, either. So they may as well just pretend I don't exist. They'd rather watch a show about someone like Clarissa Hobbs, whose problems can all be solved.

One afternoon, it's so hot I can barely stay awake. I'm lying on my bed smelling bushfire smoke, listening to the sounds of traffic on Canterbury Road. Then I have an idea. I pull my notebook out from under the mattress, and start writing:

Clarissa Hobbs: The Next Generation

In the *Next Generation* episodes, I'm one of the junior lawyers working at Clarissa's firm, helping her with the most important cases. In a later episode, it will be revealed that I'm really Clarissa's long-lost daughter that she gave up for adoption.

After a while, I look at what I've written. It's not bad, but I can't just write *Clarissa Hobbs* episodes all day during vacation. I look at the clock and realise that three hours have passed since I started writing that episode. I need some exercise.

I go down the stairs intending to take a walk, then something occurs to me. Bindi didn't take her skateboard with her, so Lyyssa put it in the storage closet with all her other things just in case she comes back. Yeah, right. Like Miss Junior High Class Hooker who's probably making five hundred dollars an hour on her back would come back here just to get a skateboard.

The storage closet isn't locked. I don't have to look very hard before I find the skateboard, propped next to a cardboard box with 'Bindi's things' written on it in black Texta. *You touch my skateboard and I'll kill you.*

Is that right, you stupid moll? This skateboard's mine now.

I close the front door behind me, set the skateboard on the footpath, and push off.

I've never skateboarded before in my life, but it's not that hard. You just have to watch out for uneven pavement. I'm whizzing along, feeling the wind in my hair and the sun on my face, just like I used to when Daddy would take me for a ride on his motorbike.

'Hey! Watch –'

Before I realise what's happening, I crash into some guy and fall flat on my face. I'm so embarrassed I want to die. The guy helps me to my feet. 'Are you all right?'

I nod, and make myself look up. What I see makes me want to cry. Not only have I done something completely stupid in public, but I've done it in front of an utterly gorgeous guy. He's about sixteen, with short blond hair, blue eyes and a deep tan. He's wearing a Ripcurl T-shirt and board shorts, like a surfie. 'You sure you're okay?' he says, looking really concerned.

'I'm okay,' I croak. 'I'm sorry I ran into you.'

He grins and pats me on the shoulder. 'Don't worry about it. Just be careful, eh?' Then he walks off.

I carry the skateboard back to the Refuge, throw it back in the storage closet, and write, 'In my room – Do not disturb!' on the whiteboard, then run up the stairs. I manage to get back to my room before I start to cry. Maybe I'd just better stay in my room and write *Clarissa Hobbs* episodes for the rest of my vacation.

Chapter 45

I calm down after a while and pull my notebook out. I put a line through each page of the *Clarissa Hobbs* episode I wrote. Only a little kid would fantasise about being a character on TV – I'm embarrassed that I penned it.

I turn to a fresh page and start writing.

It's just before Easter. Daddy has an old flyscreen door hanging in front of the fireplace. It's hanging horizontally, like a table. From each corner, a wire runs up to one central hook drilled into the ceiling. Dope is spread out on the fly screen door, drying.

Daddy is stripping the flowers away from the marijuana plant and putting them on the screen door to be dried. The leaf gets discarded. This is kind of funny. Most city dope smokers, the ones who want everyone to know that they use dope, adopt the marijuana leaf as their symbol. They have marijuana leaf T-shirts and wear silver marijuana leaf pendants strung on leather string necklaces. But it's not the leaf that really gets you high, it's the flower.

When I was little, I used to help Daddy dry the crop, and Daddy thought that was cute. Then all of a sudden he didn't want me to help, because he realised I was old enough to figure out what was going on. But I'd already figured out what he was doing, so banning me from the lounge room while he was stripping and drying didn't change anything.

'Why are you throwing the leaf away?'

Daddy pretends he didn't hear me. He runs his hand up the stalk, and pop, pop, pop, pop, pop, the flowers come off in his hand.

'Some people smoke leaf,' I persist. 'Kevvie's dad sells it.'

Daddy looks up with his 'Don't ask' look.

'Dad, I'm not exactly a kid anymore.'

Daddy drops his eyes back to the stalks and works a little faster than he was before. Daddy knows I'm not a kid anymore – I got my first period a fortnight ago. I think Daddy was more shaken up about it than I was. He got all flustered, jumped in the truck and came back an hour later with a huge bag full of tampons, sanitary pads, and panty liners.

'People who buy leaf are the kind of people who buy retreads instead of new tyres,' Daddy says, at last. 'They're cheapskates. If they don't want to pay for the good stuff, then I don't wanna deal with 'em.'

I'm starting to notice a certain evasiveness in Daddy's explanations. What he just said would make sense if he were proud of growing dope and liked the people he sells it to. But he doesn't even smoke dope, and he doesn't have a lot of respect for people who do.

'Daddy, why are you a cropper?'

That word has never been said before in our house. Daddy looks up at me, hurt and disappointed. He thinks a while before he answers. 'Remember that Neil Young song? The one that goes "The Devil fools with the best-laid plans"?'

Daddy and I don't have history lessons very often, but he used that song to teach me about the civil rights movement in America.

Daddy sighs. 'I left school at fifteen. Was an apprentice on the railway. Left home at sixteen 'cause I didn't get along with my old man. Then the Vietnam War happened, and I joined up with the Merchant Navy so I wouldn't have to fight. Came back after a few years and got a job as a sheet metal worker. It was good money, but I spent most of it on motorbikes and girls. At least I had enough sense to save enough to buy some property.' Dad picks up another stalk and resumes working.

'Then your mother caught my eye.' Daddy smiles a little. 'Before I knew it, I was a father. Your mother stayed up here and looked after you, and I worked in Sydney and came home on the weekends.' Daddy tosses aside a handful of leaf.

'Then the arse fell out of the economy. The company I worked for went broke. Nobody could get a job. At least I owned the property outright, lots of people with mortgages lost their homes. But the dole didn't pay enough to keep you in nappies and the car in petrol.' Another stalk is stripped and tossed aside.

'So when your mother said, "Hey, we've got prime, high-altitude land, what's the sense of letting it go to waste?" I went along with it. Anita used to knock around with croppers, she knew what to do. I told myself it was only going to be for one season.' Another handful of flowers is spread on the flyscreen door.

'Then two seasons went by, and there still wasn't much work around. Then your mother died, and I couldn't be bothered looking for a proper job. Then five seasons had gone by, and any job agent I rang wanted to know why I hadn't worked in five years.' Daddy throws another stripped stalk on the pile to his left.

'So you see, Poss? The Devil fools with the best-laid plans.' Daddy suddenly gets up and leaves the room. I hear the back door bang shut.

I go to my room and lie on my bed. The Devil fools with the best-laid plans? I didn't think Daddy believed in the Devil. He always laughed at Holly because she'd freak if the Devil card came up when she was playing with her deck of tarot cards.

I think I've earned a nap after writing that down. I put my notebook away.

I wake up with my heart pounding. For a second I think I can smell the dope that Daddy's drying. Then I realise that the smell is coming from down the hall.

The clock next to my bed says 8 pm. I hear the TV downstairs and Lyyssa talking to a couple of new kids in the kitchen.

I hear giggles coming from Bindi's old room. For a minute I freeze, thinking that Bindi has come back. But the voices don't belong to Bindi, or Cinnamon. It's a sharp, bossy, nasal voice, and a duller, dumber, younger voice. It's Karen and Allie. Allie has got hold of some dope and is sharing it with Karen. I think Allie wants to be caught, otherwise she wouldn't be smoking it so early in the evening, with Lyyssa still up and about.

Holly used tarot cards to read the future. I don't reckon you need a deck of tarot cards in a place like the Inner West Youth Refuge.

Allie's future is obvious. At best, she'll end up working as a barmaid in some grotty pub in Westieville. At worst, she'll end up being the moll of some guy in a bikie gang. Or maybe the moll for all the guys in the bikie gang. And Karen? She'll wait till she's about eighteen or nineteen, then sleep with someone who's too drunk or stoned to notice how fat and ugly she is. She'll fall pregnant on purpose, so she can get the single parent's pension and a Housing Commission flat. Then she'll eat all the wrong things and neglect her health so that when the kid grows up, she can get the disability pension.

What's going to happen to me? At best? At worst? Which tarot card would come up for me? I don't even have any best-laid plans for the Devil to fool with.

I wish I could get the *smell* of Karen out of my nose. The smell of her urine, her dirtiness, and now, her drugs. I get out of bed and light one of my peppermint-scented candles. In a minute, my room smells pure and beautiful. Someday, I promise myself, I will own a house where all the ceilings are painted gold, where nobody smokes dope, and I will light candles every night.

Allie and Karen have gone quiet. I turn off the

overhead light and look at the glow of the candle. For the first time in months, I'm not afraid to go to sleep.

Chapter 46

The bushfires burn out, but Sydney stays hot and sticky through to March. It's too hot to go outside much.

Easter comes late in April.

Even before the bunnies had been taken down at the stores, we got a huge box of leftover Easter candy from a grocery store – marshmallow rabbits and chocolate eggs. Lyyssa put the box on the kitchen table. I knew that Karen would scoff them all the first chance she had, so I took exactly my share and put them in my desk drawer. One chocolate a day won't make me fat. I have only one every night, after I've finished my homework.

When the evenings finally turn cool, Lyyssa brings some stale-smelling doonas and blankets from the storage closet for everyone to put on their beds. I see Lyyssa opening the closet and I get in first before the other kids, so I have first pick. I pick a goosedown comforter inside a white cover, which is embroidered with white butterflies. It looks almost new, except for a faded brownish stain on one side that someone has tried and failed to bleach out. The stain doesn't matter. I can put it on the bed with that side facing down. I also get an off-white waffle-weave cotton blanket.

Karen picks a vomity pink comforter with pictures of strawberries all over it. Then she finds a fluffy white chenille blanket, which I suppose to her represents the cream to go with the strawberries. She folds both of them and pulls them close to her chest, then realises that I'm blocking her way out of the storage closet. 'Excuse me,' she mumbles, and I step aside to let her pass. I feel guilty about bullying Karen that time, but at least she knows not to annoy me any more.

Allie is looking enviously at my white comforter, but then she finds one that is still wrapped in the thick plastic department store packaging. It has a price tag on it that shows $120, which has been crossed out and replaced with a series of lower prices, ending at $29.95. 'I found a *new* one,' she says triumphantly. I just smile and nod. Why bother telling her that a purple poly/cotton comforter cover with Asian writing all over it is tacky, which is why no one would buy it and the store gave it to us? Then she'd only be plotting how to get her hands on my beautiful embroidered pure white cotton.

I wonder what the writing says. Probably 'Screw you, white trash'.

Shane wants the dark-green Paddy Palin sleeping

bag. It has a hood that you can zip up over your head, with only a tiny hole for air to come inside. I can see why that would appeal to Shane. I got a look inside his room once. He's put up a barricade around his bed with milk crates and cardboard boxes. He still wears three shirts at a time, even in summer. At least he doesn't have to be forced to take a shower anymore.

The next day I take my doona outside to air. I throw it over the Hill's Hoist, then pull an old banana lounge into a sunny spot and lie down. The smell of the air and the feeling of the autumn sun reminds me of another time and place.

Easter. It was Eastertime last year that I was in the accident.

Where Daddy and I lived, Easter always meant that money was just around the corner. Easter candy marked down to half-price meant it was just about time to harvest that crop and sell it in Sydney. But one Easter, something went wrong. There were no new clothes or new tyres for the truck. And we went on eating tinned soup like we had been coming up to harvest. I close my eyes and let myself remember.

'They had a gun,' Daddy says.

Ernie shakes his head and looks at Daddy like he should have known better. 'Mate, you always gotta hold something back.'

'You got any left?' Ernie says, concerned.

'Every other patch I had's been ripped,' Daddy says bitterly. 'So who were these clowns?'

'The blokes I normally deal with couldn't take it. I had to offload it to someone new.'

'Maybe you need a gun,' Ernie says. 'I got a mate in Sydney, over in Burwood. He can get you a revolver.'

'What good's that?' Daddy retorts. 'Then I'd either be dead, or I'd be doing twenty years.'

'Listen,' Ernie says quietly. 'You better watch your back. Terry still has it in for you, and now he's all palsy-walsy with old mate Drury down the road. You know Drury had a patch ripped? Terry's been putting it about it that you did it.'

Daddy makes a disgusted noise. 'The prick. He did it himself. And Drury believed that? Sounds like Drury's been using a bit too much of his own product.'

'Drury's using that and just about anything else you can think of. He's a freak. He's got a houseful of firearms and the coppers in his pocket. And every day, his little mate Terry is whispering in his ear that you ripped him off. Now, are you sure about that revolver?'

'Not interested.'

'Let me know if you change your mind. Cost you six hundred bucks, but it's got karma. Fifteen hundred for one that's never done a job. You don't want one that's done a job. Ballistics.'

Daddy says he'll think about it. Ernie finishes his beer and leaves. Daddy is quiet for a long time.

Daddy was selling what was left of his crop to a dealer in Sydney, but the dealer pulled a gun on him and stole Daddy's dope.

Daddy has a rifle, like everyone around here. But Ernie thinks Daddy needs a smaller gun. One you can hide in your jacket. Ernie also thinks Daddy should pay more money to get a gun that has never been used in a crime. That way, the cops can't ever land him for crimes that someone else did with that gun.

I don't know Drury. He's new in town, he bought the old Fruin place only a couple of years ago. Daddy and I never stop at his place. Sometimes we see his four-wheel drive in town outside the Commercial Hotel, with two mean pig dogs sitting inside. Daddy told me never to touch a pig dog. A pig dog will rip you to pieces.

Something has changed in Riggs Crossing. It used to be that everybody's cropping was an open secret, and nobody stole anybody else's crop. As long as you didn't advertise what you were up to, the locals didn't care and the police would take money to turn a blind eye. Now we hear there are undercover police around. But nobody knows who they are. And we know that some locals are paid police informants. But which ones? And now, everybody who's cropping is being stolen from. But who's doing the ripping? The whole town has turned suspicious and nasty. I'm not sure Daddy trusts anybody but Ernie anymore.

I open my eyes and look at the sky. *Riggs Crossing.* Daddy and I lived in Riggs Crossing. Is anything of mine still in Riggs `Crossing? Do I still have a room there, with my own bed and a comforter that never belonged to anyone else? Or has everything I ever loved been taken to the tip?

I feel something in my chest, a sharp, twisting pain. I get up quickly and give the comforter a good fluffing, then carry it upstairs and make the bed. I grab a rag from the storage closet, get some spray cleanser from the kitchen, and wipe the skirting boards in my room until the pain in my chest goes away.

Chapter 47

'Easter Eggs?' Miss Dunn repeats, frowning.

'Yeah,' I say. 'Why do they sell chocolate eggs at Easter?'

Miss Dunn puts her pencil down on her desk and waits a few seconds before she says anything. 'Len, we are in the middle of an English lesson. I am teaching you how to write an essay. This is the third time you have asked a question that is totally irrelevant to the task at hand. Now, would you like to tell me what the problem is?'

'Sorry,' I mumble, and look down.

Again, Miss Dunn looks at me for a moment before replying. I think she knows that I don't really know what the problem is, and that I probably wouldn't tell her even if I did. Finally, she sighs and closes the textbook.

'Okay, let's save the rest of that English lesson for next time. You've mastered the basics.' Miss Dunn picks up her pencil again and taps it against the top of the desk. 'Easter eggs. Do you know much about

Christianity? Were you taken to church when you were a kid?'

After Daddy's fight with Holly, we get up very early one morning and drive to a big church far away from Riggs Crossing. Daddy sits next to me on a long wooden bench. He teaches me how to cross myself, when to kneel. Hail Mary, full of grace, the Lord is with thee . . .

'No.'

'Right. Well, Christians believe that Jesus was the son of God and arose from the dead after being crucified. Jesus rising from the dead is called the Resurrection. The Christian holiday that marks the Resurrection is now called Easter. But when Christianity started, most people were pagans and didn't want to give up certain rituals that they liked. One of these rituals was a lunar festival called Easter. LEN, ARE YOU PAYING ATTENTION?'

'Yes.'

Miss Dunn calms down. 'Good. Now, this pagan festival Easter took place during the full moon. It celebrated fertility. That's why we have Easter bunnies, because rabbits produce lots of offspring. And we have Easter eggs because eggs represented fertility to pagans. Pagans refused to stop being pagans and start being Christians because they didn't want to stop having fertility celebrations. So, the early Christian fathers invented the story that Jesus was resurrected during Easter time, and told the pagans that it was okay to have a festival every year.

But they had to say that the festival was to celebrate Christ being resurrected. Oh, and the word "Easter" has the same origin as the word "oestrus". Female animals can fall pregnant when they're in oestrus.'

Holly dancing naked under the full moon. Daddy watching her, standing to one side of the window so she can't see him watching, smiling a little.

'Does that make any sense to you?'

Daddy closes the curtains. 'Off to bed, Poss.'

'Not exactly. I mean, sort of.'

Miss Dunn sighs. 'Well, I probably didn't explain it very clearly, and what I said might not be entirely accurate. I'm not a walking encyclopaedia.' Miss Dunn scribbles something on a piece of paper and hands it to me. 'This is your English assignment for next week. Write a five hundred-word essay on the origins of Easter. Major Heath may be able to help you.'

Miss Dunn doesn't offer me tea at the end of the lesson.

Walking back to the Refuge, I turn down the street with the Nohant house. After all, the lady who owns that house has no right to intimidate me. I'm allowed to walk down that street, or any other street, if I want to. And why does she bother having a house and garden like you'd see in a magazine if she doesn't want people to admire them?

I'm almost at Nohant when I realise a car is coming up behind me. I turn my head to look. It's one of those cars that Westie boys like, with a V8 engine, blackened windows and a stereo you can hear in the next suburb. But this car is being driven very slowly and quietly, its engine pulsing at a low throb.

Then the car roars into high gear onto the footpath, hurtling straight toward me. I scramble over the picket fence and run across Nohant's garden, tripping over stones and lanterns and clumps of black mondo grass. The car ploughs straight through the fence – I can hear the wood cracking and splintering as I sprint around the side of the house. The car stops a moment in the middle of the garden, then whoever's driving guns the engine, demolishing what's left of the garden and smashing the other side of the fence to get back on the street.

I'm shaking but I come out from where I was hiding and watch as the car races off and turns left onto Canterbury Road. That wasn't an SUV, this isn't the Hamptons, I'm not white trash, and that sure as hell wasn't Lucy Grubb behind the wheel.

I'm standing there frozen when the second-floor window bangs open and the nasty bleached blonde woman pokes her head out, angry that someone's making noise. She looks down and sees me in the middle of her wrecked garden.

'YOU LITTLE BITCH!' she shrieks, her face turning a blotchy purple. She thinks it was me who left her garden looking like Darwin after Cyclone Tracy. She jerks her head back inside and I run without thinking why I'm running.

I'm still shaking when I get back to the Refuge. I run straight up the stairs to my room without even marking the whiteboard to let Lyyssa know I'm home.

I sit at my desk and take one chocolate Easter egg from my supply in the top drawer. I let it dissolve slowly in my mouth as my heart pounds.

Terry saw me in Newtown a couple of weeks ago. Was it him in that car? Or somebody worse? He's too stupid to know how to find me, but whoever he's working for would know. Find a mug with a government job, they get paid bugger-all, even less than the coppers. A bit of money will get you any information you're after.

My heart won't slow down and I start crying. I take two more chocolate eggs out of the drawer. I think I've got more important things to worry about than my weight. Like where to go if I'm not safe here.

I'm just unwrapping my fourth chocolate egg when there's a ruckus downstairs in the entryway that distracts me. Lyyssa's talking with someone, trying to calm them down. The other voice doesn't sound familiar. It's a woman's voice, harsh and loud.

'I know she's here, the Department told me!' the voice shouts. 'Why can't I see her?'

Probably the mother of one of the newbies we got last week. I can't make out what Lyyssa says, but I hear the front door close and the two of them walking toward Lyyssa's office. I put it out of my mind. I should start on the algebra homework that I was supposed to have done for Lyyssa today, but instead I take my notebook out and start writing a new *Clarissa Hobbs* episode. I know some of the episodes I wrote were pretty crap, but I can do better this time.

I've just about finished the episode when Lyyssa comes running down the hall and pounds on my door.

'Len! Len!' Lyyssa opens my door without waiting for me to answer. She never does this. I'm so astonished that I forget to be angry with her.

'Len, your grandmother's here!'

Chapter 48

Over the next quarter of an hour, Lyyssa gives me the condensed history of my life. Apparently, the police have been talking to Lyyssa all along about leads they'd got on the case.

Daddy is dead.

But I have a grandmother.

'Why didn't anybody tell me?' I hear myself ask.

Lyyssa looks uncomfortable. 'Well, the police wanted to locate any family you had. And I thought it would be therapeutic if you remembered things in your own time.'

Therapeutic. I want to slap her. Then she starts spouting some crap about how people at the hospital tried to tell me, but I didn't want to know about it. *Nobody told me nobody told me nobody told me* I chant in my head, like holding your ears and singing *la la la* so you don't hear what someone else is saying.

Lyyssa's mouth is moving but I can't hear the sound of her talking, only a roaring in my ears. That's when I know either I'm crazy, or she's telling the truth.

In the hospital, I screamed and threw something at a social worker and a nurse when they tried to tell me my father might be dead and called me Samantha. Shut up, go away, I screamed at them. My name's Len!

I remember now.

'Len,' Lyyssa says gently, 'do you understand what I'm telling you?'

I nod.

'Do you want me to tell you the rest?'

I nod again.

Lyyssa tells me that my father, Michael Patterson, was a reclusive marijuana grower who raised me by himself up in the North Coast ranges. Drug traffickers who thought he was encroaching on their territory murdered him. On the night of the accident, my father was trying to get me out of the area and away from the killers. A few weeks ago, police got a tipoff and made two arrests. Talking to the locals, they discovered that Michael Patterson had a daughter who disappeared when he did. They thought that daughter might be me.

Then someone remembered that I had a mother.

They told the police my mother's name. The police looked in their computer databases or searched the internet or did whatever police do when they're following a trail. The trail led to a Mrs Gibson of Campbelltown.

Campbelltown. Way past where my MyMulti pass will take me. Way past anywhere I want to go.

All the information they got from Mrs Gibson matched with what they knew about me. Then they did some DNA testing, matching up her blood with a sample of mine that the hospital still had. The DNA proved that she's my blood relative.

'So, where's my mother?' I say, already knowing. I'm trying to distract myself, trying not to think about my father, who I now know is dead and buried. Or maybe not even properly buried. Maybe the murderers just dumped his body somewhere.

'Your mother's been dead a long time, Len,' Lyyssa says, as gently as possible. 'Her name was Anita Gibson. It's her mother who's come to see you today. She's waiting in my office.' We sit quietly for a minute. 'Are you ready?' Lyyssa asks me.

I nod, and we start walking down the hall.

Lyyssa opens the door to her office, and I feel a stab of disappointment. The woman sitting at the table isn't a tastefully dressed mature-age lady like Clarissa Hobbs. She is skinny and wrinkled, with her hair dyed a canary yellow.

'Mrs Gibson, this is Len.'

My grandmother doesn't get up. She sits there eyeballing me while I stand just inside the door, doing the same to her. Finally, my grandmother speaks. 'Am I allowed to smoke in here?' she says to Lyyssa, as if daring Lyyssa to say no.

'Well, normally, no, but, um, let me go find an ashtray while you two get acquainted.'

Lyyssa hurries out, closing the door behind her. Mrs Gibson pulls a pack of cigarettes and a lighter out of her purse even though Lyyssa hasn't come back with an ashtray yet. I'm not even sure we have an ashtray at the Refuge.

'Mrs Gibson –' I start to say, but I can't get the rest of the sentence out.

'For Heaven's sake,' she says, fidgeting and lighting a cigarette. 'You don't have to "Mrs Gibson" me. Call me Gran.'

Gran and I go back to staring at each other. Finally, I take a seat across from her at the table.

'You don't look like Anita,' she says finally. 'Anita was slim, with dark curly hair.'

'Maybe I take after my father.'

Mrs Gibson snorts. 'Let's hope not.'

I decide to let this pass. 'What was my mother like?' I say, changing the subject.

Gran takes a deep drag on her cigarette and exhales slowly. 'Your mother was wild,' she says. 'Anita was a handful as a little girl. Not a bad kid, just always up to some mischief. When she got to a certain age, she started drinking, staying out all night, going off with boys on motorcycles. I tried to discipline her, but it always made things worse. If I took away her pocket money, she'd shoplift. If I grounded her, she'd run away. In the end, she just wore me down. I had four other kids to raise.' Gran looks at the ash on the end of her cigarette, then looks around the room. She sees a Diet Coke can on Lyyssa's desk. She scrapes back her chair, walks over to the desk, picks up the can and shakes it to make sure it's empty, then flicks her ash into it and brings the can back to the table with her.

'So what happened to her?'

'I threw her out when she was sixteen,' Gran says bitterly. 'I told her she could either follow my rules or leave, so she left. She and a school friend hitched a ride to some hippie commune up the coast. Your Aunt Cheryl heard from one of the kids at school who had an older brother at the same place. Anita sent letters to Cheryl sometimes, but not to the rest of us. Anita wasn't that close to her sister Phoebe, and Sean and Bradley were still small.'

Anita, Cheryl, Phoebe, Bradley, Sean. My mother, my two aunts, my two uncles . . . I can't put a face to any of them.

Gran's hands are shaking and her voice is harsh. 'I was married at seventeen. Your granddad pissed off after Sean was born. I raised five kids on my own. Five. I made sure Anita and her sisters and brothers had a decent home. So why was it so damn hard for her to stay out of trouble? Why was it always so damn hard?' Gran smacks the table to emphasise each word. Then she starts to cry.

I'm praying that Lyyssa doesn't walk in. This is the sort of messy emotional outburst she'd love. Gran's mascara is running down her face and her bleached hair looks like a bird's nest. A horrible, sinking feeling comes over me: people who come from families like mine don't end up living in Los Angeles and working for people like Clarissa Hobbs. In my mind's eye, I see Clarissa tossing her ash-blonde hair, slipping into her Mercedes and driving away from me without so much as a glance in the rear-view mirror.

Gran pulls a crumpled tissue from her purse, blows her nose and wipes her eyes.

'I never saw Anita again. We knew there was a baby girl born the first week of July two years after Anita left, but Anita never brought her to see us.'

I'm wondering why Gran is saying 'her' rather than 'you', then something else hits me. My birthday is the first week of July? That means I'm not a Leo, after all! I search my memory for astrological tables. First week of July is – Cancer! Placid, affectionate, home-loving, boring, boring, boring! I'm so stunned I barely notice that Gran has started talking again.

'Then we heard she'd had a fight with Mick, left the baby with him and run off. Four years later, the police show up on the doorstep and say they've found a body in a nature reserve. They wouldn't let me see it. Said there wasn't anything left to see. Asked for her dental records. It was Anita. They said that backpacker murderer did it, like he did all those other girls who hitched a ride with him.' Gran stares into the distance and takes another drag of her cigarette. 'I always knew something bad happened to her. Even Anita wouldn't have left a tiny baby with that loser.'

Somehow I don't think Gran is connecting Anita's tiny baby with me, the girl who is sitting there right in front of her.

After a minute Gran remembers that I exist. Her eyes focus on me and narrow a bit. 'Anyway, what's with this calling you "Len"? That's a boy's name.'

'When they found me, I was wearing an old jumper with "Len" stitched on it.'

Gran looks unimpressed. 'Yeah? Well, that's not your name. Your name is Samantha.'

I let this sink in. 'Any middle name?'

'Rose,' Gran says. 'My name.'

Samantha Rose Patterson. It sounds elegant, yet sensible. There is a world of possibility in that name. I don't have to be Len Russell for the rest of my life. Len Russell sounds like a grill cook or a petrol station attendant. But Samantha Rose Patterson could be a horse trainer, or a veterinary surgeon, or a fashion designer, or even a barrister at a top law firm.

Lyyssa opens the door without knocking. 'Len? Mrs Gibson? How's everything going?'

'Everything's going just fine,' I say coldly. 'And my name's not Len. It's Samantha Rose. I don't ever want to be called Len again in my whole life.'

Lyyssa smiles nervously, then speaks to me the way you would address a four-year-old who wants to be called Princess Leia. 'Well, *Samantha*, would you mind leaving your grandmother and me alone to discuss a few things for a little while? We'll come find you when we're done.'

Gran narrows her eyes, and I realise that she doesn't like Lyyssa any more than I do. 'I gotta go,' she said, shoving her cigarettes and lighter into her handbag. 'If Samantha needs me, you know where I am.' With that, Gran heaves her handbag over her shoulder and walks out.

Lyyssa watches in astonishment as Gran leaves without even hugging me or saying goodbye or asking when she can see me again. 'Right. Okay,' Lyyssa says, taking a moment to reassemble her social worker's mask. 'So Len, I mean, *Samantha*, what do you think of your grandmother?'

Just once, I decide to tell Lyyssa the truth. 'I think she shouldn't wear white socks with black leggings.'

For a moment, Lyyssa looks stunned. Then something changes in her eyes and I see myself in them. Someone mean and ugly. Someone who refuses to love her own grandmother.

'Len,' she says quietly, 'you need to learn some compassion. You're not the only person in the world who's had it rough.'

I feel the blood rush to my face in a burst of humiliation. Lyyssa's right and I don't know what to say, so I turn away and run through the door that my grandmother just passed through, catching a whiff of her cheap perfume. But I go in the opposite direction she went, back towards my room. I go straight to my scarred wooden desk, pull out my algebra book, and study until dark. I concentrate on the equations, trying not to think about Gran and trying to forget that I'm not a Leo, after all.

Chapter 49

Incident Report

Patient: Samantha Rose Patterson (aka Len Russell)

Caseworker: Lyyssa Morgan

Samantha's maternal grandmother, Rose Gibson, arrived unannounced at IWYR despite an agreement that she would let the Department arrange a meeting when Samantha appeared psychologically ready. As Samantha has recently shown markedly fewer symptoms of Attachment Disorder, exhibiting less hostility toward others and establishing bonds with mentors, the planned meeting would have occurred within the next month. This was explained to Rose Gibson, but she demanded immediate access to Samantha, threatening legal action if I did not comply. To avoid further escalating the situation, I escorted Mrs Gibson to my office and established some ground rules for her meeting with Samantha.

Samantha was understandably surprised

at Rose Gibson's sudden appearance, and demanded to know why she had not been told about her grandmother, or about the ongoing investigation into her father's death. When I informed Samantha that hospital staff had tried to do so, she reacted with shock, anger, and a return to the passive-aggressive silence she demonstrated in her early days at IWYR.

I left Samantha and Rose Gibson alone in my office for a short time, as per my agreement with Mrs Gibson. Neither Samantha nor Mrs Gibson was forthcoming as to the content or tenor of their meeting. Rose Gibson left contact details and said Samantha was welcome to call or visit, but behaved in an abrasive manner.

Samantha made a derogatory comment about Rose Gibson's appearance after she left the Refuge, and has since said that she will no longer participate in weekly psychotherapy sessions.

Samantha has been at the Inner West Youth Refuge for nearly one year. Her psychological trauma may be irreparable, but she possesses considerable intelligence and determination. She is old enough to choose to live with any of her biological family, or to move to a less-structured living situation, such as a halfway house. Samantha may continue to stay at IWYR if she agrees to comply with the weekly psychotherapy sessions that are part of IWYR's charter. I recommend that a panel including myself, representatives from the Department, and a Child Advocate explain Samantha's options to her and allow her to make her own decision.

Chapter 50

I've done a fortnight's worth of algebra homework. I can't concentrate on it anymore. I keep thinking that I'm not a Leo, I'm a Cancer. As if that matters.

I remember the book of Chinese astrology that I tea-leafed from the Refuge library but could never get into. I flip through the book and find the table that lists all of the years. Year of the Snake, Horse, Rat, Monkey. The year I was born is the year of the Ox. I look in the index and find the chapter. Key attributes of the Ox: *steadfast, solid, plodding, methodical.* Great, I've struck out with Chinese astrology, too.

I go back and find the chapter devoted to the Dragon. Passionate, confident and independent, the description reads. *Gifted with an extraordinarily intense personality, Dragons often have ambitious plans and are usually strong enough to accomplish them. This Sign's strong temper can be hard to stand against, yet Dragons are also quick to forgive. Dragons are lovers of nature and animals, and often prefer extended journeys to quick tourist jaunts.* The pages show photographs of Chinese artwork featuring dragons embroidered on tapestries and painted on to porcelain vases. I close the book. Is all astrology a crock of shit? Or was I born in the wrong month and wrong year by mistake?

I'm tired but I'm afraid to go to sleep. I light a candle, turn out the overhead light, sit on my bed and stare into the candle flame.

When I close my eyes, I see a parade of painted Chinese dragons against the purple-red background of my closed eyelids. A dragon flies through the air, soaring above the clouds, then lands on a misty mountaintop and waits in silence.

I'm supposed to sleep over with Megan Wilson, but Megan has an asthma attack and has to go to the doctor, so Daddy comes to take me home. When Daddy and I get back from town, something is wrong. Reggie isn't barking like he always does when he hears us come back, and the phone is ringing.

Daddy picks up the phone. I start to go outside to see where Reggie is, but Daddy tells me sharply to go to my room.

'Mate, I've been ringing you every five minutes for the past three hours!' Ernie's voice is loud enough that I can hear it.

I don't go to my room. I quietly walk into Daddy's room and very carefully pick up the phone.

'You'll probably find your dog's dead.'

'Yeah,' Daddy whispers.

'That's part one. The rest is like I tell you. Drury and his mongs have been waiting for you to drive past. I don't know

how you got past 'em coming up the hill. You need to get out of there now.'

'I can't drive past that bastard in me own car, he'll know it,' Daddy hisses.

'I'll send Craig. He owes us one. Matter of fact, he owes us about half a dozen. He'll be over in twenty. Be ready when he gets there.'

I put the phone down and run to my room.

Daddy comes to my door. 'Poss, we're going to Sydney for a while,' Daddy says in a strange voice. His eyes wander around the room, then come to focus on the bed. 'Put your heavy coat on. And take that blanket and a pillow.'

I take the blue blanket and a pillow from my bed. I stand for a moment looking at my bookcase full of books and the wicker basket with all the teddy bears and stuff I'm too old for now.

'Come on, Poss.'

We sit in the lounge room and wait. Daddy loads his rifle and puts an extra clip in his jacket.

'Dad, where's Reggie?'

'Reggie's over at Ernie's place.' Daddy's voice sounds raspy and broken. I know Reggie isn't really with Ernie.

We hear it at the same time. We can tell by the sound that it's not Drury's four-wheel drive. Daddy looks at me and nods. I pick up my blanket and pillow, he picks up his rifle, and we walk out the front door.

The car pulls into the driveway, right up to the house. Craig flashes the headlights twice, then lights up the inside of the car for a second so we can see it's him. Craig's about twenty. I've *seen him at Ernie's place a few times. He looks scared. Really scared.*

Daddy puts me in the back. 'Don't sit on the seat,' he tells me. 'Keep down.' There's no place on the back seat for me to sit anyway, the car's full of clothes and stuff. I lie on the floor of the car.

Daddy bangs the door shut after me and opens the driver's door. 'Move over, Craig, I'm driving till we get to Tamworth. You changed the plates on this thing?'

Craig says something to Daddy and lights a cigarette. Daddy throws the car into Drive and we roar back down the track. We're going fast, taking curves at a sickening speed and sliding out on the dirt. I can tell we're almost to town when we start driving in a straight line.

I can't get comfortable on the floor of the car even with the blanket and pillow, and I'm cold. There's a jumper in the pile of clothes on the seat, so I struggle out of my coat and put the jumper on, then put my coat on over the top.

I think we're almost to Wollomombi when headlights appear behind us, then flash to high beam.

'Christ, they're on our tail,' Daddy says.

It's the people who killed Reggie.

'Lose 'em!' Craig yells. 'You gotta do something!'

'Shut up!' Daddy hisses, then pulls over, puts the car into Park, and leaves it idling.

'Give me that thing.'

Craig hands Daddy the rifle and slides down in his seat. Daddy slides the bolt into the rifle.

'Soon as I get out, put your foot on the brake,' Daddy tells

him. *'I need the brake lights to see their car.'*

'What? Why?' Craig sounds like he's about to cry.

'I'll put one through the radiator. They won't be going far after that.'

Daddy speaks to me in a low voice without turning his head. *'Poss, get under that blanket. Don't move till I get back.'*

I pull the blanket over my head. Daddy throws the car door open and jumps out. There's a rifle shot and the sound of a windscreen shattering, and what sounds like tiny little pebbles showering down all over our car. A car door opens.

'Good shot, Drury!' Terry yells. *'I'll finish him off.'* Two more gunshots.

No.

Craig jumps out of the passenger side. There's another rifle shot.

'What the hell was that?' Terry's yelling. He's deaf from the gunshots.

'There was another bastard in there. But not anymore.' The voice is hard and ugly. Drury. The pig dog man. I don't know his face. In my mind I see the head of a pig dog on a human body. A pig dog will tear you to pieces.

'Is he dead?' Terry's still yelling. He can't hear Craig moaning and saying, *'Please, no, I don't want to die.'*

'Just finish the prick off.'

Three more shots.

No.

'Right. That's got 'im. See, Drury? Told ya I was a good shot!' Terry's still yelling. He sounds crazy.

'Wake up to yourself and chuck 'em in the trailer. NOW!

And throw the tarp over them.'

There are sounds of dragging, lifting. Another voice I don't recognise says, 'This bastard's heavy. Hey, he's pissed himself,' and someone laughs and I cry silently underneath the blanket.

'That thing's still idling, innit?' Drury says. 'Good. Pull on full left lock, then knock it into Drive. It'll go straight down into that gully. We'll deal with these two pricks up the road a bit.'

'Where's that brat of his?' someone says.

'Camped with Steve Wilson's kid, tonight,' Terry says. 'Heard it from the barman at the Commercial Hotel.'

The car clunks, the engine takes a load, and I stay quiet and still under the blanket as the car rolls forward and falls into blackness.

The dragon glides, the dragon soars. I ride on the back of the dragon, back to when I was six.

I'm in front of Daddy on the motorbike and Reggie is racing alongside us. 'Go, Dad!' I yell. Daddy stops the bike under a tree and sets me down. Reggie runs around us in a circle, because he's so happy to be with us.

The scream I've been keeping inside me ever since the car went over the cliff comes out and Lyyssa comes running up the stairs and unlocks my door with her master key. Then I'm sobbing and Lyyssa is holding me and telling me it's okay. She doesn't ask any questions or try to get me to talk. Her face looks soft and tired. I think she's been crying, too.

Daddy and Reggie are dead. Daddy may have

been a cropper, but he loved me. Reggie was just a cropper's guard dog, but he was a good dog who protected us. And no one will ever love me as much as they did ever again, not even if I grow up to be as rich and beautiful and successful as Clarissa Hobbs.

I understand now why I've never trusted Lyyssa. The way Daddy lived, he could never really trust anyone. He taught me to be suspicious. If anyone asked you too many questions, it meant they were looking to take advantage of you or dob you in or rip you off. I guess that's why he pulled me out of school, because he was afraid I'd let it slip that he was a cropper and he'd get arrested.

'Samantha, I'm sorry,' Lyyssa says. She doesn't say for what, but I understand.

I nod. 'I'm sorry too.'

Lyyssa leaves the room for a few minutes, then comes back with a pot of herbal tea and a mug. She sets them on my night table, tells me that she's downstairs if I need her, and softly closes the door as she leaves.

Chapter 51

I get up but I'm not awake. I go to sleep but don't dream. I eat scarcely anything. I watch TV but don't remember afterwards what I watched. I try to read but don't understand what I've read. I walk along University Road but don't notice anything around me. I go to lessons with Miss Dunn and can't concentrate on what she's saying to me. I know she's worried about me and has called Lyyssa to ask what's the matter.

It's six weeks since Easter. Every day is cold rain.

I ride the 355 bus to the stables at first light on Tuesdays and Thursdays, muck out the boxes, have a dressage lesson on Dex. Sometimes I cry into a horse's neck when I'm grooming it, but only if it's a nice horse, and only if I'm sure no one's around.

If Ray knows anything about what's happened to me, he doesn't say so. He talks to me during lessons and tells me what to do with the horses, but he doesn't break the quiet.

The police start coming to see me about once a week. I guess these police are the straight kind. If they were the bent kind, they would have killed me already.

They tell me they've made two arrests. One is Drury, the pig dog man. The other is nobody I know. I tell the police about the business Terry did with Daddy, and how Daddy beat him up in the bottle shop because Terry ripped him off, and how I heard Terry's voice the night of the accident. I tell them about seeing Terry in the 7-Eleven on University Road, and how I think it was him that tried to run me over in the Nohant garden. The police find Terry and arrest him. I have to testify at his trial, but I don't have to be in the same room with him.

The police ask me to tell them as much as I can remember about the shooting. They always have a female officer there. I guess she's supposed to calm me down if I start crying. But I don't cry.

They ask me lots of questions. What did Daddy say before he got out of the car? How many gunshots did I hear? How could I tell whether it was a rifle or a pistol being fired? Who said what after which gunshot? When did I feel the car start to move? Sometimes they ask me the same question several times. They can see I'm getting annoyed, so they explain to me that this is a normal part of police questioning. They need to make sure your answers are consistent. If your answers are inconsistent, it means your memory is faulty.

They listen carefully and record everything I say. I

never tell them what Ernie said about Drury having the Riggs Crossing coppers in his pocket. Ten to one on, they'll know that already. I'm not dogging on anybody who doesn't need it.

Finally, the female officer explains what they think happened. When the police arrested Drury, they looked over his car and noticed that the rego sticker was a re-issue, so the windscreen must have been a replacement. The police found the bloke in Tamworth who replaced the windscreen and interviewed him. The windscreen man said he'd never seen a broken windscreen before where there was not a single piece of glass inside the vehicle. The windscreen had been shattered outwards, not inwards. The coppers reckoned this meant that a shot was fired from inside the car. When the windscreen man asked Drury how this happened, Drury said he didn't know. The windscreen man remembered that. It was weird for someone to bring in a vehicle with a smashed windscreen, and not know how it got smashed.

The coppers also said that they found Daddy's weapon in Drury's house. Ballistic examination showed that it had not discharged a round since its last cleaning.

The female officer says that this, taken together with what I said about the sequence and number of shots, indicates that no shot was ever fired into

Drury's car. This means that Daddy never got to fire a shot.

Daddy miscalculated. He thought he was fast enough to disable Drury's car, then jump back into Craig's car and drive away. It shouldn't have taken three or four seconds on a lever action or a repeater. He thought that if Drury was going to try and shoot him, that he would get out of the car first. But Drury knew not to muck around. He shot Daddy from inside his own car, as soon as he could aim. He didn't care about shattering his own windscreen. He was playing for bigger stakes than windscreens.

Then Terry shot Daddy at close range with a pistol even though Daddy was already dead. Then Drury shot Craig the second he jumped out of the car. Terry fired the shots that killed Craig.

Drury was a real crim and an expert shot. Terry was a little thief and a wannabe who couldn't have hit the side of a barn from six metres away, but Craig was less than three metres away. And even then it took Terry three shots to do the job.

They never found the trailer from Drury's vehicle. Drury would've burnt it to get rid of the DNA.

The police also tell me that there was an article about the accident in the *Tamworth Advocate*. The article mentioned that an unidentified girl, me, had been found in the wreck. That's most likely when Drury and Terry realised I'd been in the car. Terry probably thought he'd make a hero of himself to Drury by getting rid of me. Or maybe Drury told him to find me and kill me. We don't know yet.

It didn't take long for people in Riggs Crossing to figure out that the girl in the car was Mick Patterson's kid, but everyone was too scared of Drury to say anything.

The police finally go away. They give me their business cards to call them if I need to. They also give me a card for a professional counsellor to call. I keep the police officers' business cards and throw the counsellor's card in the trash.

Lyyssa and a man from some government department tell me that the land Daddy owned has been sold, and the money put in trust for me. The house we lived in burned down. I nod and say nothing.

One day I'm walking home and see a fruit bat dead on the street. I look up and see another fruit bat, dead and hanging by one leg from the power line. They were mates, and were both electrocuted when they landed on the power line. One fell, the other didn't. In death, their eyes are open, staring at each other. The one hanging from the power line stares downward at his wife. Maybe he saw her fall just before he died. The one on the ground stares up at her husband. Maybe she died just after she hit the ground. I start to wonder why I couldn't have died along with Daddy.

This is the way things have been for the three weeks since my grandmother came, since I found out what happened to Daddy and Reggie.

Then another visitor comes.

'Samantha?' This time when Lyyssa comes for me, I'm not writing a *Clarissa Hobbs* episode. The day after my grandmother came to visit, I ripped the *Clarissa Hobbs* episodes out of the notebook, tore them up, and put my notebook at the bottom of my desk drawer. I'm staring out the window at nothing when Lyyssa knocks.

I open the door.

'Samantha? There's someone here to see you.' Lyyssa has changed in the last fortnight, too. Her eyes are darker, her face thinner, her skin paler. All her bounce and cheer has gone, because I made her feel like she couldn't possibly help me, no matter how hard she tried. I told her I was sorry afterwards, but that doesn't really change anything. Now, I feel like I've just told a five-year-old kid that there's no such thing as Santa Claus. I wish we had the old, silly Lyyssa back.

'It's a man named Ernie,' Lyyssa says. 'He knew your father. He's waiting in my office, if you'd like to see him.'

Ernie. I thank Lyyssa and run down the hallway and down the stairs. Ernie is standing in Lyyssa's office, looking out the window.

'Ernie!'

Ernie turns. It's the face I remember, only sadder.

'Sam.' He opens his arms and I run to him and start to cry. Ernie holds me for a while, then when I've calmed down we sit on Lyyssa's couch.

'I didn't know where you were,' Ernie tells me. 'I knew what happened to your dad, and I knew who did it. But I didn't dare go to the cops.'

I nod. I know what Ernie means. Daddy told me that you can never really trust the police, because you never know which cops are bent. Suppose Ernie had told a cop which drug dealer murdered my father, and the cop was being bribed by that very same drug dealer? Then Ernie would be dead, too.

'They burned our house down, didn't they? And they killed Reggie.'

'Aw, Sam.' Ernie's face creases. 'They shot him, it was over in a second. He died protecting you. That's the way a dog like Reggie would've wanted to die.' Ernie swallows hard and wipes his eyes. 'Bastards.'

I think of the outside dunny overlooking the Nymboida River, the kettle that I burned my hand on, the blue blanket on my bed. 'I don't ever want to go back there again.'

Ernie shakes his head. 'No, Sam. You stay in Sydney. Riggs Crossing's for ferals and croppers. I sold up and moved to Gosford. I run a garage now.'

'Can I come stay with you?'

Ernie looks embarrassed. 'Sam, you're a young lady now. A guy like me can't have a young girl living in his house, it wouldn't look nice.'

A slideshow of Ernie's girlfriends flickers through my mind.

'Sam, you're a smart kid. They tell me they've got university professors teaching you stuff that most eighteen-year-olds can't get their head around. You buckle down and study.' Ernie hugs me again, says he'll keep in touch, and then he's gone.

Chapter 52

Ernie drops by to see me every few weeks. Ray gets a job up north training the horses for a movie, so I have two months break from the stables. I start playing tennis at the Community Centre, sometimes playing against someone, sometimes just smashing balls over the net, practising my serve. My shoulders get broader and my waist gets smaller. Guys start to look at me. Every morning just after I wake up, I lie in bed for a while thinking about guys I see at the Community Centre, guys I see on the street, guys I make up in my imagination.

Allie is caught shoplifting and gets the usual round of scoldings from the usual collection of dickheads. We get a new kid named Stuart who arrives with the usual baggage: doona, backpack, junkie single mother, alcoholic stepfather, scars from beltings he's been given and scars from razor blades that he gave himself. Karen and Shane stay the same.

The new season of *Clarissa Hobbs* starts. I still watch it every week, when I don't have too much homework. I still go to see Miss Dunn twice a week, and once a week I go to see someone in the mathematics department. I start to wonder why Miss Dunn is teaching me. I know she likes me, but it obviously takes up a lot of her time, and I know she's busy. One day, when I can see she has dark circles under her eyes from staying up late working on something, I ask her.

'Why am I teaching you?' Miss Dunn says, seeming surprised that I asked.

'Yeah. I mean, you obviously have a lot of stuff of your own to do.'

Miss Dunn hesitates a moment, then gets up. 'How about we discuss this over a pot of tea.' She puts the kettle on, and we wait in silence for it to boil. Then she puts three bags of mint tea into a pot and brings it to the desk, along with two cups.

'Why am I teaching you? Well, it's like this. As you know, Paul, that's Mr Brentnall — the education officer who gave you tests — is my partner. He knows I'm doing research on highly intelligent kids from disadvantaged backgrounds, trying to figure out how to get them to do their HSC and get them into university even if they don't have much support at home. After testing and interviewing you, Paul knew you'd get bored in a public high school. He approached me with the idea of teaching you, I got approval from the university, he got approval from DOCS.'

Miss Dunn rolls her eyes and shakes her head.

'Don't repeat this, but DOCS were the biggest obstacle. They were all worried that you wouldn't get enough "interaction with your peers". Paul and I convinced them that you got enough interaction with your peers at the Refuge.'

Miss Dunn doesn't know how right she is. I get more than enough interaction with my loathsome peers at the Refuge. Any more, and I'd commit suicide.

Miss Dunn pours the tea and sets a cup in front of me. 'So, in a way, I suppose I'm using you for my research project. But I think that I'm giving you a better education than what you'd get in a public school.'

I can't think of anything to say. I take a sip of my mint tea and look around. I see a picture on the wall that I've noticed before. It's Asian writing, kind of like the writing on Allie's duvet cover. It's painted on a creamy white background, and framed in black.

'What does that picture mean?' I ask.

Miss Dunn looks to see which one I mean. 'That one by the window? That's Japanese calligraphy. That character means "eternity".'

'How do you know it doesn't mean, "Screw you, white trash"?' This comes out of my mouth before I can think about how it sounds.

Miss Dunn chokes on her tea, flushes red and starts howling with laughter.

'I mean, what I meant was . . .' I'm confused

and embarrassed, trying to figure out where to start explaining about Lucy Grubb or Allie's duvet cover.

'I know, Sam, I know.' Miss Dunn is still laughing, searching through her bag for a handkerchief and mopping up the tea that she sprayed over her desk. 'That's just the point. Most people who buy calligraphy can't tell good calligraphy from bad, and they wouldn't have a clue what it meant unless someone tells them. They really wouldn't know if it said "Screw You, White Trash". They just want something exotic-looking to decorate their walls.'

'But you do know what this picture means?'

'Yes. I know that it means "eternity" because I studied Japanese language and lived in Tokyo for a year. And I know that it's good calligraphy, because I took calligraphy lessons.' Miss Dunn takes out a piece of paper and pencil. 'Here's how you write it.' She demonstrates. 'It's similar to the sign for water,' she says, counting out the strokes of her pencil, 'One, two, three, four. But to write "eternity", the middle stroke is slightly different, and there's a small stroke over here.' Miss Dunn draws a second character. One, two, three, four, five.

I watch Miss Dunn as she writes. She looks like Ingrid Bergman, an actor from old black-and-white movies. Daddy liked the sort of women you see in old movies. He said that back in those days, movie stars weren't all silicone and collagen and botox.

'But if you go back to the character for water, and

put that last stroke over *here*,' a tiny flick of the pencil, 'it means "ice".'

Water, ice, eternity. Miss Dunn folds up the paper and hands it to me. 'But we don't need to worry about teaching you Japanese just yet.'

'Can I learn Japanese if I want to?'

Miss Dunn thinks for a minute. 'Well, I'm not a qualified teacher of Japanese language. But I'd be willing to teach you the basics, providing it doesn't take too much time away from your compulsory subjects. You'll need very high marks if you're serious about veterinary medicine.'

'Can I learn calligraphy?'

Miss Dunn looks at me and takes a sip of her tea. 'Why would you want to learn that?'

'So I can make signs that say, "Screw you, white trash" and sell them at a stall at the markets.'

Miss Dunn bursts out laughing again. Fortunately, she doesn't have a mouthful of tea this time. 'Then I'd get fired and you'd get sent to Ramsay. No, you will not get any calligraphy lessons, at least not from me. Anyway, calligraphy is for little old ladies.'

As I walk back to the Refuge, I start writing a kind of TV episode in my mind. This time it's not a *Clarissa Hobbs* episode. It's a daydream where Renate Dunn is my older sister, or maybe even my mother. I won't ever write it down, though. I'd be too embarrassed if someone found it.

More great reading from Ford Street Publishing

By Jenny Mounfield

One summer afternoon three boys play a prank on the ice-cream man. This one decision sets into motion a chain of events that will forge a life-long bond, testing each boy as never before.

Three boys united by fear and their need for friendship.

Three boys united against the ice-cream man.

Also by Jenny Mounfield: *Storm Born* and *The Black Bandit*.

www.fordstreetpublishing.com

FORD ST

More great reading from Ford Street Publishing

CROSSING THE LINE

Being abandoned is nothing new for Sophie. But things look up when she moves in with Amy and Matt.

So how come she ends up in a psych ward? And aren't therapists supposed to help?

'Drama, pathos, nail-biting stuff –
this is Dianne Bates at her best'
MARGARET CLARK

'A profoundly sensitive exploration
of emotional agony . . .
an engrossing read'
ELIZABETH FENSHAM

www.fordstreetpublishing.com   FORD ST